YOU CAN RUN

MARY MILLS MYSTERY - BOOK 2

WILLOW ROSE

Contents

Books by the Author   v

Prologue   1
Merritt Island   3
Merritt Island   5

Part I   9

Part II   89

Part III   181

Afterword   249
Copyright   251
About the Author   253
IT ENDS HERE   255
Order your copy today!   269

Books by the Author

MYSTERY/THRILLER/HORROR NOVELS

- IN ONE FELL SWOOP
- UMBRELLA MAN
- BLACKBIRD FLY
- TO HELL IN A HANDBASKET
- EDWINA

MARY MILLS MYSTERY SERIES

- WHAT HURTS THE MOST
- YOU CAN RUN
- YOU CAN'T HIDE
- CAREFUL LITTLE EYES

EMMA FROST SERIES

- ITSY BITSY SPIDER
- MISS DOLLY HAD A DOLLY
- RUN, RUN AS FAST AS YOU CAN
- CROSS YOUR HEART AND HOPE TO DIE
- PEEK-A-BOO I SEE YOU
- TWEEDLEDUM AND TWEEDLEDEE
- EASY AS ONE, TWO, THREE
- THERE'S NO PLACE LIKE HOME
- SLENDERMAN
- WHERE THE WILD ROSES GROW
- WALTZING MATHILDA
- DRIP DROP DEAD

JACK RYDER SERIES

- HIT THE ROAD JACK
- SLIP OUT THE BACK JACK
- THE HOUSE THAT JACK BUILT
- BLACK JACK
- GIRL NEXT DOOR
- HER FINAL WORD
- DON'T TELL

REBEKKA FRANCK SERIES

- One, Two…He is Coming for You
- Three, Four…Better Lock Your Door
- Five, Six…Grab your Crucifix
- Seven, Eight…Gonna Stay up Late
- Nine, Ten…Never Sleep Again
- Eleven, Twelve…Dig and Delve
- Thirteen, Fourteen…Little Boy Unseen
- Better Not Cry
- Ten Little Girls
- It Ends Here

HORROR SHORT-STORIES

- Mommy Dearest
- The Bird
- Better watch out
- Eenie, Meenie
- Rock-a-Bye Baby
- Nibble, Nibble, Crunch
- Humpty Dumpty
- Chain Letter

PARANORMAL SUSPENSE/ROMANCE NOVELS

- In Cold Blood
- The Surge
- Girl Divided

THE VAMPIRES OF SHADOW HILLS SERIES

- Flesh and Blood
- Blood and Fire
- Fire and Beauty
- Beauty and Beasts
- Beasts and Magic
- Magic and Witchcraft
- Witchcraft and War
- War and Order
- Order and Chaos
- Chaos and Courage

THE AFTERLIFE SERIES

- Beyond

- SERENITY
- ENDURANCE
- COURAGEOUS

THE WOLFBOY CHRONICLES

- A GYPSY SONG
- I AM WOLF

DAUGHTERS OF THE JAGUAR

- SAVAGE
- BROKEN

There is only one difference between a madman and me. The madman thinks he is sane. I know I am mad.

~ Salvador Dali

Prologue

THE KIDS ARE SITTING in the living room. The youngest boy, Jack Jr., is on the floor. He is watching TV, the same movie he always watches on Saturday mornings. Kimmie, his older sister by three years is on the couch, a blanket wrapped around her legs, even though it is not cold.

"Could we watch something else?" she complains. "We always watch *How to Train your Dragon*. It's so boring!"

"You don't have to watch it if you don't want to," Jack Jr. says. "I love this movie."

His older sister rolls her eyes with a deep groan. "Come on. You've seen it seventeen times. Don't you get tired of watching everything over and over again? You're such a baby. Stupid little baby."

Her ten-year-old brother looks up at her, then bursts into a loud wailing sound. Seconds later, their mother, Lisa, is in the room with them.

"Quit shouting!" she yells. "Dad is trying to sleep in. He had a late meeting last night."

"She called me stupid!" Jack Jr. cries.

"Kimmie!"

"But, Mooom," Kimmie complains.

"Kimmie! You be good to your brother now. You're the oldest."

"But I didn't do anything."

"You called me stupid!"

"Did not!"

"Did too. Moom she's lying."

Lisa sighs and closes her eyes. She is tense. Jack's many late evening meetings are tearing on her and on their marriage. Mostly

1

because of how they make her feel. Not knowing what he is up to, after…after that time with the secretary, when Lisa walked in on them, bringing him lunch as a surprise. Jack insists it's over, that it ended when he fired her, but how can Lisa be sure? She knows her husband and worries every day what he is up to. She hasn't been to his office since that day. She knows she won't be able to stand the pitiful looks from his colleagues. Not anymore.

"We always watch that same stupid movie, Mom. I want to watch *Harry Potter*!"

"That is not for your brother," Lisa says. "I don't want him to watch those movies yet. We have so many TVs in this house. Why don't you go watch *Harry Potter* somewhere else? You have your own TV in your room. How about going up there instead of arguing with your brother down here?"

"Why do I have to be the one to leave?" Kimmie shouts angrily. Her voice sounds like it's about to crack. Tears are in her eyes. "You always pick Jack Jr. over me, Mom. It's not fair."

Lisa clears her throat in a deep exhale while Jack Jr. throws his sister a triumphant glance. "Just do it, will you, Kimmie? Be the big sister for once? I can't really deal with this today."

Kimmie lets out an annoyed gasp. She is thirteen and getting worse every day, Lisa thinks to herself, right before she feels that overwhelming sensation of anger well up in her stomach and yells, "Just do as I say. NOW!"

Lisa points towards the hallway and the stairs. Kimmie lets out another annoyed sound, gets up, and walks, dragging her feet ostentatiously. Lisa decides she will deal with her later. Right now, she is looking forward to getting her coffee.

As silence falls upon the big house once again, she walks to the kitchen, and pours herself a cup, knowing she'll probably need more than one to get through the day. Maybe she'll even need something stronger later. But not before noon.

Never before noon.

She drinks her coffee, while glancing out at the lake with the water fountain, through the window that extends from the floor to the twenty-foot ceiling.

Upstairs, she hears Kimmie slam a door. Lisa puts down the cup and turns to walk up the stairs and have a word with her.

She doesn't even notice the figure staring at her from the window in the kitchen door, the same door Lisa left unlocked after taking out the trash earlier. Nor does she hear it when the door is opened and the person enters.

It's just not the kind of thing you'd expect to happen on an ordinary Saturday morning.

Merritt Island

DECEMBER 2010

"Sh. Don't make a sound or everybody dies."

The cold gun is pressed against Lisa's cheek and a hand is placed to cover her mouth. The fingers on her lips leave her with a taste of cigarettes.

Lisa gasps while fear grabs her heart. She is struggling to breathe through her nose. The panic is spreading like cancer through her body. The intruder is speaking close to her ear.

"Where is your husband? Show me to him. Nice and slowly. No sudden movements. No screaming. Do you think you can do that?"

Lisa nods carefully, while focusing on her breathing.

"Alright. Show me to him."

With the intruder still holding her mouth, Lisa starts walking towards the stairs. All she can think about is the children. She is hoping, praying, that the intruder won't know about them. She is hoping that the intruder has come for her husband or for valuables. They can give those away easily. They won't miss any of the things they have in the house.

As long as no one is hurt.

They walk into the master bedroom, where Jack is still sleeping. He grunts and turns in bed when they approach. Lisa is crying, whimpering behind the hand.

"Rise and shine," the intruder says. "You have company, Jack."

Jack opens his eyes and terror slams through his body as he sees his wife. He jumps to his feet fast. Something in the way he acts tells Lisa this intruder isn't a complete stranger to Jack.

"What the hell…?"

The intruder shows him the gun and places it on his wife's

3

temple. "You can try and run…but I don't recommend it. Now, get dressed."

Jack wants to speak. Lisa can tell he wants to object to this treatment, and she throws him a pleading look not to.

Just do as you're told, Jack.

"Who…what…who the hell do you think you are? You can't just come here and…this is my house."

"Are you done?" the intruder says. The intruder is agitated. Lisa can tell by the shivering hand holding the gun.

Please, just do as you're told, Jack. Don't put up a fight. Don't puff yourself up like you always do, telling them who you are and how important you are. Just don't be your usual self. Think about the children, Jack.

"I will not put up with this," Jack continues. "I…you can't just… come in here and…"

"You do realize I could kill your wife—and don't get me wrong, I will do it—if you don't get dressed and come downstairs with me right away," the intruder says, then turns the gun and releases a shot at a painting of Jack's mother on the wall. The gun makes hardly any sound when it goes off, and Lisa realizes it has a silencer on it. It makes it even scarier.

"Okay. Okay," Jack says, finally realizing the seriousness of the situation. "Just give me a second. Just don't hurt her, alright?"

Jack picks up his pants from the chair behind him. Lisa is crying heavily now behind the hand. The taste of the intruder's fingers in her mouth makes her nauseated. The fingers are hurting her jaw. She wants to scream. She wants to scream and yell for help, but she can't, and she doesn't dare to.

Please, God. Please don't let the children be involved in this. Please keep them out of it.

When Jack is finally dressed, he looks at the intruder. "Now what? What do you want?"

"Take me to the children."

The neighbors will hear us. They must have heard Kimmie scream when the intruder came into her room, right? Didn't they? They heard Jack Jr. when he screamed for his mommy, didn't they? They'll come to our rescue, won't they? Of course they will.

They have to.

Lisa is trying to convince herself that the neighbors have already called for the police to come. She tries to calm herself down by thinking about it, by imagining the police cars arriving outside the house.

But she still can't hear them.

They have been lying on the floor of the living room for what feels like forever. She still can't really grasp what happened after she heard the voice behind her in the kitchen, after she felt the gun being pressed against her back and the voice spoke into her ear, talking with a low, almost whispering, snakelike voice.

Maybe if the neighbors were paying attention—just for this once in their busy lives—to what is going on right down the street from them in their quiet neighborhood, then maybe they'd hear me if I screamed.

"Please!"

Still, nothing happens. No wailing sirens in the distance. No officers yelling outside or even footsteps approaching. The neighbors haven't heard anything.

Maybe someone else will hear me. A passerby will call the cops. Maybe they'll hear our cries for help, maybe they'll hear us, if only…Please, God…Please.

Lisa is praying silently while lying on the floor. She looks at her son, Jack Jr., who is lying face-down, a gun pressed to the back of his head, the intruder sitting on top of him. His entire body is shivering in terror.

Please, not my son. Please, don't take him from me. He's all I have.

"Fifty-thousand dollars or the son gets it," the voice says. "Get it here within the next hour. And no police, or the boy dies."

The pressure on Jack Jr.'s back is loosened and Lisa watches as her husband gets to his feet and—hands shivering—picks up the phone.

"Richard? It's me. Could you bring fifty-thousand dollars to me within the hour? Yes. Discreetly, please. Thank you."

Jack Jr. looks at his mother lying on the floor next to him. She tries to smile and hide her fear. She can almost touch him, but she doesn't dare to, afraid she might anger the intruder. Jack Jr. is crying, sobbing heavily. She wants to protect her son, she wants to hold his hand or hug him, tell him it's going to be okay, tell him that once Richard brings the money, it'll all be over.

Richard.

Richard will do something, won't he? Of course he will. He's Jack's accountant and best friend for ten years. He'll know something is wrong. He'll hear it in his voice or maybe they even have a word, something he is supposed to say in case something like this happens. Of course they do.

Reassured that Jack will somehow handle this, Lisa throws a glance at her daughter. Their eyes meet and she sees nothing but utter terror in hers. It frightens her. Nothing is worse than seeing fear in your kid's eyes and not being able to do anything about it. Nothing.

"It's done," Jack says, looking at the intruder.

"Good. Now call for pizza. I'm hungry."

"Pizza? But…"

The gun is pointed at Jack's face. "Just do it."

"Just do as you're told, Jack!" Lisa screams.

The eyes of the intruder are filled with madness as the gun shifts to point at her instead.

"Shut up, bitch! Shut the fuck up! Don't speak unless I tell you to, okay? Just…just don't!"

"Alright. All right. I'll call for pizza. Just…just don't hurt anyone, okay? We'll do anything you tell us, just don't hurt us." Jack hurries to the phone and dials a number.

"Pepperoni," the intruder says.

"One pepperoni pizza," Jack repeats, his voice shivering, his eyes fixated on the gun in the intruder's hand. The hands don't seem stable enough to carry such a mortal weapon.

"What? Nothing for the rest of the family?" the intruder asks.

"Make that two pizzas. Yes, both pepperoni. Thank you."

The intruder shakes their head, holding a finger in the air. "No.

No. No. Not pepperoni. Ham. I want ham! I told you I wanted ham! I can't stand pepperoni. Can't stand it. Simply can't!"

Jack stares at the intruder, not knowing what to say. The gun is placed on Lisa's temple. She whimpers. The intruder growls and puts a hand over her mouth while whispering, "Shut up! Or I'll kill your kids. I swear, I'll kill them."

"Sorry. Could you make that ham instead? I must have heard wrong," Jack says. "Thank you."

"Now, lay back down!" the intruder yells, as soon as the phone is hung up. The yelling is loud, inconsistent, angry and mad.

Lisa studies the intruder's pale face. There is something about the eyes that tells her this person isn't well. The manic eyes, the constant rubbing of the hair, the hands that won't stay still.

It strikes Lisa that the intruder hasn't covered their face. They'll be able to identify the intruder for the police when it is all over. What does this mean? Could it be that the intruder simply forgot? That the intruder didn't think everything through? Or…? Or does it mean…could it mean that this person doesn't intend to release them when the money or the pizza arrives? That it was never the intention?

What if it isn't what the intruder came for?

Part I

WITH A LITTLE HELP FROM MY FRIENDS

1

January 2016

"LET'S GRAB A TABLE OUTSIDE."

I follow Sandra through the doors of our favorite breakfast place, Café Surfinista. We have both ordered the Acai Bowl, which is amazing. The weather is nice and chilly, the winds blowing in from the north making it dryer and the air cooler. I like it. I like January in Florida.

Sandra receives a glance from a passerby. She tries to hide her face underneath her cap. I feel a pinch in my heart. She has been used to people staring at her all of her life, but for a different reason. I'm wondering if she will ever get used to the stares she gets now. I fight the urge to yell something after the passerby.

People can be so rude.

Sandra's skin has healed, but she is still disfigured from the acid my brother threw in her face three months ago. On the day he got away with murder. I still hate myself for not being able to stop him. I was so close, and then it happened. He did this to my best friend and ruined her life completely. Having a great career as a model, her looks were everything. They were her entire life. Her recovery afterwards was long and filled with many more trips to the hospital. At home, she was forced to wear a plastic mask twenty-three hours a day to help her wounds heal. For weeks, she had no reason to get out of bed. The crew and I took turns visiting her and getting her up. Still, she hardly ever leaves the house alone anymore. She cries a lot, even though she tries to hide it. She still isn't herself at all, and I wonder if she will ever be.

"So, how are you doing?" I ask her, as we sit down and the passerby is gone. I can tell from her eyes that the stares hurt her.

Today is a victory. It took a long time of convincing her it would be good for her to go out for breakfast with me. She had all kinds of excuses. I can't blame her. Every time she walks outside, she is reminded of what happened. There is no way she can escape it.

She answers with a scoff. "I'm okay, I guess." She pauses and finally looks me in the eyes. "I removed all the mirrors in my house yesterday."

"Good for you." I say, almost choking on some granola. I cough and try to shake the feeling of guilt, but it's eating me up. I can't believe my brother got away with this.

I haven't given up on catching him and Olivia. None of us have. We want him to pay for what he has done. But finding him is proving to be a lot harder than expected.

So far, we don't know much. We know they ran away together. I've followed the police investigation closely, but so far, there has been no sign of life from either of them in two months. Not since a surveillance camera at a gas station in Ft. Lauderdale spotted my brother in November. The police, with Detective Chris Fisher in charge, lost track of him after that. Meanwhile, Chloe is using all her skills to try and track them online, tracking his and Olivia's credit cards, but so far without any luck. I fear they could be anywhere by now. The police found the car that Blake escaped in, in Melbourne, abandoned. It's my theory that he was picked up by Olivia there; her phone records show she received a phone call from a phone booth in the same area that day, and no one has seen her since. Both of their phones were found in a trash can near the Melbourne Mall. Chloe thinks Olivia might own a credit card or a bank account under a different name, and right now she is working on that angle. Meanwhile, the rest of the 7th Street Crew are doing all we can to keep our eyes and ears open. The two months of silence is eating me alive. Seeing Sandra suffer the way she does is tearing me up.

"But you have no idea how many things you have in your house where you can see your own reflection," Sandra says, sucking in her breath. "Just using my silverware or putting a pot of water under the faucet in my kitchen won't let me forget. Every freaking second of my life, I have to face it."

"What about surgery? What do they say?" I ask, knowing she has been through a marathon of reconstructive surgeries already.

A couple walks past us on the street. The woman stares at Sandra. The disgust is oozing from her eyes. Yet, she can't stop looking.

Sandra turns her head away and closes her eyes.

"You ain't exactly a looker yourself, lady," I say. I sound like an idiot, but I am so frustrated, I can't help myself.

Sandra places a calm hand on my arm. "You don't have to defend me," she says. "It's okay. It's not their fault."

She sighs and removes her hand before she continues.

"They can't do anymore. The damage is too severe. This is it for me. This is what I am going to look like for the rest of my life. I just have to learn to live with it. The worst part is Ryan. I can tell he is trying hard, but just looking at me still makes his eyes water. He has that look of disgust that I see in everyone who looks at me. And he definitely doesn't want to touch me. He used to be all over me, but now he tries to avoid even looking at me. He works constantly, and I think he might be avoiding being home because it makes him feel uncomfortable. I can't blame him. I would run away too. But I can't. I'm right here. All the time. I can't run away from myself."

"I am sorry, Sandra." I say. I am at loss for words and try with a joke instead. "I can beat him up for you, if you want me to?"

Sandra chuckles, but she isn't smiling.

2

January 2016

MARCIA LITTLE WALKS across the street at Minutemen Causeway. She hurries up and a car misses her as it rushes by, honking its horn.

"Ah, come on," she yells after it.

The driver throws a finger out the window. Marcia blows raspberries and laughs. In her hand, she is carrying a bottle of gin. It is wrapped in a brown paper bag. She has just bought it at ABC Wine, and now she is heading for the beach by Coconuts. The air is chilly today. The scarf she always wears doesn't keep her neck warm enough. Too much wind. She knows the others won't be in the usual spots.

Billy is the first one she sees. He is sitting in front of the Beach Shack, in the dunes, a guitar in his lap. He smiles and yells her name. Where he is sitting, you can't feel the wind when it is in the north.

With the sun in a clear blue sky, it will be nice to sit on the sand, she thinks to herself and joins him. He is finishing up a beer. Neither the Beach Shack nor Coconuts on the beach have opened yet. It's nice and quiet right now. Just the way Marcia likes to start her day. Especially since she lost her job at CVS on 520, the third job in just as many months.

Billy is playing a tune, and after a couple of sips from her bottle, Marcia is humming along. She used to be a great singer, back in high school, and everyone thought she would pursue a career in music, but…well it never happened. She played bars and venues all over Brevard County for nothing but free beer and food for years. That's how she met Carl, the father of her four children. He owns a bar in Orlando, where she would play regularly. He liked her and kept asking her to come back. Soon, they hooked up, and she never

14

got any further with her career. As soon as their firstborn came along, she was done singing anything but nursery rhymes.

Marcia had always been fond of drinking. Ever since her teenage years, when she had her first beer, she had known she liked it. But it was also what killed her marriage. Carl liked to drink too, and over the years, he turned violent. Finally, one day, it became too much for Marcia. That was when she caught Carl beating their youngest, who was only two-years-old till he was bruised on his entire back. That was when she knew she'd had enough. Carl could beat her all he wanted to. That she could handle. But not when he took it out on the children. That was it for her. So she left and came back to her hometown with the heavy load of having to raise four children on her own. She often wondered where the years went, how come her breakthrough never came, why she never got the career she had thought she would. Where did it all go wrong?

Well, you can't have it all. At least she has a place to live. She doesn't have to sleep on the beach or the streets like Billy and most of the other guys she hangs out with. At least she has a roof over her head and a bottle in her hand. Who needs a career?

It's all overrated anyway.

Marcia sips her bottle and lets the alcohol settle the uneasiness she always wakes up with in the morning. The mornings are the worst. Until she is able to send the kids off to school on the bus, she strives just to stay upright. Her entire body is usually shaking in withdrawal. That's why she normally starts the day with a couple of painkillers to keep her going until she can make it to the gas station, where she has her first beer of the day. After that, she is up and running again.

Today is a special day. Today, she is celebrating the fact that the court has told Carl to pay her a thousand dollars a month in alimony. Not that he will feel it. His bar is doing really well.

About time he pays up. After all, they're his kids too.

But the extra money means Marcia doesn't have to hurry up finding another job. She lost the condo two months ago when the bank took it and they moved into a small townhouse across the street from the beach instead that was much cheaper. The money from Carl is enough to pay her rent and groceries, so it's only the extra stuff she needs to make herself. With the money she borrowed from her sister last week, she'll get by for a couple of months, even if she doesn't find a job. It suits Marcia, since she hasn't been doing so well lately. She needs a little time to get better.

October 2005

"I KNOW he's in there somewhere, Mom. I'm certain. Why won't you listen to me?"

Daniel looks intensely at his mother. Her eyes are tired, exhausted even. "I am telling you, Daniel. We've tried everything."

"I refuse to believe that my brother is going to have to live like this. I am the one who knows him best. I am the one who has been the closest to him all of his life. I know he understands what we tell him. He might not be able to speak, he might not be able to communicate, but he is in there. Behind those eyes is an adult who needs to be heard, Mom. There's got to be some sort of treatment."

His mother, Michelle, sighs deeply, then closes her eyes while shaking her head. "You've got to stop this, Daniel. Peter has Cerebral Palsy. He hasn't spoken a word in the twenty-five years he has been on this planet. He is and will always be impaired. You've seen how he is getting worse every day. You've seen the muscle spasms in his face, his neck, his torso and his arms and hands. You know it's hard for him to stay in one position, that muscle contractions sometimes twist his spine and clench his fingers in a useless ball. He can hardly make eye contact and keep objects fixed in view. He wears a diaper, for crying out loud. He can't even dress himself. He can walk only if someone steadies him; otherwise, he gets around by scooting on the floor. All we have ever been able to communicate with him is by his screams when he's unhappy and the chirps when he's excited, but he can't control his vocal cords. His last assessment shows he has a very low IQ. That guy, the clinical psychologist, that Wills fellow, assessed Peter and found that his comprehension seemed to be *quite limited*. Those were his words, Daniel. Quite limited. Remember that? He also said that Peter's attention span was very short and he lacks the *cognitive capacity to understand and participate in decisions*. Peter can't even carry out basic, preschool-level tasks."

Daniel's mother grabs his hand in hers and smiles. "I know you love your brother. I know you want what's best for him. We all do. But we have fought this fight since he was a small child, trying to find treatment for him. Back when your father was still alive, we had him tested constantly; we refused to face the fact that Peter is severely handicapped and he will never be able to communicate with us."

"But…" Daniel tries, but his older sister sitting at the end of the dining table stops him.

"Leave it, Daniel. You heard Mother. We have tried everything. Peter is our brother, but he will never be able to communicate with us."

"Just leave it alone," his older brother chimes in. It annoys Daniel how they always stick together.

His four siblings sitting around the table in their parent's old estate seem to all agree.

"Am I the only one who hasn't given up?" Daniel asks.

"He is twenty-five now, son," his mother says. "I'm getting old. We have help here day in and day out, and he can stay here till I die, but as I said earlier, I want us to take a look at his other possibilities for when I'm not here anymore. All of you have jobs and families. You can't take care of him as well."

Daniel grunts. He wants to say something, but he knows it won't help. They've all made up their minds. Their mother has made all of them legal guardians of Peter when she dies. He will be their responsibility when their mother passes away. Daniel has feared the day for years. He is the one who has been closest to their youngest brother. Being only five years old when he was born, Daniel always felt responsible for him. Unlike the others, who were a lot older when Peter was born. Their oldest brother was nineteen and their sister sixteen. None of them have the same relationship with him that Daniel does. Not even the two other brothers who were seven and nine when Peter was born. They just don't get him like Daniel does. Still, he knows he can't take Peter in either once their mother dies. His wife would kill him for it.

Daniel looks to Peter, who is sitting in his wheelchair in the corner, his chin touching his chest. He wishes deeply that Peter could speak for himself. That he would speak up right now. Tell them they are wrong, that he can still have a life. That it is wrong of them to simply hide him away in a home somewhere after the death of their mother.

What if he hears everything? What if he understands everything? What if he just can't tell us?

The very thought terrifies Daniel. He hates the fact that his brother is trapped in his body like this. He has seen it in his eyes. Peter isn't stupid. He is smart, he is intelligent. The doctors have told them it is impossible. Over and over again, they have told them that Peter is out of reach. Yet Daniel stays convinced that all it will take is someone else besides him who believes it to be possible. Someone who knows of another way to reach into Peter's deeper inner self, inside where his thoughts are trapped.

January 2016

"MARK YOU KNOW you're not allowed to wear a hat indoors. Please, take it off."

Mark tries to avoid looking at his teacher, Miss Abbey. She is standing in front of his desk. He stares at her jeans while holding onto his cap.

"Mark. I told you to take off the hat."

Mark bows his head even further down. The entire class is staring at him. Some are whispering. He feels his face blushing.

"Mark!"

Mark doesn't react. He is holding onto the cap like his life depends on it. It sort of does. For an eighth-grader, this type of thing can ruin your life.

"Mark. I am not going to tell you again. You're being very disrespectful towards me right now. I am going to count to three and then you'll take off the hat or I see no other choice than to send you to the principal's office…again."

Mark closes his eyes and wishes it would all go away. His mom used to tell him it was possible.

"If only you want it enough, then you can change everything with your mind. Isn't it amazing?"

Mark opens his eyes, but she is still there. He doesn't understand why he can't make the teacher go away or even just this awful situation. Maybe he doesn't want it enough, like his mother said?

"One…two…"

Mark draws in a deep sigh and looks down at his desk.

"Don't make me say three, Mark."

Carefully, he lifts his cap and finally looks up at his teacher.

When she sees what is underneath, her expression changes completely. A loud wave of laughter bursts through the classroom.

"Mark, what have you done to your hair?" Miss Abbey exclaims.

Mark's eyes hit the floor in embarrassment. "I…I…cut it."

He's lying. It wasn't him. It was his mother who did it that very morning, right before school. She came running into his room with the shaver in her hand, held him down on the bed, and shaved his hair off in big clumps, yelling weird things about some angel visiting her at night and telling her that Mark's hair was infested with flesh-eating bugs and that she needed to cut it off before he infested anyone else. Mark screamed and tried to fight her. He ended up running out of the house, grabbing his backpack and a cap on the way out. At school, he had looked at himself in the mirror in the bathroom and realized it was all uneven, that here and there big clumps of hair were still sticking out, while it was completely shaved off in other areas. That was why he didn't want to take off the cap.

"Mark…I…I…why would you cut it like this?" Miss Abbey says, baffled, while the laughter and giggling continues mercilessly. "And, come to think of it, what…are you still wearing your pajamas?"

Another wave of laughter rushes through the class. Mark blushes again. "I…I…guess I forgot to get dressed."

"Why…I never…" Miss Abbey's upper lip is getting tighter. She lifts both of her hands in the air. "I simply don't know what to do with you anymore. Last week it was that awful smell from that bug-spray you had used as deodorant all over your body. The other day your math book was completely destroyed, and now this. What is going on with you, Mark? Are you trying to get out of school or just annoy me? 'Cause I don't know what to do about you anymore."

Mark nods and keeps looking down. He knows what it sounds like, but he wants to avoid the truth at all costs. He doesn't want the school to know his mother was so afraid of bugs one morning she sprayed him all over his body with bug-spray, or that she was the one that had used his math book for killing imaginary bugs at the house, slamming it against the walls for hours and hours while screaming at the government that they'll never get her.

There is no way he is ever going to tell them that. No way.

Instead, he takes a deep breath, and once again bends his head in shame.

"I know, Miss Abbey. I'll try and get better. I promise."

January 2016

BLAKE WATCHES the blonde as she walks out of Walgreen's. He is sitting in his car, hands tight on the wheel, his knuckles turning white when he sees her, his jaw clenched. The blonde doesn't notice him. She has a bag in her hand. She walks to her car and gets in. Blake starts the engine and follows her closely, like he did on the way there from her house. He has watched her all day. On the display of his new phone, it says that Olivia has called him five times. He was supposed to go pick up some beers this morning, but then he saw her, the blonde, and couldn't take his eyes of her since. He doesn't know what it is about her. She reminds him of someone, someone he wants to hurt.

For the past three months, while they have been on the run, Blake has been able to keep his urges down. But the last couple of days or so it has been bugging him. That nagging feeling that keeps him awake at night, that makes him wake up bathed in sweat if he finally dozes off.

He has managed to keep it a secret from Olivia, how he really feels, but he is not sure he can keep it that way. All she thinks about is keeping a low profile, to not draw any attention their way. Blake knows she is right. He knows it is dangerous, but that only makes it even more tempting and the feeling even more overpowering.

As he parks outside the woman's house, his phone rings again. It doesn't say her name on the display, but he knows it's her. She is the only one who has his number. They bought the phones from a guy they met at the motel where they are staying. No one will ever know they have them. Just like no one will ever find them where they're hiding. Blake is certain of it. They're being too smart. They pay for everything in cash. It's his luck that Olivia saved up for years for her escape from the general. Month after month, she would stash away cash to make sure the general would never track her when she left. She even has a credit card that no one knows about. She had it all planned and figured out so many years ago; she created a fake identity for herself using her dead aunt's name. When her aunt died, Olivia stole her passport from the house when they cleaned it out, thinking it would be useful one day. And it sure has been. Especially for Blake.

The phone is still ringing insistently, and he finally picks it up.

"Where are you?" Olivia growls from the other end. "You've been gone for five hours!"

"I know. I know," he says, while watching the blonde get out of her car and walk up to the small house, if you can call it that. Looked more like a bungalow to him. "Just needed to check on something. I'll be right back."

"You better. What is it with you lately? You make a beer run at nine in the morning and then don't come back? What if someone sees you?"

"Baby, no one sees me. I can assure you of that."

Her voice calms down and she sighs. "Okay then. I guess I was just afraid since I didn't hear from you. I feel like there are police everywhere these days."

"We talked about this. You're just being paranoid. The plan is working. For all I know, they've already stopped looking for us. I mean, have you seen anything on the news about us lately? Anything?"

"No."

"Trust me, Olivia. They have no idea where we are, and as soon as someone else does something bad, they'll forget about us."

"What if that manager at the motel rats us out? I don't trust him much," Olivia says.

"Randy? Pah. He's harmless. He's had his own share of run-ins with the cops in his life. Besides, after we gave him that envelope of money from selling the watch my dad gave me, I think he is pretty satisfied. He won't talk."

Olivia exhaled. "I know. I know. You're right."

"Now crawl up on that bed and get naked because daddy's coming home soon and he's in the mood for a little action. Alright?"

Olivia giggles, then hangs up.

Real smooth Blake. That's how they like it.

Blake puts the phone back on the passenger seat as he pulls out the binoculars that he bought at Walgreen's while the blonde shopped. They work perfectly, and soon he is able to see her up close. The blonde is unpacking her groceries and putting them away one by one. Blake likes the parts when she is bending to reach the lower cabinets. He feels himself getting aroused and jerks off while watching her every move.

6

January 2016

JOEY IS home when I get back from breakfast. Salter has started at Roosevelt Elementary and loves it. It was the same school that both Joey and I went to, and I love it there still. It feels like I have come home.

"Home already?" I say with a smile, lean over and kiss him on the lips. Bonnie and Clyde are running after Snowflake, chasing him out the door into the backyard. They come back a few seconds later. Bonnie in the front, holding the ball in her mouth. The pig grunts victoriously. Clyde is barking, and I have a feeling that he and Snowflake are ganging up on the pig.

"Have you finished the fence job so soon?" I ask, leaving the animals to their little game.

"Yeah. I did as much as I could today. The rest of the wood won't arrive until tomorrow, so there isn't much I can do for now."

I nod, feeling a little sorry for him. There hasn't been much for him to do lately. I keep telling him it's because it was Christmas and people have been spending their money on presents and not on rebuilding their houses. Joey doesn't seem to think it'll pick up any time soon.

"I'll go work on the beach house after lunch," he says. "Help out Ryan's people a little."

My dad and I have hired Sandra's husband's company to rebuild my childhood home after a fire destroyed it three months ago. The same fire that hurt my dad and left him paralyzed from the neck down. Joey likes to go over there and see if they need his help. I have offered to pay him for his hours, but he won't hear of it.

"Is he still sleeping?" I ask, and nod in the direction of the room that we have made into my dad's room, since he was released from the hospital. Joey's place is only two bedrooms, so that means we all sleep together in the other bedroom. Salter, Joey, all the animals, and me.

"No. He asked for water a little while ago, so I gave him some and read the newspaper to him," Joey says.

"That was sweet of you. Thank you."

"No problem. I feel bad for him. Must be terrible to not be able to move a muscle in your body. I can't imagine what it must be like."

I nod. I feel bad for him too. Only his face is fully functional. He has regained the ability to speak, smile and blink, but not effortlessly yet. That is all. At least, so far. I refuse to give up on believing he will one day be able to walk again. I have hired a physical therapist who stops by three times a week and tries to work with him. But he still doesn't feel anything.

"I'll go check on him," I say, and walk to the door and knock. "Dad?"

"Come in," he says.

I walk in. My dad seems even smaller than he did the day before. Lying in bed like that makes him lose all his muscles, the doctor explained to me. And he is not eating much.

"How are you today?" I ask and sit on the edge of the bed. I take his hand in mine and lift it up. He has a nurse that comes in every day and washes him and turns his body so he won't get bedsores. His hand feels limp. I squeeze it, hoping he will feel something.

"Nothing new," he says, fighting to get the words out. He speaks three words at a time, then stops to catch his breath. It is good for him to keep talking, training his facial muscles to obey, the therapist explained to me. The more he speaks, the better it gets. It's always worst in the mornings.

"But you brought...a nice breath...of fresh air...with you when...you came in...I enjoy that."

I smile and touch his cheek gently. It is strange to watch your once-so-strong father like this. Devastating. But at least I can talk to him and he can answer me. I feel very grateful for that.

"It's nice and cool out today," I say. "Just under seventy degrees and sunny. Do you want me to open your window and let some of the air in?"

"That would be...nice. Thank you." He takes a break, and when he speaks next the words come easier. "So we're having a cold spell...these days, huh?"

"Yes."

"I miss those days...when the air cools off and everything is so...so..."

"So crisp," I say. I bite my tongue. I know I am supposed to let him find the words himself.

"The beach is usually the best place to be…I used to love walking…on the beach on days like this. It was fun to watch…all the tourists jumping…in the water when you felt like it was freezing."

"That's winter for you in Florida," I say. "Socks and flip-flops and all that."

My dad chuckles. "You hated it…as a child. Blake loved it…You were so different, the two of you."

He stops himself and looks down. We haven't talked much about Blake the past few months, but I know it is troubling him. I wonder if he is blaming himself for things turning bad like they did.

"I thought it would be enough…to give him what he wanted… what I believed he needed," he suddenly says. "Guess I gave him all…all the wrong things. I guess I…just didn't know how to handle him…you know…after your mother died."

I open the window and a breath of fresh air hits my face. I close my eyes and swallow the lump that seems to be stuck in my throat these days. I turn to look at him. "So, is Laura coming today?" I ask.

7

January 2016

"Hı. I'm here about the room. I called earlier?"

Marcia stares at the man in front of her. In his hand, he is holding a suitcase. Everything is blurry and has been since she finished her bottle and left Billy and the beach. She can't remember much from the past few hours and has no idea what time it is. She stares at the man, trying hard to focus.

"My name is Harry Hanson. You told me to just drop by and take a look at the room."

"Ah. Harry," Marcia says, pretending like she remembers talking to him. She is gesticulating wildly while speaking. "Yes. Yes. Come on in. Take a look."

Marcia finds the key to her small townhouse in her pocket and opens the door. As she walks inside, she remembers placing the ad on Craigslist for a renter for one of the rooms. It's a three-bedroom house, so the kids will have to bunk up in just one room.

"It's right in here," she says, and shows him to the room. "It has its own back entrance, so you can come and go as you want." She stops at the end of the stairs. "It's right up here. On the second floor."

Marcia grabs the railing and walks up the stairs, almost loses her balance, but regains it and looks back at the man with a goofy grin before she continues. "There's a bathroom right across from it that's all yours. Me and the kids stay in the rooms downstairs and use the bathroom down there. You'll have the entire floor to yourself," she says with a smile, trying hard to seal the deal. Getting a renter in would mean she wouldn't have to work at all anymore. With the money she's getting from Carl on top of it, she could make it work if they keep their expenses low, which they are very good at. The kids all qualify for the food-program and eat at the school for both breakfast and lunch. Her sister offers them hand-me-downs of clothes and toys.

"It's right in here."

Marcia opens the door to the room and walks in first. She hurries to the window and opens it to make sure it doesn't smell. The man follows her with his suitcase in hand. He throws a glance around the small room and takes in the twin bed up against the wall.

"There's a nice-sized closet and a desk too," she says proudly, wondering if the man has a computer in his suitcase. "No pets and no smoking," she adds.

He puts it down and looks at her.

"Three-hundred a month, you say?"

Marcia nods excitedly. "Yes. I know it's a lot, but it's beachside. Right across the street. When you open the window like this, you can hear the waves. Doesn't get any closer to the ocean for this price."

"I went down to the beach when I got here. It looks very nice."

"You're not from around here, are you?"

The man turns away from her and doesn't answer.

"Do you have a car? I didn't see one in the driveway," she says.

"I didn't bring one."

"You don't have a car? All right. Neither do I," she says with a rough laugh. "You don't need it much around here. You can bike everywhere. The path outside of this window leads right to downtown Cocoa Beach. If you continue, it will lead you all the way to Cape Canaveral. Where do you work? At least tell me you have a job. You're not one of those losers who moves in and never pays the rent, right? The types I can't get rid of? Is that why you don't have a car, because you don't have any money?"

Harry turns to her with a smile. Even through her daze, she can see that he is different. He is not dressed like the typical no-good surfer type. He is wearing nice pants and shoes and his white T-shirt is tucked neatly in his pants. His hair is cut short and he is freshly shaved. He is quite the looker.

"I work from home. I don't need a car."

"Ah. I see."

"And the price includes everything?"

"Water, electricity and feel free to use the kitchen downstairs as often as you need to. And don't mind the kids. They're a wild bunch, but they mean well," she says with a nervous laugh. She knows four noisy kids can be a bit much for a neat guy like Harry. Especially if he needs quiet time for working. Well, that's not her problem. As long as he pays the rent on time.

"I'll take it," he says.
Yes!

October 2005

THE AUDITORIUM at UCF is packed. Daniel manages to squeeze himself into the back row just as the doors are closed. He stands behind a man taller than him, so he can barely see the woman whom he has wanted desperately to hear for months, ever since he watched her Oscar-nominated documentary. The film describes a non-verbal girl with disabilities and an IQ of only thirty-two, who learns how to type and use facilitated communication, and somehow manages to put herself through college. The documentary has taken Daniel completely by storm, and the girl in the movie reminds him so much of his brother Peter, he can hardly believe it. Since he watched it, Daniel has read everything he can find that Kristin Martin has written, and he is stunned to realize that there actually is someone else who believes there can be more to his brother's world.

After the lecture is done, the crowd starts to move for the doors, but Daniel is not moving with them. He has a mission. He has to speak to her, to Kristin Martin. He manages to elbow his way against the moving crowd, and soon he finds himself standing in front of her. She is younger than he expected. And more beautiful. She is speaking to another man before him who wants her to sign his book. She does so, then looks up at Daniel with a smile.

"Hello."

Daniel swallows hard, his throat is suddenly dry, and he can't get the words to leave his lips. She continues to stare at him.

"Do you have a book for me to sign…or?" she asks.

Daniel shakes his head in embarrassment and clears his throat. Finally, he manages to speak. "No. No. I…I'm here on behalf of my brother."

"Your brother?"

"Yes. He has Cerebral Palsy. Never spoke a word in his life. I think he can. I think he desperately wants to. I think he is trapped in his body and that he could speak if only given the right tools. Do you think he could be able to use a keyboard like Maggie in your movie?"

Kristin Martin's smile widens. It makes Daniel feel comfortable. She has kind eyes and doesn't seem to want to reject him.

"Cerebral Palsy, you say?"

"Severe. Developed in early childhood and is getting worse still. His spasms prevent him from walking or even holding utensils. He can't do anything on his own. And he has never spoken a word. But I think…I mean with this…like that girl in the movie. I believe…if only someone gave him a chance. Somehow…I have seen it in his eyes, Miss Martin…I…I don't know much of how this works, but I do know I'll do anything for my brother. When I look into those eyes…I…I am sure I have seen him react. There's a want in there, a longing. He wants to speak."

Daniel stops himself to catch his breath. He is too agitated now; talking about Peter will do that to him. He wants Kristin Martin to believe in Peter like he does; he wants it more than anything in this world.

"Do you think using this keyboard could help him?" he finally asks.

She nods. A sigh of relief goes through his body.

"I don't see why not," she says. "Give it a try."

The woman reaches into her pocket and pulls out a business card. "Here. Give me a call next week. I think I might like to take a look at him. I have never had a patient with Cerebral Palsy before. Could be interesting."

She hands him the card and their eyes lock for a few seconds before someone from the university pulls her away from him and she is engaged in a new conversation. Daniel stares at the card in his hand and can't seem to hold it still.

As he leaves the university, he is filled with a hope and belief in the future for his brother, unlike anything he has ever had before.

I'm gonna hear what you have to say, baby brother. Don't you worry. You'll finally get your voice.

January 2016

My things are in boxes everywhere in Joey's house and it is all a mess. I can't find anything. I don't want to unpack either. We haven't really talked about our situation and if we are ready to move back in together or not. And, to be frank, I am not that thrilled about living here in this small townhouse that he has rented. There isn't enough room for all of us. I don't really know what he wants yet, and so far I am planning on moving back in with my dad once the house is done. He needs my help. I don't know how much my stepmom Laura is going to be there for him. So far, she is still staying at the Hilton using my dad's money and only stops by a few times a week to visit him. My dad keeps making excuses for her and tells me she has to get over the shock first, that she'll come around soon, just wait and see.

It's been three months.

Joey has given me a corner of the living room where I have put up my desk and I call it my office. I have started writing the blog and Chloe is doing the design and all the practical stuff that I know nothing about.

I started out three months ago writing the story about how I was fired from the *New York Times* because I wrote the wrong story, and to my huge surprise, the thing went viral. The next day, I had twenty thousand followers on the blog and even more on Twitter and Facebook. A few weeks later, I had a million. Now I am closer to four million. It has grown faster than I could have ever imagined, and I have to admit, I feel a little intimidated. My next story about the serial killer roaming the streets of Cocoa Beach killing off old high school friends after they mutilated her went crazy viral. Newspapers and magazines all over the world picked it up, and I was quoted everywhere. Later, I wrote about how a general from the air force base had taken in a fugitive, wanted for murder, and changed her name, her identity, and hidden her when she was supposed to face justice for killing a woman, my mother. That was an article people liked. I wrote it with a personal touch and it received more comments and shares that any of the others. Next thing, Chloe tells me some companies want to sponsor my site, and it is suddenly crawling with ads, and I am making money. I can hardly believe it myself, but that's what happened. Now, Chloe wants me to start making video clips with interviews or me trying to get a comment from some of the bad guys I write about, and small video blogs for my fans where I tell them what I am working on. It's kind of taking over my life, and I'm trying hard to keep it down. Chloe, on the other hand, is all over it. I am so lucky to have her helping me. She has given me a few stories about online child porn-sites and how bigger companies fund them, especially the gun-industry, that I have published as well, causing the companies to pull back their funding in fear of bad publicity. In that sense, we try to help out each other, trying to make the world a better place, one story at a time. That's actually our motto.

Today, I start working on the story of my brother and how he fooled all of us and is still on the run, wanted for murder. I have wanted to write the story from a personal perspective for a long time, but every time I sit down to write it, I just can't get the words onto the paper. It hurts so badly. I can't stand the thought that it was my fault. That I was so naïve, that I believed him. I was the one who got him out of jail, and then when I realized what I had done and tried to stop him, he poured acid over my best friend and mutilated her for life.

Just thinking about it again makes me want to throw up. I stare at the blank page in front of me and suddenly get the urge for chocolate. I find a Snickers in my drawer and pull off the wrapping. Eating it makes me calmer, but I still feel awful. I keep seeing Sandra's face when I dropped her off at her house after our break-fast, and I feel terrible. I open the drawer and look for more choco-late. The dogs and the pig are being noisy, running around the house again. I go through the drawer, but find nothing more. I get up and walk to Joey's kitchen and start start to open all the cabinets. I feel like a drug addict looking for her next fix. Finally, I find some of Salter's Oreos and start to gulp them down one after another, while the dogs bark at Bonnie, who once again has outsmarted them, and runs into the yard with the ball in her mouth. I look at myself in the mirror while eating another cookie.

How am I supposed to write this story without gaining fifty pounds?

10

January 2016

AFTER FINISHING the pack of Oreos, I turn on the TV, while the white computer screen with the blank page is staring at me, almost mocking me. I try to ignore it, thinking a little distraction might help my inspiration. I fall into an old episode of *Friends* and watch that till it ends. I am in the mood for popcorn all of a sudden, so I walk back to the kitchen and microwave a bag while a new show rolls over the screen. It's one of those crime shows with unsolved crimes from real life.

I love those, so I hurry back to the couch as soon as the popcorn is done. My dad is sleeping, but he is usually a heavy sleeper, so I turn up the volume to better indulge in the story they're unfolding. I tell myself it's okay to take a little break. After a few minutes, I realize I know the story. I watched the video clip they're showing a thousand times, over and over again, several years ago when it was all over the news back in 2010.

It's the story of the Elingston family. The footage taken by a neighbor's surveillance camera outside their mansion on South Merritt Island shows a person in a dark hooded sweatshirt leaving the house seconds before it bursts into flames. The last part always makes me jump. Knowing the family, and especially the children, are still in there, bound together, after what the police believe to be almost twenty-four hours of being held captive by the suspect, maybe by several of them. They still don't know much about the circumstances, the reporter says. All they have is the footage of the person in the hoodie and a missing Porsche owned by the family. It is believed the intruder escaped in that car, which was later found in the Indian River.

An old picture of the couple at a banquet comes up on the

screen, while the reporter tells of the couple in their mid-fifties and their two children that were found dead in their two-million-dollar home. It is believed that gasoline was poured over their bodies before the fire was set. All four were found in the remains of the living room, all close together. Investigators found no signs of forced entry and believe the suspect or suspects were able to gain access to the Elingston home and stayed overnight. It is believed that they must have known the family, as they seemed to know how they lived their day-to-day-lives.

The next pictures are of the children. I forget all about the popcorn as I watch the old photos and listen to the reporter talk about how young Jack Jr. Elingston loved to play baseball and had a game on the Saturday they were held captive that he never showed up to and that had the teammates and the trainer concerned. A small clip follows from one of his Little League games, then a quote from the trainer, stating it was odd that he didn't come, since Jack Jr. was always there at the games.

Next, we see a school photo of Kimmie Elingston, the oldest child. We hear about her success on the school's debate team, how she was a straight A-student and wanted to be a vet. Police records show that friends and relatives tried to reach the family on the Sunday morning when they didn't show up at church, just hours before the house was set on fire and the bodies were discovered. It also shows that Mr. Elingston called their housekeeper around noon on Saturday and left a voicemail where he told her not to come in today, since they were all sick and didn't want to infect her.

"He sounded tense and very strange," the housekeeper says in a small statement. She also says she tried to call back to confirm, but no one answered.

The police believe the intruder entered the house on Saturday morning. By late afternoon, Mr. Elingston called the local Papa Johns and ordered two large pizzas first with pepperoni, then changed the order to ham. The pizzas were delivered to the property forty-five minutes later. The delivery boy spoke shortly to Mr. Elingston as he paid him in cash, but didn't noticed anything strange going on at the house.

On the same afternoon, Mr. Elingston also called his accountant and friend of many years and had him withdraw fifty-thousand dollars in cash. The money was later delivered to the house, where Mr. Elingston greeted the accountant at the door and took the money.

"It wasn't unusual," the accountant now says in a new interview. The first one he ever agreed to give. "I worked for the man and knew to do as I was told and never ask questions."

"So, what do you believe he needed fifty-thousand dollars for on a Saturday afternoon?" the reporter asks.

"I…I don't know. As I said. I never asked questions."

"So, you didn't think that something could be wrong?"

The accountant sighs and shakes his head. "I know I should have. But how was I supposed to know? Jack sounded completely normal on the phone."

"So, you didn't think he looked or sounded tense?"

"Jack was always tense. If you ask me if he was more tense than usual, then no. I don't believe he was."

January 2016

"Surf's building. Do you want to go?"

Joey rushes into the house and I turn off the TV in the middle of the accountant's sentence.

"I've watched it over the last hour from your dad's lot while working and I can't stay out anymore. It's getting better by the minute."

I jump up from the couch. "Let me get suited up."

"I'll wax our boards."

I walk to the bedroom and look at all my boxes that are stacked in there with a deep sigh. I know my wetsuit is in there somewhere, but how do I find it? It hasn't been cold enough yet this winter to need it, but today the temperature has dropped below seventy, and that is my limit.

I open a box and start looking, then another, and go through that as well. I look at the clock. I still have two hours before Salter comes home by bus, just enough for a good surf session. If only I could find...

"Found it!" Joey yells from the garage. "It was in one of the boxes out here."

He walks into the house and throws it at me.

"Hurry up. The others are already down there."

We meet them at the crossover at 7th Street. Alex and Danny have both left work early, using some dumb excuse that their bosses know perfectly well is not true. That's how it works in Cocoa Beach. When swell is good, people call in sick or leave early. Everyone does it and it is accepted in most workplaces. That's just the way it is in a community where everyone surfs.

"How's the article coming?" Chloe asks me, as we put on our

leashes. In front of us, the waves are crashing in two feet overhead high sets. I close my eyes and enjoy the sound.

"It's alright," I say.

"Mary," she says, and grabs my arm.

"What?"

"If it's too hard for you, then let me write it for you. It's an important story. Who knows? Maybe someone will read it and help find them."

"Their pictures have been all over the news," I say and look at her.

"The way the world works today, you're more likely to have them listen to you than what is shown in the news. You have a big voice and it's not just in this area. It's all over the country. For all we know, they could be hiding in a different state where they will never see their pictures on the news."

I hadn't thought about it that way. That my article could actually make a difference in finding them, but Chloe is right. It fills me with motivation.

"I'll get at it," I say, and look back out at the waves. A gorgeous one rolls towards us. A surfer catches it. "Later."

Chloe laughs. Danny grabs his board under his arm. "Shall we?"

Joey, Chloe, and Danny run towards the ocean, while Alex and I walk. Alex turns to look at me before we hit the water.

"Where is Marcia?" he asks.

I shrug. "Joey tried, but couldn't get ahold of her."

Our eyes meet. We don't have to say anything. We both know it. Marcia isn't doing well.

"Has anyone seen her this week?" I ask, concerned.

He shakes his head. "I met her last week in Publix."

"Was she…?"

"Wasted? Oh, yeah. I don't think I've seen her not wasted in the past three or four months."

"It's that bad, huh?"

"I think it's getting worse. She's hanging out with all the homeless people down by Coconuts or at the Sportsbar."

"I thought she was in AA?" I ask.

"She was. She had to. It was court-ordered after her DUI, but I don't think she's actually following the program. Well, I know she isn't because every time I see her she's drunk."

We walk in silence and our feet hit the water.

"Have you heard from Sandra today?" Alex asks.

"I took her to breakfast."

"Wow. You actually got her to go outside? That's great. I've tried for days to just get her to take a walk on the beach with me."

"I know," I say.

"How was she?"

"So-so."

"I went to see her yesterday," Alex says. "I feel bad that she can't surf. Missing out on this swell must be killing her. They're just her type of waves; look at them."

"I know. It must be killing her. But she'll be able to surf once the doctor says it's okay."

"Maybe I'll stop by after we've surfed, and ask her again if she'll walk with me on the beach," he says, jumps up on his board, and starts paddling.

I follow in his tail. The others are already out in the back. I regret having eaten so much today. It makes me feel heavy. I promise myself to cut back.

Tomorrow.

12

January 2016

MARCIA WAKES UP WITH A GASP. She looks around. Where is she? She is outside somewhere. She sits up and realizes she's on a bench at the bus stop outside of Publix. How did she get here? She never takes the bus.

Where is my bike?

Marcia has a bad headache and she is shaking all over. Is it because of the alcohol or maybe because she is sobering up? Or is it the dream that is still lingering with her? She can still hear the screams as she sits up on the bench. Those screams that she keeps hearing again and again. It doesn't matter if she is awake or asleep anymore. She doesn't know if she is losing it or what is going on, but she is afraid she might be.

Those images. Those awful images of screaming faces, people in pain. They haunt her still as she gets up and starts walking in the hope she might find her bike somewhere.

But you know they're real, don't you? You know they are.

"No!" she says out loud, to silence that annoying voice in her mind always nagging at her, lying to her. "You're not real."

Marcia starts walking faster when she realizes it is late in the afternoon. The kids have to be home by now. She'll have to look for her bike later. Marcia starts running down A1A. Soon, she is wheezing to catch her breath and has to stop. She really should stop smoking. And drinking. But how can she? It's all she has. It's all that keeps those awful images and voices away.

She can't run anymore and has to walk the rest of the way. She sticks her hand out and tries to catch a ride, but no one stops. They never do anymore. They used to. In Cocoa Beach everyone used to hitchhike. But now people don't dare to pick up anyone anymore.

Fear has destroyed everything. Even our little paradise.

Marcia's head is aching badly now. And so is her arm. She pulls up her sleeve and realizes she is hurt. Badly. A long wound stretches from her shoulder to her elbow. Like she has been cut with a knife. It's not deep, though.

It's probably nothing. You probably just fell while drunk like usual. Ripped your arm.

Marcia is used to waking up with strange bruises on her body and not knowing how they happened. The blackouts are getting more and more frequent, though, and it concerns her. It's not a comfortable feeling to not know where you've been or what you've done.

She reaches the townhouse just before sunset and enters the front door.

"Mom!" one of the kids exclaims. "What happened to your arm?"

"Where have you been?" another one asks.

Too many questions, Marcia thinks and avoids looking at them.

She storms past them into the bedroom, where she takes off her bloody shirt. The wound is still bleeding and she tries to wipe it off. She doesn't care if it leaves a scar. As long as she doesn't have to go to a clinic and have to pay for that. Not now that she is finally on top.

What have you done? You don't even know, do you? You have no idea where you've been. Aren't you ashamed of yourself? You should be.

Marcia throws a glance at herself in the mirror. It's been a long time since she recognized her own reflection. She gave up on herself a long time ago. Now all she can think of is when and how to get drunk again so she won't feel the pain or hear the screams.

There's a knock on the door and her daughter Rose sticks her head in. Her beautiful, strong daughter. Is she really twelve already?

"Mom?" she asks carefully.

Embarrassed that she should see her like this, Marcia growls at her, "Give me some privacy!"

The girl's eyes water. "But…but I just…"

"I know! You want food, right? I can never get a moment alone. I'll be out and feed you birds in a minute, all right?"

"I…I just wanted to tell you we already called for pizza, that's all. We had a coupon for a free pizza," she says, then slams the door behind her.

Marcia looks at the closed door, tears welling up in her eyes. She wipes them off, telling herself that she's an idiot before she bends over and opens the bottom drawer in her dresser. She pulls out an emergency bottle of gin and places it to her lips. She doesn't remove it until it is empty.

13

January 2016

MY ARMS ARE SO sore I can hardly lift my fork to eat dinner. After we had surfed for two hours, Joey went to get Salter at the bus. He then brought him out to us, and we continued for two more hours before we finally had to cave in to the hunger and pain in our bodies. There is nothing like dinner after an afternoon of surfing. I have the biggest appetite in the world and we're all shoveling in our take-out from Cocoa Beach Thai and Sushi, while discussing who had the greatest ride.

"Did you see my turn off the lip on that last wave, Mom?" Salter asks. "Did you?"

"Of course I saw it," I lie. I saw most of his waves, but that one I missed.

Salter takes his plate out and takes the dogs for a walk. Bonnie stares disappointed at the door as he leaves with the dogs on their leashes. She is not allowed to be walked in the streets, the police have informed Joey. So, she stays at the house. I pour her some milk in her bowl. She doesn't even notice. She stands by the door and stares at it, like she is waiting for it to open and the dogs to come back. It's like she is completely lost.

"That's cute," I say with a chuckle.

Joey looks up at me. "What is?"

"The pig. I love how she can't live without the dogs."

"Yeah. It used to be only Clyde that she couldn't do without, but lately it seems that Snowflake has taken an even bigger place in her life. We might even be looking at real love here. Just sayin'."

I laugh and Joey springs for the refrigerator, where he grabs two beers. He hands me one and takes the other himself. He walks up to me and kisses me. I close my eyes and enjoy it. He pulls his chair up next to mine and we sit close for a little while without saying anything.

"I was thinking I would put up a TV in your dad's room. Give him something to do when he's in there all day. I kind of feel bad for him."

"That would be awesome. Thank you. That's very thoughtful of you," I say. "Say, have you seen Marcia lately?"

He drinks from his beer, then shakes his head. "Nope. Not for several weeks I believe. Why?"

"I don't know. I have a feeling she's not doing so well. I'm just worried, that's all."

"Well she has been hitting the bottle pretty hard the last couple of months."

"I just wonder if there's anything we can do for her. I mean, can't we help her? What about the children? Is she even capable of taking care of them? I really don't like it."

Joey nods pensively. "I know. Maybe we should check in on them tomorrow? Maybe stop by in the afternoon when they're home from school and make sure they're alright?"

"I think that would be a very good idea."

My dad calls for me and I walk into his room. He looks at me and asks me to close the window, since it's getting too cold now. I lift him up and fluff his pillow to make it more comfortable for him. He smells nice, since the nurse was here earlier and gave him a bath. She was worried about some pressure sores he was getting on the lower part of his back. They looked like they might be getting infected, she told me just before she left.

"Are you ready for your dinner?" I ask.

"Not really," he says with a sniffle. "I'm not...hungry."

"You've got to eat, Dad. You haven't eaten anything all day. You've got to get some energy or you'll never get better."

His facial expression tells me I said something wrong. "What's wrong, Dad?"

He shakes his head. "Don't you realize...I am never going to get...better? I can't...feel anything. I am a...vegetable. I hate being such...a burden to you all."

"Don't say that, Dad. You know you can get better. The doctor said it's possible. A lot can happen with physical therapy. You can't give up hope, Dad. You can't."

He shakes his head in disbelief. "I don't want...to be chained to...a bed for the rest of my...life. I don't want to lie here and watch as my body...deteriorates in front of me and not...be able to do anything about it. I would rather...be dead."

I bite my lip in frustration. I want so badly to do something to help him, but I can't. Just like Sandra, I can't heal him; I can't make all of this go away, no matter how much I desperately want to.

"I'll make you some soup," I say, my voice breaking. "All right, Daddy? Dad?"

"Laura was here earlier," he suddenly says. "She…stopped by."

"That's nice. Weren't you happy to see her?"

He exhales. It isn't a good sound. "She's…leaving."

My heart stops. Literally.

She is what?

"Excuse me?"

"She's leaving. Tomorrow…she'll be driving back to Orlando… where she grew up. She is moving in…with her brother." My dad pauses and catches his breath. I can tell he is struggling to find the words. "Says she can't handle…seeing me like this, that she too needs a life and…and…and that it can't stop here. I…I can't blame her. I can't…offer her anything anymore. I don't…want her to… waste her life here…here with me."

I stare at my dad, not knowing what to say. I feel all kinds of anger flushing through my body. There is so much I want to say, but I don't. I can tell my dad is hiding how broken he really is over this.

"I'll make you that soup," I say, and walk out the door.

In the kitchen, I cover my face and cry. Joey is watching TV when Salter comes back home with the dogs, much to Bonnie's joy. The animals reconnect like they haven't seen each other for years, and soon they're back to playing with the ball again, the dogs chasing after Bonnie.

"What's wrong, Mom?" Salter asks, as he hangs the leashes up and takes off his shoes.

I wipe my eyes and force a smile. "Nothing, sweetie. I was just making soup for Grandpa."

"He's eating? That's great."

"I know. It's good."

Salter walks to his dad and sits on the couch with him. The news is talking about how the police still have no clue who killed a fifty-seven year-old woman whose body was pulled out of Indian River two weeks ago, just two days before Christmas Eve. I sit with my family while the microwave is heating the soup that I ordered for my dad from the Thai-place. I am not listening to the TV. I am thinking about Laura. I can't believe anyone could act like this. How you can pretend you love someone and then just leave them in their biggest hour of need? So what if my dad can't offer her anything. Maybe it is her turn to offer something. Maybe it is her turn to take care of him; maybe he needs her and not the other way around. Isn't that what love is all about? Isn't it all about sacrifice?

I look at Salter and Joey, while thinking how happy I am that I made the decision to stay here and to give Joey a second chance. My dad's house is supposed to be done in a month, if everything goes according to schedule—which it probably won't—but I still have to decide at some point what to do next. Should Salter and I move with my dad so we can help him, or should we stay here with Joey and be a family?

I know in my heart what I want the most, but I also know my dad needs me more than ever now. I can't just think about myself.

14

January 2016

"MOM. I HEARD A LOUD BANG."

Kelly blinks her eyes in the darkness. She can only see the outline of her daughter as she is standing by the foot of their bed. Kelly sighs, still half a sleep. Next to her, her husband, Andrew grumbles sleepily.

"What's wrong, honey? What are you doing out of bed?"

"I heard a loud noise. It woke me up and now I'm scared."

As she is speaking, their Beagle, Max, jumps into their bed. Max usually sleeps with their daughter. He runs to Kelly and starts licking her face. Kelly groans. She is so tired. It's still pitch dark outside.

"Just go back to bed, Lindsey. It's probably nothing."

"It was really loud, Mommy. I'm afraid that someone came into our house. I'm scared."

Andrew groans. He looks at his phone. "We still have three hours till we have to get up. Please just let us sleep a little longer."

"Go back to bed, sweetie," Kelly says. "I'm sure it was just a dream."

"But there was a loud noise, Mommy," the girl insists. "And now the light is on in the living room."

Kelly opens her eyes now. She sits up straight and looks at her daughter. She can barely see her in the darkness. "The light is on in the living room?"

"We probably just forgot to shut it off last night," Andrew says. "Lights don't just turn on and off on their own."

"Maybe we should check it," Kelly says.

Andrew groans ostentatiously. He knows where this is going.

"Would it make you feel better if Daddy checked it out, sweetie?" Kelly says.

"Yes," the girl says with a slight whimper.

"Okay. Come up here on the bed and lie down while Daddy checks it out."

"Seriously?" Andrew says.

"Just do it for her sake," Kelly says. "To give her peace of mind."

Andrew exhales deeply, then sits up. "You do realize I have an important breakfast meeting, right?"

"Yes. I know perfectly well about your meeting, but this is the only way we can get some sleep. So, if you would please…?"

"All right," he grumbles and pulls off the covers. He plants his feet on the carpet. The bed moves when he lifts himself off it. Andrew is no lightweight. Not like he was when Kelly met him. In a brief second, she misses those years.

Andrew leaves, and Kelly pulls her daughter closer. She kisses her forehead and holds her tight. "Shh. It's probably nothing, sweetie. You can sleep here. Just close your eyes. Daddy will take care of it."

Their daughter finally relaxes and closes her eyes. Kelly caresses her hair, while wondering if she will be able to fall asleep again. Their daughter has been known to sleepwalk from time to time, and Kelly now wonders if Lindsey dreamt she heard a bang, then walked into the living room and turned on the lights. Kelly chuckles to herself. That is probably what happened. Lindsey did and said the strangest things when sleepwalking. One morning they had found her in the living room, sitting on the couch, with all the lights turned on, sleeping with her eyes open. It had scared Kelly like crazy, until she realized the girl was just asleep. This was probably just another one of her stunts.

Lindsey is sleeping now and Kelly puts her head on the pillow next to her daughter. She likes to listen to her heavy breathing. Such peace.

Must be nice, she thinks to herself. *To be able to just let go of all your worries like that and enter that deep of a sleep.*

Kelly can't remember when she had last had a good and worry-free night of sleep. Not since she had her child probably. She wonders if she will ever stop feeling that anxiety deep in her heart, that deep worry that soon all of her happiness will be ripped out of her embrace, that it was all just a joke life played on her, a vicious game to make her allow herself to be happy, and then in an instant when she is not worrying or being aware it'll all be ripped from her. After all, she has everything. Finally, after many years of trying and waiting for a child, she has one. She has a beautiful family, a big house, four cars in the garage, money enough to last her a lifetime. Is she really allowed to have all this? Is anyone?

"I've checked the entire house. There's nothing."

Andrew closes the bedroom door behind him and turns off the flashlight. "Now, maybe we can finally get some sleep?"

15

October 2005

KRISTIN MARTIN'S office is a mess. The room has high wooden ceilings, and books cover the walls from top to bottom. There are piles of newspapers and magazines. Clipped out articles cover her desk. It is just as Daniel has imagined it. The absent-minded professor in her right element.

"Ah, Daniel, come on in," she says, looking up from behind her desk. She takes off her glasses and gets up.

Daniel pushes Peter in his wheelchair in front of him. Kristin walks towards him with a big smile on her face. She looks at Peter and bends down.

"And this...I take it, must be...Peter. It's a pleasure to meet you Peter," she says, and touches his hand. Peter doesn't react.

It's rare that people talk directly to his brother, and it warms Daniel's heart. Kristin looks directly into his eyes while talking to him.

"I am so glad you are here, Peter."

Daniel feels a tug at his heart. For so many years, he has dreamt of finding someone like Kristin. His family doesn't know he has brought him there to see her, since they would only tell him it is a waste of time. He wants to give Kristin a chance; he wants it to work before he presents it to the rest of the family.

"Let's get started, shall we?" Kristin says, still addressing Peter. It's like she actually believes he understands what she is saying. Daniel is usually the only one who talks to Peter this way.

"If you will bring him over here. I have prepared a little game for us. Just to get to know each other a little bit, alright?"

Daniel nods, but she isn't looking for his approval. She is looking into Peter's eyes, waiting to see his reaction.

"Alright," she says again, after Daniel has placed Peter where she wants him. On the table in front of him, she places a series of pictures and index cards.

"Let's do this. Are you ready? In what room would you find the refrigerator?" she asks, laying out a card showing a bedroom, a bathroom, and a kitchen. "Please, don't be offended by this," she adds. "I am sure these questions are very easy for you."

Kristin looks at Peter like she is waiting for his response, waiting for him to talk or point at one of the pictures.

"He can't..." Daniel interrupts, thinking Kristin doesn't understand how bad Peter's condition really is. "He can't do that."

Kristin pays no attention to Daniel. She puts a hand in the air to stop him from talking. Daniel is afraid that he might have made a mistake. This woman knows nothing about treating patients with Cerebral Palsy. He should have known better. Daniel feels his heart drop as the last hope threatens to leave him.

"Wait," Kristin says with a slow voice. "Did you see that?"

"See what?" Daniel asks.

"He is trying to communicate."

Daniel shakes his head. "He's not doing anything."

"Yes. Yes, he is. You're just not seeing it."

"Those are just spasms," he says, disappointed. "He has those constantly."

"In my eyes, it looks like he is trying to move his arm. His eyes are focused on the picture over here, the one of the kitchen, but when he tries to move his arm, it's like it...it locks, like it shuts up like...like a rabbit trap. It snaps back against his face."

A rabbit trap? This was a mistake.

"So, you think he's trying to answer?" Daniel asks skeptically.

"Yes. I've read about this. They helped a girl in Australia using this new technique. Here, let me."

Kristin places her hand beneath Peter's elbow. "This is to stabilize his arm," she explains to Daniel. "This is what they did to the girl in Australia and had great success with it. I think this might help. This way, I help to keep his arm balanced. I need to be acting as a responsive item of furniture, not moving his arm, but simply facilitating his own movement. Now, Peter, if you would point to the picture of the kitchen, please."

Daniel is holding his breath while watching his brother suddenly move his arm towards the picture. Kristin now uses her other hand to tuck Peter's pinkie, ring and middle finger lightly under hers, spooning their hands, with just his index finger sticking out.

"Great, Peter. Now point to the picture of the ocean, please."

Slowly, but steadily, the arm moves while Kristin is assisting it towards the photograph of an ocean. Daniel doesn't know what to say.

"And now for the hard one," Kristin says, and puts out three pictures. "Please point to the picture of the President of the United States."

"He doesn't have any chance of knowing who is..." Daniel starts, but stops himself when Peter's arm starts to move. It stops and points to the picture of George W. Bush.

Daniel is still speechless when Kristin smiles and looks up at him. Her eyes are sparkling with joy. Daniel thinks it makes her look stunning. He feels such a close connection to her in this instant. So many years he has been alone with this, thinking there was a way for Peter to express himself. Could it be? Could it really be true? Daniel is watching it happen and he is overwhelmed with the belief that it is in fact true. He wants to believe it, he has to.

"See! You did see it, didn't you?"

Daniel nods while biting his lips. He doesn't know whether to cry or laugh. Does his baby brother really know who the president is? What else does he know?

Excitedly, Kristin is now pulling out index cards with letters on them, and one after another, Peter identifies the letters.

"He even knows the alphabet!" Kristin exclaims, as they go through all the letters, and seconds later she asks him to put together words, and he does. Daniel holds his breath while Peter spells his first word, by pointing at the letters and Kristin writing them down. Soon an entire sentence emerges.

"I...am...hungry," Kristin reads out loud. She looks up at Daniel. "He just spelled *I am hungry*. Daniel, your brother's first sentence, the first thing he ever told you is that he is hungry. Isn't that wonderful? He *is* smart. Peter is smart! He does communicate. We just have to learn how to listen."

She looks back into Peter's eyes while Daniel's eyes fill with tears. He can't wait to tell his mother and siblings. Now they have to believe him.

"I believe I can teach you to speak, Peter," Kristin says. "Not with your mouth, but with your hands. It's about time your family hears what you have to say."

16

January 2016

I WORK on the article for the next several days and manage to write something that I end up trashing by the weekend. On Friday night, we decide to put on a movie for all of us to see. We even roll my dad's bed into the living room, so he can join us. We rent the new *Mission Impossible* and I make the popcorn and find the candy. I feed my dad while we watch it. Salter is allowed to stay up late. It's not something I let him do often, since he doesn't do well with not getting his sleep. Halfway through the movie, I look at Joey, and realize he is not watching. He's on his phone.

"Tom Cruise just died and you missed it because you were texting," I say and poke him with my elbow.

"Sorry," he says, and puts the phone away.

A few minutes pass, but I'm not watching the movie anymore. Something in his expression worries me. I know it is silly, but I have to ask. So, I do it as casually as I know how to.

"So, who was it?" I ask without looking at him. I pretend to watch the movie.

"Nobody," he says.

Not the answer I am looking for.

"You mean it's nobody that I know?" I ask, still looking at the screen.

Salter is hushing me now. I feed my dad a cookie. He enjoys it. One of the few joys he has these days. I can feel my heart is beating faster and it annoys me immensely. I recognize this feeling from back when we lived in New York. Back when I found out about him and that girl from the coffeehouse. It's the awful feeling that your beloved is hiding something from you. After this many years together, you just know something is off. And then comes the feeling of guilt for thinking like this. Because, what if you're wrong? What if it really was nobody?

But it is somebody. You saw the look in his eyes. He is hiding something. He doesn't want you to know who it was.

Oh, my. I can sense how the paranoia is running away with me now and I don't like it. I am not paying any attention to the movie anymore, especially not when Joey's phone vibrates again and he picks it up. I pretend not to notice he is reading something, and soon after, answering it. It makes my blood boil. I have no idea what to do. Should I ask again? I don't want to be this obsessive woman who wants to know and control everything he does, but I can't stop thinking about it. No matter what I do, I am screwed. If I don't say anything, I'll be wondering about this all night, and Joey will sense it and think I'm mad. I'll tell him I am not angry, and he'll just be annoyed with me because he can feel that I am. If I do say something, he'll get angry and think I am possessive and that I don't trust him. Which, I don't. To be perfectly honest, I don't. He did it before and, yes, I know the circumstances were different; he was in a terrible place, he was bored and feeling left out of my life. I know it was different, but still. What if? Why does there always have to be a *what if?*

Out of the corner of my eye, I watch as Joey finishes the text and puts the phone away. I try not to think about it anymore and feed my dad another cookie, while eating one myself. Soon, I can't stop. I have eaten four, five cookies. I had promised myself no sweets tonight, but now I can't stop. It's like I am trying to stuff my emotions back into my body by putting food on top of them. Like I am pressing my tears back with cookies. It makes me feel slightly better, but only for a few minutes.

"That is so cool!" Salter exclaims. "Did you see that, Mom?" he looks at me and I blush because I have no idea what happened in the movie. I nod.

"Pretty cool, huh?"

"You know that Tom Cruise does all of his stunts himself, right?" Salter says. "I think that is awesome."

"That is awesome," I say, and look at Joey. I swallow the lump in my throat. Joey smiles at me.

"Come here," he says, and pulls me closer. He starts to kiss me on the neck and nibble my ear.

I sigh and try to enjoy it, while Tom Cruise jumps on a motorcycle.

"I was wondering when he would do that," Joey says.

"Do what?" I ask absent-mindedly. I keep thinking about his phone and wondering if I can somehow get to look at it without him noticing it. I feel so silly for thinking like this, but if it is just an old friend he is texting, if it is just nobody, then it would certainly comfort me knowing so.

"The bike. I was wondering when he would ride one. He always does at some point."

"Ah, I see. Well, I don't think he rode one in *Edge of Tomorrow*," I say.

"Yes, he totally did," Joey says.

"I don't think he did," I repeat.

"Well, he did."

"Wanna bet?" I ask.

"Sure. You do the dishes the next two days if I'm right," he says. "And you give me a massage before bedtime."

"That's a lot," I say. "If I win, you do the same for me."

We shake hands on it, and as we let go, I put out my hand. "Give me your phone. I'll check it."

"Why don't you use your own?" Joey complains.

"My phone is in the kitchen, charging. I'll miss out on the movie."

"We can stop the movie."

"Come on. I don't want to have to get up," I say. "Just give me yours and I'll check it."

Joey looks at me like he doesn't want to. It makes it even harder on me. "What? Are you afraid I'll win?"

He chuckles and shakes his head. "I'll do it," he says, and takes out the phone.

Damn it. He didn't fall for it. And here I thought I was being so clever.

"We'll do it together," I say and crawl up next to him, so I can look at what he is doing.

He opens the Internet and starts the search. It doesn't take him long to find something about Tom Cruise and the movies he rides a bike in. As he opens the link, he receives a text again. I see it on the top of his phone. I can't see what it says, but I do manage to see that the name of the sender is Jack.

"You got a text," I say. "Don't you want to read it?"

"Nah. It's not important. Just some work I might get."

"That is important. Are you kidding me? That's great."

He shrugs. "You know how it is. I'm not celebrating till I'm sure I have it. Too many times I've been disappointed."

"I understand," I say, but feel like celebrating myself. I was just a fool for being suspicious. Never have I felt so relieved. For once, I did the right thing in not making an issue out of it. Jack is just some guy Joey knows, and it is probably just about work. Joey was right. It is just a nobody.

17

January 2016

"WHO ARE YOU? What are you doing in my house?"

Marcia is staring at the man in front of her. Her nostrils are flaring. Her blood is rushing through her veins. In her hand, she is holding a kitchen knife. The kids are all out, except the youngest, Tim, who is sitting on the couch coloring in a book. She's wondering if she will be able to protect him if this intruder tries to grab him.

"Get out!"

The man in her kitchen shakes his head. "But…"

Marcia is swinging the knife in front of her. "I swear, I'll hurt you. Don't come any closer!"

The man looks startled, almost desperate. "Don't you recognize me? I'm your renter. Harry Hanson? I moved in almost a week ago?"

Marcia stares at the man. She is baffled. What is this? A joke? "Renter?" she says.

"Yes. I live in the room upstairs. You told me I could stay there and use the kitchen when I needed to."

Marcia's pulse lowers.

A renter? I have a renter? How is this possible?

"But…I just put the ad in yesterday," she says. She lowers the knife a little, then pulls it back up with a grunt. "Is this a trick? You're not fooling me."

"No! It's not a trick! I paid you three hundred dollars. All my stuff is upstairs. I'm beginning to think you're the one trying to trick me."

"Don't turn this around on me," Marcia says. "You're just trying to confuse me and trick me. What do you want from me? I don't have any money, if that's what you think."

"I don't want your money. I just came down to make myself a cup of coffee," the man says, and shows her a jar of Nescafé in his hand. "I brought my own coffee, if you're afraid I'll take yours."

"It's true, Mom," Tim yells from the couch. "Don't you recognize Harry? He made us lasagna yesterday when you didn't come home for dinner."

Marcia looks at the boy, then back at the man. "But yesterday we went to Beef O' Brady's. Kids eat free on Tuesdays. You had chicken wings, remember? You spilled on your white shirt?" she says.

"It's Saturday today," Harry says.

"Yeah. That was last week, Mom," Tim says.

Marcia feels dizzy and stumbles backward. She sits on a chair and puts the knife down. "It was last week? But…but…"

"It's okay, Mom. You're just forgetful." He looks at Harry. "I told you she's forgetful. Sometimes she even forgets to come home."

Marcia looks at her boy. She understands nothing. It's a horrible feeling. What happened? Where has she been? What has she done? She remembers nothing. Not even Harry.

What the hell is happening to me?

She bursts into a loud fit of laughter and points her finger at Harry. "Gotcha. I was just kidding. Of course I remember Harry *Handsome*," she says, and winks at the boy. The boy shrugs.

"It's true," he says, addressed to Harry. "You are kind of handsome." The boy then turns around and returns to his coloring book.

Marcia avoids looking at Harry. She really doesn't remember him at all, and wonders how this could have happened. She turns her back on him and puts on a kettle of water.

"It should be done soon," she says. "I have to…"

Harry steps aside and Marcia hurries to her bedroom and closes the door behind her. Breathing heavily, she goes through her drawers, but finds no bottles. She curses and throws her clothes on the floor angrily. She is so sure she hid a bottle in the bottom drawer. She always has an extra, an emergency bottle. Who took it? Could it be this Harry-figure? There is something about him she doesn't like.

Instead of the bottle, she finds a bottle of pills, and she swallows some quickly and washes them down with an old glass of water from her bedside. She looks at her bed. It doesn't look like anyone slept in it last night. She doesn't remember making it this morning. Did she even sleep here last night?

18

January 2016

I GO to Sandra's and ring the doorbell around noon. I have Snowflake and Clyde with me on leashes, and they are both jumping up and down with excitement. I think they can smell Sandra's dog, Lucky the Chihuahua. She opens with a smile and I am surprised to see her this happy.

"Hey. I was wondering if you would take a walk with me on the beach today? I know Ryan is working at my dad's lot, so I thought you might have some time. We could bring all the dogs and hope the cops don't catch us? What do you say? Let's be daredevils for once."

Lucky is barking on the other side of the door. Snowflake can hear him and gets overly excited. I can hardly hold him. Clyde is barking back.

"I would love to, but I have someone here."

"Oh. Well, that's good. I'm glad you're not alone."

"Sorry to disappoint you, though."

"Nah. Don't worry about it. So who is it? Who's here?"

"Alex. Alex is here." She sounds funny when she says his name.

"Alex? Well I won't disturb, then," I say.

"Oh, you're not disturbing. We were just talking about you, as a matter of fact."

"About me?"

"Well. No. Not really. I don't know why I said that. We were talking about back in the days when you and I were best friends and…and Alex and I were…well, you know," she says with a nervous laugh.

I get a feeling I don't like. "Listen, Sandra," I say with a whisper. "I know that things haven't been easy lately, but this is not the answer. You're both married."

The look in her eyes changes drastically. "What are you imply-ing? Why would you say such a thing?"

"I just don't want to see you make a mistake you'll later regret."

"I...I really don't appreciate this, Mary," she says, and comes out and pulls the door closed behind her. "Alex and I are friends, nothing more. Besides, do you really think he would be interested in me, that anyone would be interested in me now that I look...like this...like this...monster. Do you?"

I feel embarrassed. "I'm sorry, Sandra. I just worry about you, that's all. I don't know what it is about me lately. I seem to think everyone is having an affair. Last night I was certain Joey was texting with some girl, and it turned out to be this guy named Jack. I am sorry...I see ghosts. I guess I'm damaged after what happened to us in New York."

Sandra's eyes calm down as well. "Well, no one could blame you for being suspicious. It must be difficult to trust him again."

"I try, but it really is," I say. "Say, do you want me to take Lucky with me to the beach? He sounds like he would enjoy a good walk and playtime with the others."

"Would you? That would be awesome," Sandra says. "I haven't been out with him much lately, and he really loves the beach. Just don't get him arrested, though," she says with a small laugh.

"I won't," I say. "I'll take his place if needed."

She finds the leash and hands me Lucky. Minutes later, I have crossed the street and am standing with my toes in the sand watching the waves. It's pretty flat today, so no surfing, but that's okay. I am still very sore. As I walk, I wonder once again about Joey and me. I really hate that feeling I had the night before, and I don't want to live a life constantly being afraid of what he is up to. I want to trust him, I really do. But am I able to?

I put my feet in the water and walk the three dogs all the way to Sixteenth Street and back. I enjoy the fresh air and the dogs running playfully around my feet.

When I get back to Sandra's house and walk past the kitchen window, I see them. I stop with a small gasp as I watch Sandra and Alex engaged in a long, deep kiss.

19

January 2016

KELLY IS STANDING in her kitchen. She is looking at the ocean outside her windows. This fall has caused a lot of beach erosion, and the water is coming up closer to the house than usual.

Melbourne Beach. She never did like it much down here. Being from upstate New York, she thinks it's too hot and humid down here in Florida. But her husband loves it, and when they married this was where he wanted to live. This is where he grew up. For his sake, she pretends to enjoy it.

Andrew loves to fish on his boat, and today he has taken their daughter Lindsey with him. Kelly hates it when they go together. She always worries that something will happen to their fragile daughter.

"She's not a strong swimmer," she constantly tells him. She doesn't feel like he understands how delicate their daughter is. She's afraid that Andrew wants her to be the boy he never had, and she can't be. The girl suffers from severe asthma that has destroyed many nights of sleep for them, especially when she was younger.

Kelly feels a chill go through her bones. Not because it's cold, but because she can't stop imagining Lindsey hurting herself on a hook or a spear. She looks out at the raging ocean, while peeling an apple with a small knife in her hand. She is making a fruit salad for herself for lunch. She looks at the phone next to her on the counter, waiting, anticipating it ringing and a voice telling her that something has gone wrong, that her daughter is in the hospital. She goes through all the scenarios in her mind, thinking of all the things that could go wrong. Maybe they didn't even make it to the boat. They could have been in a car accident. What if there's a thunderstorm while they're on the ocean? Even though thunderstorms are rare in January, they do appear sometimes.

Kelly doesn't understand this sudden worry. She's not usually the worrying type. She just can't escape this unease. She has been feeling it ever since that night when Lindsey came to their room and told them she heard a loud noise and that there was a light on in the living room. She knows it's silly, but Kelly can't escape the thought that something bad is about to happen.

Evil forebodings, the Bible calls it. Do not let your heart get worried or troubled. You know it's all in your head, Kelly. Gotta shake it.

The morning after the incident at night, Kelly had realized that their telescope in the back of the living room, by the window, was tipped over. Naturally, Kelly couldn't help wondering if that had caused the loud bang that Lindsey talked about. But who had tipped it over? Lindsey while sleepwalking? That was the logical explanation, but Kelly didn't feel so sure. Why didn't it wake her up? Was she also the one who had turned on the light? And then what? Gone back to bed again? It was possible, but didn't satisfy her.

"What if someone was in our house?" she asked her husband, but he didn't want to hear about it.

"You're seeing ghosts," he simply said, then left for his important meeting with another client whose land he is going to develop into yet another massive area of houses and lucrative condos.

Maybe she was. But, then again, maybe she wasn't. She decided to let it go till two days later when she came home with her groceries, and as she put the key in the lock, she heard a loud noise in the back. She walked inside and realized the door to the porch was wide open. There was sand on the floor in her bedroom, and one of the drawers was open. Nothing was stolen.

"There's always sand on the floor of our house," Andrew argued. "That's what you get from living on the beach. And maybe you just forgot to close the back door; maybe the wind blew it open."

Kelly listened to her husband, but didn't agree. She knows she remembered to close that door. She always does when leaving. And it is no longer just those two incidents that make her uneasy. It's the feeling of being watched. When she goes to the library or the grocery store, she sees the same car. It was even parked outside of the gym this morning when she came out after her spinning-class. It appears to be everywhere she goes.

She noticed it the first time a couple of weeks ago, and since then, she seems to see it everywhere. In the beginning, she thought she was being paranoid. After all, there are a lot of brown trucks, but soon she noticed it had a dent on the right side of it, and now she recognizes it everywhere. She doesn't dare to approach it, at least not yet, but it scares her like crazy.

Kelly shakes the thought and cuts up the apple. She puts it in the bowl with the rest of the fruit, and then starts to eat while her stomach is still in a knot. She closes her eyes and takes in a deep breath to calm herself down.

You have to relax. You can't live like this. Expect good things to happen to you. Life is good.

She looks down at Max, the beagle who is sleeping on the floor. "You're not much of a watchdog, are you? You're more likely to lick any burglar to death should he enter, am I right?"

The dog doesn't even react. That's when the phone on the counter starts to ring, and Kelly looks at it with a loud gasp. The display says it's Andrew.

Please tell me she's all right. Please let nothing have happened to her!

"Hello?" she says, picking it up. She tries hard to sound normal, but her voice is shrill.

"Something happened," Andrew says.

Oh, my God! Please don't. Please don't take my baby from me!

Kelly gasps and clasps her mouth. "What happened, Andrew? Is it Lindsey?"

"Yes," he says. "She…she caught the biggest redfish I have ever seen in my entire life! It's bigger than her!"

Kelly stumbles backwards as Andrew yells the last part and follows up with some loud cheering.

"I am so proud of her!" he continues. "She wanted to tell you, so here she is."

"Mom? Did you hear?"

Kelly slides slowly to the floor, her back against the cabinets, while her heart is pounding in her chest.

"Mom?"

"That's…that's wonderful news, sweetie," she finally says, while relief goes through every muscle in her body. "That's awesome. I am so proud of you."

"Thanks, Mom."

They hang up and Kelly starts to laugh. She sits on the floor, holding the phone in her hand, and simply laughs at her own stupidity. To think that she let herself get carried away with fear like that. It is ridiculous.

You're ridiculous, Kelly. As always, it is nothing. Everything is fine.

Kelly shakes her head while finishing her fruit salad. She puts the bowl in the sink and looks down at the beach, when she spots someone down there. Someone with a set of binoculars pointed straight at her. As she sees them, the person puts the binoculars down and moves on.

20

January 2016

HE IS IN HER HOUSE. Blake is going through the blonde's drawers, looking through her underwear, and decides to keep a pair. He puts it in his pocket before closing the drawer. He looks at the closet and opens it. Rows of her neatly hung dresses appear in front of him. Blake smiles to himself. The blonde sure is a nice dresser. She likes to show off her legs, he has noticed. She does have nice legs, and she makes sure to stay fit. Blake has been watching her as she goes for her run every morning. Usually, he watches her as she runs through the park, but today he decided to go into her house instead. He wants to get close to her, to get to know her, every little detail about her. Why? He doesn't know. All he knows is that he can't stop thinking about her. When lying in bed at night with Olivia by his side at the motel, all he can think of is her, the blonde with the long legs. What it is about her, he can't explain. He just knows he wants her; he wants to be so close to her he can smell her skin. He keeps obsessing about her skin and how it tastes.

Blake is not popular with Olivia these days. She annoys him. All her constant nagging. He had no idea that's what it would be like to be on the run with her. He would never have brought her with him if he had known. She is constantly on his case, telling him he goes out too much, that they'll get caught if he doesn't stay in the motel room. Blake doesn't care. He can't stand it in there anymore. He needs to get out. He needs to see the blonde girl.

Blake smells her dresses one by one, and goes through an old shoebox of her private stuff. Mostly old pictures of the blonde and her friends. Blake laughs when he sees a picture of her from when she was a teenager with braces and big hair.

"Even then you were special, dear. I bet the boys were all over you," he whispers to the photograph, then puts it back in the box.

Blake picks up a postcard from the Philippines. It's from the guy she's dating. He's some army-guy and is away a lot. Reading the words on the card makes Blake's blood boil. He loses his temper and rips it to pieces.

As the pieces fall to the carpet, he hears the front door slam. Blake gasps. He picks up the pieces of the broken postcard, puts the lid back on the shoebox, and puts it back on the shelf, then turns off the light in the closet and closes the door. He hears her steps in the hallway as she gets closer to the bedroom, and seconds later, he watches her through the door as she enters. She is still wearing earplugs and humming to some song. She is sweating and panting from the run and wiping her face on a towel. Blake enjoys watching her. He especially likes those short shorts. She sits on her bed and pulls out her phone. Blake can still hear the music playing in her ears. She is looking at the display on her phone while Blake studies her. His breath comes in ragged bursts. His body is trembling. He has never been this close to her before. He can almost touch her, almost smell her, almost taste the salty sweat on her skin.

The blonde turns off the music and starts to undress. Right there, in front of him, she gets completely naked. Blake can't believe it. He can hardly breathe as he watches her move around the bedroom. She walks to the bathroom and he can hear the shower being turned on before she comes back, grabs her phone and writes something, sitting on the bed all naked.

Blake is holding his breath to not make a sound. He doesn't want to ruin this special moment. This moment that he will cherish for the rest of his life when thinking back on this day.

The girl leaves the phone on the bed, then gets up and walks into the shower. Blake waits for a minute before he makes his move.

Enjoy your shower, gorgeous, he thinks to himself, while watching her silhouette through her shower curtain. *You can run all you want to, but you can never ever hide from me.*

21

January 2016

I KNOCK ON THE WINDOW. Startled, they let go of each other and look at me.

"What the hell are you doing?" I yell.

They stare at each other, then back at me. Embarrassed, Sandra looks down, and then goes for the front door. I walk up to her and hand her the leash.

"Here's your dog. He pooped twice. Now, would you please tell me what the heck is going on? And don't try to make me feel all guilty and embarrassed again. I know what I saw."

"Mary, please. You don't know what it's like…"

"Well, I know what it is like to be on the other side of that. And that isn't funny, I can tell you that much. I really never thought you would be…how…how Sandra, how are you able to do that and live with yourself? How long has this been going on?"

Her eyes are avoiding mine. "Only a few days."

I sigh deeply. "I can't believe you."

"You don't know what it's like to have your husband look at you like you're some monster, Mary. To have him shiver in disgust every time he tries to touch you. You don't know what that is like."

"Alright, I don't. Then, leave him. Divorce him, and then you two can fool around or whatever it is you're doing. But not while you're still married. That's just wrong. No matter what you look like. I feel for you, you know I do, Sandra. But it's still wrong. It's not fair to Ryan."

Sandra looks at me. I can tell she is embarrassed. I grab her shoulder and pull her close in a warm embrace. "I won't tell Ryan. Don't worry," I say. "My loyalty is with you. But you have to sort out your mess."

Sandra promises me she will and I leave her house. I walk back with the dogs to Joey's place. Salter and Joey are engaged in a game on the Xbox and barely notice me. Bonnie grunts delightedly as she sees the dogs again. Snowflake and Clyde are equally happy to see her and get all tangled up in each other's leashes as they run around excitedly wagging their tails and sniffing Bonnie. As I let them all go, they storm towards the couches and jump up on them. Bonnie can't get up there, so she stays on the floor while Clyde and Snowflake play tug-of-war with a brown teddy bear. Joey yells at them, and I decide he can deal with it while I take a shower after the long walk.

When I get back out, the boys are still on the Xbox. I decide to work a little and sit by the computer, going through my notes. The trashed article is still in the trash can next to me and I pull it out and read it. I shake my head. No. Still won't do. Chloe is going to get mad at me. I have never been this long writing anything. She wants me to post on my blog every day, just anything to keep the site active.

"You can't lose momentum," she keeps saying. "Gotta strike while the iron is hot."

So, I decide to make a small video instead. Just to have something. I walk to our bedroom to find a quiet corner, and then turn on the camera on my laptop.

"Ah. This is hard," I say with a deep sigh. "But I am going to try anyway. As some of you might know, my brother is wanted for murder. As far as we know, he has killed one woman here in Cocoa Beach about three months ago. He was arrested for it, but tricked us into believing in his innocence. He fooled me into believing him, and not just me. The whole system. And now he is free again. He is on the run. The police are looking for him and his girlfriend, who was also present when he killed the woman. Now, I am trying to write an article about it. Trying hard to get the words onto paper, but I can't. I don't know what it is. It just hurts so badly to even think about it," I say.

"It's hard to put words to it. You see, my best friend was badly injured and almost lost her life while we tried to catch him. My best friend's life has been destroyed ever since, and I don't know how I can live with myself knowing this. She was a model. A gorgeous woman with a great career. My brother poured acid on her face, and now..." I stop and press back my tears. I try to keep my tone in check. "Now she can't work anymore. Her career is destroyed. All I know is I want to see him punished for what he did, and I'll do anything, give *anything* to find him. He is out there somewhere. What is he up to? Is he killing again? I don't know. It is up to us to catch him, hopefully before he hurts anyone else."

I turn it off and decide that it will have to do for now. I put the video on YouTube and then post it on my blog, along with a picture of my brother and Olivia, the same two pictures that have been shown on TV here in Florida.

At least I posted something, I think to myself, as I leave the computer and join the boys in the living room.

"What have you been up to?" Joey asks, as I lean over and kiss him.

"Just striking some iron while it was hot," I say.

January 2016

LATER IN THE DAY, I take my bike to Marcia's place. I have wanted to check in on her for days. I park my bike outside her townhouse and walk up to the door. I knock, and seconds later, the door is opened.

By a man I have never seen before?

"I…I'm looking for Marcia?" I say, worried. Who is this guy and what is he doing here?

The man smiles. He is annoyingly handsome. "You're probably wondering who I am," he says.

Well…just a little bit!

"Hi. My name is Harry. I've rented the room upstairs for a couple of days. Are you one of Marcia's friends?"

"Yes."

"Alright. Come on in."

"I didn't know Marcia rented out a room," I say, and shake his hand before I follow him inside. The place looks better than I had expected. Cleaner and tidier than usual. Two of the kids are sitting in the living room, reading books, I am surprised to see.

"She's not here right now," Harry says. "But I thought maybe we could talk for a little while. Do you have a minute?"

"I have many minutes," I say awkwardly. What is it about this guy? He makes me all goofy.

"Coffee?"

"Yes! I love coffee. Drink it all the time. Can't live without my coffee."

What's the matter with you? Why are you rambling?

"Milk?"

I shake my head. "Black. I prefer black. I mean I like white too…it's not a racist thing or anything…"

Will you stop talking? What are you? Twelve?

"Here," he says with a chuckle. I can see his muscles through his tight white T-shirt. I blush and look away, but not without thinking that Joey never had a chest like that.

"Thank you. You're very nice...I mean, it's very nice of you. You're very...handsome."

Did you just call him handsome? What's wrong with you!

Harry chuckles. Even his chuckles are sexy. We sit in the kitchen. The coffee is hot and steaming. So is Harry.

Will you stop it now?

"So, have you known Marcia for long?" he asks.

"You could say that. We've known each other since preschool," I say.

He nods seriously. "Good. Then it won't be too much to talk to you about this. I won't be overstepping my boundaries here."

I feel my heart drop. "It sounds serious. What's going on?"

"I have only lived here for about a week, but I have to say...your friend...Marcia is in need of help. She is hardly ever home, and when she is, she is...well, not really there."

I sigh and sip my coffee. "Is it that bad, huh? I know she has been drinking a lot since the divorce, but I thought she was getting by."

"Some nights she doesn't come home at all; other times, she comes home and then leaves again not long after. The kids pretty much have to take care of themselves," he says. "I have been cooking for them the past couple of days and taking care of the home, since she is in no condition to do so."

It feels like a punch to my stomach. All kinds of emotions go through me right now. Guilt being the biggest one of them. How had I not seen this?

"I had no idea it was that bad."

Harry nods. I can tell he is concerned. Genuinely. "Yesterday, she attacked me in the kitchen with a kitchen knife. She said she had no idea who I was. It appeared she thought I was here to rob her or something."

"And you've been living here all week?"

"Yes. It had me quite concerned."

"I can imagine," I say pensively.

"And then, there is this," he says, and places a letter in front of me. "I know I had no business opening it, but seeing who it was from, I had a feeling it was important."

"Oh, my," I say, when reading it.

"Apparently, she was court ordered to go to AA meetings when she had her DUI, but hasn't been showing up the last three months. "She risks going to jail if she doesn't do it."

I look at the children. "She's going to lose her kids, then."
"I am afraid so."

23

January 2016

"WE NEED TO FIND MARCIA. She needs help."

I look at the others. I've called everyone and asked them to meet me at Joey's house. Sandra and Alex still look guilty, but keep a distance between them. I can tell by their stolen looks that they're in deep trouble. I really hope for them that they figure things out before it gets messy.

"What's going on?" Danny asks.

"I spoke to the guy who is renting a room at her house earlier in the afternoon," I say.

"Wait. Wait. She has a renter?" Alex asks.

"I nod. I know. It was a surprise to me as well. But, yes, she rented out the room upstairs. Nothing wrong with that. Great that she'll get a little extra income. That's not why we're here. Harry, her renter…"

"His name is Harry?" Chloe asks.

"Yes. Harry Hanson," I say.

"What? His name is Harry Hanson?" Joey asks. "That sounds like the name of a cartoon character."

"It does sound like it's made up," Chloe adds.

"Whatever," I say. "It's his name. Anyway, he told me that Marcia hardly ever comes home anymore, and that he has been taking care of the children for the past several days, since Marcia is not there. I think she might be on a heavy bender."

The room grows silent. The seriousness is printed on the faces of my friends. They all know it is bad. We have all known for a while.

"But, that's not the worst part," I say. "She hasn't been to her court ordered AA meetings, and now she risks going to jail. She might lose the kids. It's bad, people."

"That is bad," Danny says.

"What do you suggest we do?" Joey asks.

"It's Saturday night, so my guess is she'll be in some bar around here. I say we spread out and hit all of them till we find her."

Everyone in the room nods.

"I can take Cape Canaveral," Danny says. "I'll hit Grills, Rusty's and Milliken's. They're like pearls on a string."

"Don't forget Fishlips," I say. "The deck upstairs."

"I'll take Sandbar and the Irish pub by 520," Joey says.

"What about Salter?" I ask and nod in his direction.

"Your dad is with him?"

"My dad can't move. He won't be of any help if anything happens."

"He's turning ten next month, Mary," Joey says. "He can stay here for the hour that it takes."

"Yes, Mom. I can be alone for an hour," Salter says with a deep sigh.

"I can stay with him," Chloe says. "I'll try and track her phone from your computer."

"Thank you, Chloe," I say. I know Joey is right. Salter is big and a very responsible boy. I am just not comfortable leaving him home alone yet.

"I'll take Slow & Low," I say. "Then hit the Sportsbar."

"Alex and I can take Coconuts and the Beach Shack," Sandra says.

I stare at them, wondering if I should say anything. I decide they're not children and don't make an issue of it. This is not the time. Right now, all that matters is finding Marcia and getting her sober.

24

January 2006

THE NEW TECHNIQUE works brilliantly for Peter. A few days after Kristin starts working with him, he is able to pick out word-blocks and form sentences, asking for a newspaper or something to eat. Just three weeks into his training, Kristin introduces him to a keyboard, and soon he is spelling things on his own, supported by Kristin's hand under his arm.

To Daniel, it is a miracle. Every time he drops Peter off at Kristin's office, he waits excitedly outside, wondering what new things his brother has told her, what wonders have been revealed about the world he lives in.

It took some convincing, but eventually the rest of their family has understood the miracle that is taking place in their youngest brother's life. Only their old mother doesn't seem to trust this new technique fully yet. It doesn't matter, Daniel tells himself. Peter has been given a voice, language. He has freed himself, and that is what is most important. Their mother will learn to see it with time.

Now, three months later, Daniel is waiting excitedly outside Kristin Martin's office, as always on Saturdays, as the door opens and she comes out smiling. For the first time, their mother has agreed to come and see it for herself.

"I believe we reached a milestone today," Kristin says. "Come and see for yourselves."

"Come on, Mother," Daniel says to his mother, and grabs her hand to help her get up from the chair. "Now you'll get to see it. Then you'll understand why we are all so excited for him."

Holding his mother's arm, Daniel walks into the office, where Peter is sitting in his chair. It's hard to tell that he is actually five feet tall the way he sits, with his skinny arms and legs and his drooping head. He is rocking from side to side and bangs his face against his hands again and again. Seeing Daniel and his mother makes him agitated, and, as always when excited or upset, he puts his hands in his mouth and bites them, leaving open sores.

"Peter seems to have a lot to say to us," Kristin says, as they approach him in his wheelchair.

Kristin helps their mother to sit on the leather couch, while explaining to her how the training works.

"At first, when we began this, his messages were simple and often misspelled, but his skills have improved as has his fluency. By a lot. You should be very proud of him. Now he hits a letter every second. It's truly amazing. I have given him books to read. He reads very fast. We're going through the books very quickly. And they're not just easy books. He's reading about everything from politics to fiction, and gobbling it all up, I might add. I should know because I turn all the pages for him. And then we talk about the books after-wards, and he tells me what he thinks of them. His knowledge of politics is quite extensive. And his math skills are amazing. We worked on fractions today."

Daniel sits next to his mother and holds her hand. Her hand feels stiff in his. She looks skeptically at the professor.

"We had no idea," Daniel says. "Did we, Mother?"

Their mother doesn't answer; she looks at her son in the wheel-chair and Daniel can sense her hostility towards the professor. It makes him uncomfortable, irritated as well. All he wants is for her to see what he sees.

"Isn't it wonderful, Mother? Aren't you happy that he finally is able to communicate with us? To think that he is that smart, but never has been able to express it. I can hardly believe it."

"I understand if it takes a little while for you to get used to the fact that your son is communicating after all these years. I can't blame you for being skeptical. It is very remarkable," Kristin Martin says. "But it is vital that he learns to develop his skills and not just treat his illness. That's what I believe, and what I want to tell the world. In fact, our results here are so stunning, I want the world to know about it. I was wondering if I could borrow Peter for a couple of weeks. I want him to write an article about his progress. I want him to go with me to a conference next month, and together, we'll present this article to a room of professors and scientists like me. What do you say? Will you let me borrow him?"

"Under no circumstances," the mother replies. "My son is not a guinea pig."

"Now, wait a minute, Mother," Daniel says. "Peter's progress has made a huge difference in his life. For the first time in twenty-five years, he can actually talk to us, tell us that he is in there; he has opinions, and he is a lot smarter than we thought. What if him attending this conference could help others like him? Don't you want that?"

His mother stares into Daniel's eyes. "I know my son," she says. "I gave birth to him. I have been taking care of him for twenty-five years, every day. Peter likes to play with PlayDoh and mash it between his fingers. Peter likes to eat, he loves to be taken to the ocean, he likes the fresh air, and the highlight of his day is staring out of the big window and watching for the mailman to come driving in his small truck up the road. Peter doesn't know about politics. He doesn't do fractions or read books."

Daniel watches as his mother gets to her feet. She walks up behind the wheelchair and starts to push it. "Now, if you'll excuse us. Peter and I are going to our favorite place for ice cream."

25

January 2016

"Heey, Mary! What's up?"

I look at Marcia. Her eyes are hazy and blood-shot, her speech slurred. Even more than usual. I find her sitting in the bar at the Sportsbar on A1A. She is smoking a cigarette and kills it in the ashtray.

"You want a beer?" she asks. "Com' on have a beer with me. Hey, my friend here is a famous writer," she yells to the people in the bar. Everyone turns to look at me. Marcia is loud and clumsy. "It's true. A reporter in New York, and now she writes this awesome blog that has like millions of followers. She's really awesome. Isn't she awesome? I think she is…awesome."

"We have to go, Marcia," I say.

"Where are we going?"

I try to speak in a low voice, but the music and the people are being very noisy. "You need to go home."

"Home? But we just got here. Now, have a beer with me."

Her behavior angers me. I try to stay calm. I can't believe she sits here all drunk while some stranger takes care of her children. Who does that?

"Say, why don't we go outside?" I say. "It's easier to talk. Too much noise in here."

Marcia laughs and a beer lands in front of me. I grab it and signal for her to follow me outside. Finally, she does. She almost knocks over the barstool as she jumps down.

"Be right back," she says to the other drunks in the bar. They don't seem to care. I wonder what makes her want their company instead of that of her children or us. Why has she chosen this life?

We sit at a table outside. The air is nice and warm. Today has been a warm day for January. The cold spell has come and gone, and now we're back to temperatures in the eighties. It feels good outside. And less noisy.

"So, how have you been, Mary?" she says as we sit down. "I can't believe we haven't seen you in twenty years. How time flies, huh?"

Suddenly, she seems less drunk. Maybe the fresh air sobered her up a little.

"I'm good," I say. "But I am worried about you, and so are the others."

"Ah, I'm fine. Never been better, as a matter of fact. Say, what are you doing back anyway? Are you here on vacation?"

I look at her. "What do you mean? I moved back, Marcia. Three months ago. Don't you remember?"

Marcia shakes her head with laughter. "Of course I remember. Duh. Guess I've had enough to drink, huh? It just slipped my mind."

She doesn't seem convincing. For a split-second I am certain I see great fear in her eyes, but it is soon replaced with something else.

"So what did you want to talk to me about?" she asks.

I show her the letter. She grabs it and reads it. She looks up at me, surprised. "What is this?"

"Marcia. You haven't been going to your meetings. They're going to put you away if you don't go."

"Yes, I have."

"Marcia. Stop lying. It says here you haven't, and by the looks of how drunk you are, I don't believe you have been to any meetings."

She looks like she doesn't understand. She puts a hand on her forehead and shakes her head slowly. "I don't know what is going on, Mary. I swear, I remember going to the meetings. I can't seem to…it's like the days…they are so blurry."

I grab the beer in her hand and take it from her. "Because of this," I say. "The drinking is destroying you. You haven't been to a meeting in months. You risk losing your kids if this continues. You have to act now. We're all here for you, but you have to do your part."

Marcia looks at me seriously. Her speech is less slurred, but her eyes still give her away. She puts her hand on my arm.

"I want to get better. Tell me what to do."

"We need to get you sober," I say. "You have to quit drinking."

26

January 2016

"I swear, there was someone with binoculars watching the house."

Kelly looks at Andrew. It angers her that he refuses to take this seriously. But that is so him. He never worries about anything.

"Worry is like a rocking chair," he always says. "It gives you something to do, but never gets you anywhere."

"You've got to relax," he says this time. "You're winding yourself up. It's not healthy. How do you even know he was watching our house? It was probably just some guy who likes to watch birds, or maybe a tourist. It's not illegal to look at our house, you know."

Andrew sits on the couch. Lindsey is asleep upstairs after a long day of fishing with her dad. Kelly grunts, irritated.

"And what about the truck I always see, huh? And the phone calls when I pick up there's no one there, huh? Is that also a coincidence? Or the tipped over telescope on the night Lindsey heard a loud bang?"

"Come on, Kelly," he says, and puts his feet up on the coffee table. He knows she hates when he does that. He leans back in the couch with a smile. "I am exhausted after a long day. I just want to relax with a beer and watch some TV. Can we talk about this later, please?"

Kelly groans, annoyed, and walks back to the kitchen, where she starts to clean up after their dinner. She washes a pot and slams it on the table so it makes a loud noise. She slams the doors to the cabinets when she shuts them and grunts in anger. Andrew doesn't seem to even hear her. He is watching a game. Either that or he is simply ignoring her outbursts. It makes her even angrier.

How can he not take this seriously? How can he keep telling her she is being paranoid? How can he ignore her like this?

What if he is right? What if it is all just in your head? You know how you get carried away sometimes.

There was the time when Lindsey had an allergic reaction to the new piercings in her ears. The doctor said she was just allergic to nickel, but Kelly was certain she was going to die from a blood infection and refused to let her out of her sight for three days. Kelly even slept with her, waking up every hour to check if she was breathing.

Kelly draws in a deep breath and tries to calm herself down. Maybe he is right. Maybe she is just imagining things. Who would want to stalk her anyway?

Kelly chuckles and puts the last pan into the cabinet and closes it normally. She looks at the kitchen with satisfaction. It looks clean. She then turns off the light, and as she does, she notices the full moon right outside of her window. It is hanging beautifully over the water, lighting up the ocean. It is so bright she almost wants to go outside. She walks to the window and looks down at the beach, when she notices a figure down there again. She stumbles backwards, then calls out.

"Andrew!"

Her husband runs to her in the kitchen. "What's going on?"

"He's down there again," she says, her voice shaking. She points to the window. Andrew moves closer and looks down.

"He's standing right down there, wearing a hoodie, looking up at us with his binoculars."

"I can't see anyone," Andrew says.

Kelly walks closer and looks down as well. But the figure is gone.

"No one is there," Andrew says.

"But there was. Someone was there a second ago. I promise you. I am telling the truth. I saw it!"

Andrew looks at her, just as the phone starts to ring. Andrew picks it up. "Hello?"

He looks at Kelly with troubled eyes. "Hello?" he repeats.

He hangs up.

"Alright now," he says and grabs her trembling shoulders. "Take it easy. Tomorrow, we'll talk to the police, okay?"

27

January 2016

SUNDAY MORNING, I go to pick up Marcia. I knock on the door and Harry opens it, wearing nothing but shorts and sneakers. He is sweating.

"She's almost ready," he says with that handsome smile of his. "Just got back from my run; sorry if I am sweaty and smelly."

"Great," I say with a smile, and walk inside trying to avoid looking at him. This guy is unbelievable.

Marcia comes out of her bedroom. She looks terrible. I can tell she has been crying. I am glad to see that she gets the seriousness of her situation now. She seems sober, but with her, I am never sure.

"Are you ready?" I ask.

She nods with a sniffle.

"Are you here in case the kids need anything?" I ask, addressed to Harry.

He nods on his way up the stairs. I watch him from behind as he disappears. I feel like I am cheating on Joey and turn to face Marcia again.

"Shall we?"

Marcia grunts something, then follows me to my car. I drive us there, and we walk in together. A small flock of eight people are already there, speaking amongst each other. As we enter, a woman around fifty, or maybe older, it's hard to tell, approaches us.

"Marcia!"

The woman opens her arms and hugs Marcia warmly.

"This is my sponsor," Marcia says. "She's also the therapist here."

"Hi. I'm Jess," she says.

We shake hands.

"I'm Mary. I'm a friend of Marcia's."

"That's wonderful. I'm glad you have such good friends, Marcia. We haven't seen you here for a while."

"Well, I haven't been doing so well," Marcia says.

Jess puts her hand on Marcia's shoulder. "I know how it is. But I am glad you're here now."

"I'm going to get some coffee," Marcia says, and walks away.

"She needs help," I say, addressed to Jess when Marcia can't hear us anymore. "She's in deep trouble."

"I know," Jess says. "She'll get what she needs here. But we can't force anyone to get better if they don't want to. She has to want it. I did try to help Marcia when she first came here, but I can only do so if she'll let me. I hoped she would come back. We haven't seen her in three months, I believe. She has to come to the meetings."

I nod and look at her as Marcia fumbles with her cup. I can tell she is not well. It breaks my heart. "It's just...it's been really bad lately. She hasn't been able to take care of the kids and it's like... yesterday, she didn't even remember that I moved back here three months ago."

Jess sighs. "That is not that uncommon, unfortunately. Alcohol is a slow killer, but it will destroy your body from the inside. The brain is no exception."

"So, you'll help her?" I ask.

Jess smiles warmly at me. "Of course. I am glad she has such a good friend in you. Many of us barely have any friends left. Now, if you'll excuse me, I have to begin the meeting, and I have to ask you to wait outside unless you yourself are struggling with an addiction?"

"Me? No. I eat too much, but hey, who doesn't, right?"

"Food can be an addiction too, you know," she says with a smile and a wink. Then she leaves me and starts the meeting.

28

January 2016

THE SCREAMING WON'T STOP. Marcia's head is about to explode as Mary takes her home. The only thing that usually makes it stop is the alcohol or the pills, but she hasn't had any all morning and it is killing her.

The meeting went great. Marcia told about how she had fallen in and how she wanted to get back on track again. She managed to not say anything about the blackouts or the screaming. The images and the voices in her head, she keeps to herself. They'll only think she is insane, that she has lost it.

"So, how did it go?" Mary asks with a smile.

Marcia looks out the window as Minutemen Causeway drifts by. She spots Billy walking next to City Hall towards the beach, guitar in one hand and a brown bag in the other. It is warmer today, so he'll be hanging out on the beach in front of Coconuts instead of in the dunes. She wonders who else will join him today. Marcia likes to hang out with them. Most of all, she likes who she is when she is with them, when the world is all fuzzy and warm and she doesn't have to worry about the screams or images in her mind.

"It went okay," she says.

"Good. So I'll take you again tomorrow, then?" Mary asks.

Marcia freezes. The thought of having to stay sober for even longer kills her. Can she do this?

You have to. Or you'll lose the kids.

The kids. Marcia feels awful that the kids have been suffering under this. She thought they were doing fine. Every time she saw them, they seemed fine.

You knew they weren't. You just chose to ignore it, you coward.

"I think I'd like that," she says, looking down at her shoes.

There's a hole in the right one and one toe is sticking out. Her clothes are dirty and smell weird.

How did it come to this? How did I become this bum?

"Great," Mary says, and drives up in front of her townhouse.

Marcia stares at the front door. Does she really dare to walk in there sober? To face all the misery, her guilt, her own disaster?

Mary places a hand on her arm. "Listen. I can't say I know how hard it is to be you right now, because, let's be frank, I have no idea what you're going through. But I can tell you that I will be here. No matter what. You call me in the middle of the night. Anything. I'll take care of the kids for a few days if you need to get away. Anything, as long as you don't start drinking again."

You don't deserve her as a friend. You don't deserve to be loved like that. You're not worth it.

"Shut up," Marcia says.

"What?" Mary says.

Marcia hides her face in her hands. "I'm sorry," she says. "I am so sorry. I'm such an awful person. I don't deserve you."

"Hey!" Mary says. "Don't you say that about my friend. Besides I think I am the one who will decide whether or not you deserve me. Now, come here."

Mary grabs her around the shoulders and pulls her close. She holds her in a warm embrace for a long time, while Marcia tries to pull herself together. In her head, the voices are all screaming at the same time. When she closes her eyes, she sees these awful images of people in pain, in excruciating pain, people pleading for their lives. Where do those images come from? She doesn't dare to think about it. She is terrified of learning the truth.

"What do I say to them, Mary? How do I face them?" she asks, and looks at the house.

"You just do it, I guess," Mary says after a little while. "They'll be happy to see you sober. Maybe do something fun with them today. Play a game. Talk with them. Especially Rose. She needs you."

Marcia nods. She is not so certain that anyone needs her.

"So, same time tomorrow?" Mary asks.

Marcia nods and opens the door. While Mary drives away, Marcia walks up towards the front door. She grabs the handle, but hesitates before finally opening the door.

They'll never forgive you. No one will ever love you. Not when they learn who you really are.

Two young faces look up as she enters the room. Their eyes are wide, scrutinizing, wondering who it is that they're greeting through the door. Will it be drunk Mommy? Will it be yelling Mommy? Will it be sweet and funny Mommy or angry mean Mommy?

A third set, belonging to her daughter Rose doesn't even dare to meet her eyes as she closes the door behind her.

Marcia forces a smile. It feels terrifying to stand like this in front of them. It's like being naked; she feels like they can see straight through her, see her for who she really is.

You can't do it. You can't. You're not strong enough. Not without drinking. You won't make it You're too weak.

"Anyone up for a game of charades?"

29

January 2016

MY STOMACH IS in knots when driving home from Marcia's. I can't bear seeing her like this. I feel guilty for not having reacted sooner. Those poor kids.

"How'd it go?" Joey asks from the couch when I enter the house. The dogs attack me and Snowflake licks me incessantly.

"All right, I guess," I say and sit next to him.

"Where's Salter?"

"A buddy from his school stopped by and asked him to go to the skate park with him."

I smile. "That's great. He's making friends," I say and lean back. I feel exhausted. Mostly emotionally.

"So, you think she'll get better now?" Joey asks.

I shrug. "I think we have taken the first small step, but there is still a long way for her. It's tough. Makes me appreciate what I have more, though."

Joey sits up straight, then leans over me and kisses me. I close my eyes and enjoy his kisses. Soon, his hand is inside my shirt. He is touching my breasts.

"Are we in a hurry?" I ask.

"You do realize we're childless, right?" he says. "It's been awhile."

I chuckle and look into his eyes. "I know. There has just been so much. With my brother and all that. It's getting to me."

Joey keeps kissing my neck and chest, and now he pulls off my shirt. He is not listening anymore, and soon I am not talking either. We make love on the couch and I feel so close to him, closer than I have in a long time. I am so blessed. So happy I made the decision to take him back. Especially for Salter's sake.

"By the way, Chloe has been trying to reach you. She came over earlier and said she needed to talk to you. Apparently, you don't answer your phone," he says, panting, when we're done.

"I had it on silent when I went with Marcia to the meeting," I say, and kiss his nose. I get dressed and find my phone.

Fourteen calls from Chloe. I call her back.

"What's up?" I ask.

"What's up? What's up?" she says on the other end. "Are you kidding me? Don't you know by now?"

"I am sorry. No, I really don't…"

"You're exploding; that's what's going on."

"Exploding?"

"Your numbers are. The little video you made went viral. It's a worldwide trending topic on Twitter!"

"What? Why?"

"I don't know why. Who knows why anything goes viral these days. But my guess is that people want to help find that brother of yours, so they share the video. It got picked up by one of the really big names on twitter, *RCThomas* and he wrote that we should all help her find this bastard, *so please share*.

"RCThomas? I have no idea who that is."

"I figured you didn't. But he's this famous YouTuber and tweeter. He's like Bono. Just on the Internet. People listen to him. If he says people should share this video, then they do it."

"Bono?"

"Okay, bad example, Lady Gaga then, argh you know what I am saying, right? The important part is everyone is tweeting your brother's picture now, and soon the entire world will know he is wanted. It's the best thing that could ever happen to us. We've already received a bunch of emails from people claiming they have seen him and Olivia. I am telling you. We're going to get him. He can run but…"

"We'll track him down no matter where he runs to," I say. "I'll be right over."

30

January 2016

MARK IS SITTING on the pavement next to his skateboard. He is waiting for his friend, David, who is eating dinner with his parents. They asked him if he wanted some and he really did, but he didn't want them to think he didn't get fed at home, so he said no and told David he would go home and eat as well, and then they'd meet back in front of his house. Not knowing what else to do, Mark stayed outside the house, his stomach growling with deep groans.

He doesn't want to go home. He doesn't like to be at the house in case his mother is there. The older he gets, the more Mark tries to stay out as much as he can. Sleeping over at friend's houses or even sometimes staying on the beach all night if it's warm enough. Anything to not have to go home.

He stares at a fire-ant crawling on his shoe when he hears the door to his friend's house open and David comes storming out.

"Let's go to the park," he yells, his mouth half full. "I have to be home at ten. Parents! They're so annoying."

"I know!" Mark says, but he doesn't mean it. The truth is, he would give anything to have someone give him a curfew. He would love to have someone want him home for once. But no one does. No one worries about him staying out all night.

They stay at the skate park for three hours, until David has to go home.

"Yeah, me too," Mark says. "Don't want to get in trouble with the old lady, right?"

He follows David home and then skates to the river and sits by the bank till midnight and he figures his mother is in bed.

Finally, he decides to head back. He enters the house as silently as possible and closes the door behind him. He takes two steps before he realizes someone is in the living room. His mother is sitting in the recliner, a is gun pointed at him. The streetlamp from outside lights parts of her face and the gun.

"Mom?"

"Shhh. They're listening, aren't they?"

"Mom. It's me. It's Mark."

Still, she is not lowering the gun.

"I am not giving in to them," she says.

"To who? What are you talking about, Mom?"

"You know damn well who!" she yells.

It startles Mark and he whimpers. "Mom? Please?"

"The government thinks they can get to me, but they won't. You can go back and tell them that."

"Go back? What?" he says, his heart throbbing.

"I know you're one of them. They got to you, didn't they? They had you place cameras everywhere, right? Don't you think I know they're watching me? Tonight they even spoke to me through the television. The guy on the news told me they would come for me tonight when I am asleep. But I am not going to sleep. Oh, no. I am not falling for that. And you better tell them that. I know you're with them."

"But, Mom. It's me. It's Mark," he repeats again and again with a shivering voice.

"It's not you. I know how these things work," she says. The gun remains steady between her hands. Mark has no idea what to do.

If I run, will she shoot? Will she shoot me if I stay?

Mark is crying now. "Mom. Please, you got to know it's me. I am your son. There is no one after you. No one is out to get you. Please, just lower the gun …"

He doesn't get to finish the sentence before the gun goes off.

Part II

TWINKLE, TWINKLE LITTLE STAR

31

February 2006

"WHAT HAVE YOU DONE?"

Daniel's mother looks at him, her eyes icily cold. On the couch by the fireplace sits his older sister and one of his brothers.

"I sent him to the conference with professor Martin." His voice is shaking as he speaks, but he stays determined. He knew this would happen, he knew their mother would confront him about this, and he had the entire speech prepared. Only now, his tongue betrays him and the words don't come out the way he wants them to. He no longer feels so certain of his arguments.

"How? How could you have done this when I told you I wouldn't have it?" his mother says.

"It's the right thing to do," he says. "Think of all the other people out there living like him, trapped in their bodies like him. They need him, Mother."

"And what about what Peter needs, huh? Did you think about that? He doesn't need a flock of nosy professors and scientists observing him like he is some…some monkey in a laboratory. Peter needs stability. He needs surroundings that he knows, he needs to follow his schedule. I am supposed to be protecting him."

"I am his guardian too, Mother. You made all of us guardians, remember? We have a say in his future as well."

"No!" his mother yells.

It startles Daniel. Their mother has been weak for years and spoken only with an almost whispering voice. Her yelling feels over-powering, and Daniel becomes a little boy again. At least that's how it feels to him. He looks at his shoes. All his siblings are present in the room, but they aren't saying anything. They avoid even looking at him.

Cowards, Daniel thinks to himself. *We agreed to do this together. We took a vote and now they won't stand by it.*

"As long as I am still alive, I make the decisions of what is best for my son. Not you. Not any of you," she says and points at the others.

She walks to her chair and sits down. Daniel can tell she is in pain. He knows her leg has been bothering her. Her heart is not very strong, the doctor says. He suddenly feels overwhelmed by guilt and sadness from making her this upset.

"I just don't understand why you would do this to him, to your brother?" she asks as she regains her strength.

"Because it is good for him, Mother. Don't you see it?" Daniel says.

"No. I really don't. The boy is sick, Daniel. He needs his family. He needs his mother."

Daniel sighs. "But, Mother. That's the thing. He's not. He's not a child anymore. He's a grown man. And he knows stuff. He is smart and he wants to share that with the world. He wants a life, Mother, and that's what we're trying to give him. If you keep treating him like a child, he'll never be anything else. He has skills. He can communicate. Besides, he wanted this. He wanted desperately to go, am I right?" Daniel asks, addressed to his siblings. They're annoyingly quiet. Finally, his sister nods.

"It's true, Mother. He really wanted to go. He told us."

"He told you? He told you?" their mother says. "How?"

"He wrote it on the keyboard," Daniel says.

Their mother shakes her head heavily. "The boy has never been able to speak, and all of a sudden, this professor, this woman, comes along and holds his elbow and suddenly you believe he speaks? That he knows politics and math? It's ridiculous. Can't you see it?"

Finally, their oldest brother rises to his feet. "We took a vote, Mother. We believe in giving Kristin Martin a chance. It's the only shot he'll ever get at a normal life. We made a decision, and now it's done. Peter is in California, and he'll be back in three days. You just have to trust us."

32

January 2016

I WORK with Chloe until around midnight, going through all the emails and tweets arriving from people who believe they have seen my brother and or Olivia. Most of them are bogus and easily thrown away, but some, a good handful, sound plausible, and slowly we narrow them down to four possible places they may have been seen.

Chloe puts up a big map on the wall and pins down the four places.

"Tucson, Arizona; Savannah, Georgia; Charlotte, North Carolina; or St. Petersburg, Florida," she says.

"Sure would make the most sense if he's still in Florida," I say.

"I'm not so sure," Chloe says.

"He was last seen in Ft. Lauderdale?"

"Right, but he's not dumb. Neither is Olivia. They know people are looking for them all over the state. It would make more sense to get as far away as possible."

"So, you think he's in Arizona?" I ask.

She shrugs. "It's a guess. Maybe they're planning on going across the border. Maybe they already have."

"Mexico?"

"Yeah, I know," she says. "Sounds like a bad movie, but still. They can hide there easily."

"They have to live too," I say. "How do they still have money? It's been three months, and neither of them has used a credit card."

"I don't know," Chloe says. "But there are ways."

I look at the clock on the wall. "It's getting late. I should be getting back home."

"I want to take a closer look at the tip that came from Arizona. I think I'll continue all night and sleep tomorrow," Chloe says. "This is the time I usually think the best. No distractions, you know?"

I smile. I do know. Chloe has always been like that. I wonder how she still manages to live a life like this. Taking care of her mother and staying awake all night. I, for one, get completely out of balance if I lose just a few hours of sleep.

"Salter has school in the morning, so I have to get up at six thirty to get him on the bus. I need some shut-eye. I'll see you tomorrow."

I ride my bike back to Joey's house. I park it outside and walk in. Joey is sleeping on the couch, a half empty beer on the table. I check on Salter in his bed. He is sound asleep. The dogs and the pig are in there with him, all sleeping in his bed. He looks so happy, so safe, it makes me feel good. I walk back to Joey, and as I do he receives a text on his phone. It's from that Jack guy again. I decide it's none of my business and go to the kitchen and grab myself a donut that they have left out. It's a little dry, but I'm starving, so I eat it anyway. Joey is grunting in his sleep and sounds exactly like Bonnie. It makes me laugh. As I finish eating, there is suddenly a knock on the door.

It startles me, while Joey doesn't react. I walk to the window to look outside. I spot a girl, a young woman in a light dress, a small jacket over her shoulders. She has long blonde curls that bounce off her shoulders when she moves. She is stunning.

Thinking she probably came to the wrong house, I open the door. Her smile freezes as she sees me.

"Hello?" I ask.

"Hi. Is Joey home?"

As the realization sinks in, my heart goes cold. I have a lump in my throat. "He's sleeping. Who are you?"

"I'm Jackie."

Jackie as in Jack?

"Sorry. I've never heard of you…Jackie. What did you want with my husband?" I ask. It's technically not a lie, since Joey and I are only separated.

She looks baffled. "Husband? I…I didn't know…he told me he was separated." She takes a few steps backwards. "I'm…I am so sorry."

"Yeah, well, you should be." I say, and slam the door behind me. The noise wakes up Joey. He blinks his eyes and looks at me.

"Hey. You're back. I missed you."

33

January 2016

"WHAT'S THE MATTER?"

Joey looks at me. I realize I am shaking. I can't speak. I can't shape the words or push them across my lips. Yet there is so much I want to say. So much I need to get out of me. So many emotions, so much anger.

I can't believe he did this to me again. I can't believe I let him!

"What's going on, Mary? Why…what's…" Joey jumps up from the couch while I sink to the floor, slowly sliding my back against the door. I am staring at him, my mouth open, my heart pounding.

"Did something happen at Chloe's?" he asks, and kneels in front of me. "Talk to me, Mary."

I stare into his eyes. I want to cry, but I can't. I want to scream. I want to yell at him, but nothing happens. I feel so lost. So betrayed.

"Mary! You're scaring me," he says. "What happened?"

Do I even bother talking to him? Do I even want to hear him explain himself? I am fed up with excuses. I am fed up with trying to understand. Yet I do it. Yet I ask him, "Who's Jackie?"

As her name leave my lips, Joey's face changes. The corner of his mouth droops. The air is still for several seconds before he finally speaks again. Rage is swelling inside my chest. Joey pulls away. His hand touches his face.

He's trying to come up with an excuse. Wondering how to tell me, to say this gently and not make me mad. To not lose me. Doesn't he realize it's too late?

"I …" he says.

"You know what? I really don't want to know," I say, and get up on my feet. I feel slain, conquered, but I haven't lost everything. I still have my dignity. And my son. I don't have to keep living like this.

"But …"

"I don't need any more excuses, Joey. I don't need explanations. I needed to be able to trust you again, but clearly, that was a mistake."

He grabs my arm and forces me to look at him. "She is no one, Mary. I promise you."

"*No one* doesn't come knocking on your door at midnight, Joey," I say.

He exhales. I can tell he is struggling to find the right words. He's afraid of pushing me further away, of losing me. He's right. At this point, there pretty much isn't anything he can say.

"You have to believe me, Mary. I only saw her for a little while, when you were still in New York. You threw me out. We were separated, Mary."

"Oh, my God," I say and pull my arm out of his grip. Finally, I lose it. "Do you even listen to yourself? You know who you sound like? Do you? You sound like Ross! *We were on a break?* Is that the excuse you're going to come up with?"

"What's wrong with that? You threw me out. I found comfort with Jackie. She was nice."

"Nice? You destroy your family over nice?"

Joey points his finger at me. "Hey. You were in New York. We were separated. You said you wanted a divorce. Yes, I saw another girl for a few weeks, but it ended as soon as you and Salter came down here."

"You ended it? What about all the texts, then?"

Joey sighs. He is panting in agitation. "She wouldn't stop. I couldn't get her to stop texting me, all right? She wanted to see me and I told her not to come. I don't know why she would be so stupid as to come here in the middle of the night."

"I don't believe you. You even lied about it when I asked. I just don't understand why you would do this to me again. After all we have been through, Joey."

He grabs both my shoulders and turns me to look at him. His eyes are filled with tears. "Believe me. I want this. I want us, Mary. I am not losing you again. I can't lose you and Salter once again."

"Well, maybe you should have thought of that before you crawled into bed with the first hooker that came along," I say, and pull away from him. I walk to the bedroom and open the door. I don't look back at Joey before I walk in. I don't want to see his face.

"That's not fair and you know it," he yells, just as I close the door with a loud bang.

34

January 2016

I CARRY Salter into my bed and snuggle with him and all the animals all night, but don't get any sleep at all. When the alarm goes off, Salter opens his eyes and looks into mine. I can't think of anything more beautiful to wake up to.

"What's wrong, Mommy?"

I kiss his forehead. "I'm just a little sad, sweetie. It'll be okay. Don't worry about it. Now let's get you to school, alright?"

"Is it Dad?"

I sigh. "We had a fight."

Salter's eyes turn hard. I don't like to see that in him. I know he feels protective of me ever since we lived alone for four months. I know I have to be careful. I want him to love his dad, no matter what happens.

"Don't worry about it, okay?" I say. "We're grown-ups. We'll do the worrying and the problem solving. You focus on getting to school on time."

He nods, but I can tell he doesn't agree. He wants to solve everything. I know he does, but he can't. He can't fix this, no matter how bad he wants to.

We get out of bed and get dressed. I prepare his breakfast, while wondering where Joey is. I thought he would be sleeping on the couch in the living room, but he is not there. I am glad I don't have to face him, but still I wonder if he went to her place instead. The thought makes me miserable.

Am I that easily replaced?

I make Salter's lunch and hand him his lunchbox when he is ready to leave. I kiss his forehead and wave at him as he walks to the bus. My stomach hurts from worry that he'll be sad all day. He is so happy that his mom and dad are back together again. To have to take that away from him again is just simply devastating.

When he is gone, I make myself some coffee and make a tray for my dad with coffee and breakfast. I walk into his room. He's already awake.

I put the tray down and force a smile. "Ah, don't give me that," he says.

"What?"

"I heard you...last night."

"Oh."

"What's going on...with you two?" he asks, while I feed him scrambled eggs. He spits some of it out when he talks, and I wipe it off his bed.

"I don't know, Dad."

"You're not splitting up again...are you?"

"I said I don't know."

"You're being...way too hard on him. Always have, Mary." My dad is agitated and has to take a break before he can continue. His breath is ragged. "You...expect too much...He tries...I have seen him. He tries...his best. Nobody is perfect."

"He slept with someone else, Dad. Not just once," I say.

My dad falls silent for a few seconds. I can tell he is wondering what to say. "Well, maybe there's an...explanation."

"Really, Dad?"

"I like...the kid. Look at...look what he did. He took all of us in and took...care of me. He put up that...TV and...finally I have...something to do while lying around here. He cares, Mary. Not many...men do."

I know he is right. Joey is a sweet guy and a great father. I truly love him. I think I have loved him since we went to preschool together. I can't remember not loving him. But is it enough? I need more than that. I refuse to be one of those women that simply close their eyes to their husband's constant cheating because they don't have the strength to deal with it. Or to make the unpopular decision. I have to be able to trust him, and so far, he hasn't earned my trust.

"All I am asking...is that you give him...a chance, Mary. Don't...throw away what you have...because of one...or two...little mistakes. You have no idea...how lucky you are to have a man... love you like that." My dad looks at me intensely while catching his breath again. "I miss...Laura...every hour of the day...but she never loved me...not in the same way. There is no doubt...Joey... loves you."

"I won't, Dad. I promise," I say and kiss his forehead. I don't want to talk more about it with him. I turn on the TV and find something he wants to watch before I walk to the door. "You have physical therapy at three today," I say before I leave.

In the kitchen, I put down the tray when my phone starts to vibrate on the counter. I am certain it is Joey and pick it up. It's a text. It's not from Joey. It's from Marcia.

MEET ME BY OUR OLD SECRET SURFSPOT ASAP. COME ALONE.

January 2016

I TEXT Marcia back and ask her what's going on. What about the AA meeting? She doesn't answer back, so I try to call her, but her phone is shut off and I leave a voicemail. I can't help but get angry with her. This is not the time for her to go surfing. She's supposed to be working on herself and going to the meetings. Does she think I'll just forget about it? This is odd, even for Marcia. I wonder if she has fallen off the wagon already or if this is just her way of trying to get out of going to the meeting. I won't let her. I am determined to help her, even if I myself am I mess. I am not giving up.

I decide to go to our old spot and convince her to go to the meeting with me instead of surfing. When I open the door to go to the car, I spot someone coming up the driveway. I recognize him immediately. The long legs, the brown waving hair, the gorgeous blue eyes. But there is something different about him today. Something desperate and bleak that I haven't seen in him before.

"Harry?" I say. "What are you doing here?"

"Mary. Finally," he says with a deep sigh. "I've tried to get ahold of you all morning. But I don't have your number, and all the kids knew was where you lived. I had to get them out of the house before I could get down here…"

"I don't understand. What's wrong, Harry? Has something happened?" I ask, the feeling of dread quickly spreading throughout my body.

What is going on here?

"It's Marcia," he says.

Uh-oh!

"Marcia? What happened?"

A series of images run through my mind. Marcia driving drunk on her bike to our secret surf spot with her board under her arm. Marcia being hit by a car and lying on the asphalt. Is she dead? Is she unconscious? Is she alive?

Harry looks at me and shakes his head. It's bad. I can tell by the look in his eyes that he has no idea how to tell me.

"Last night...I have no idea how it could have happened. I was upstairs in my bed, sleeping, when I heard the shot."

The shot? Oh, my God, it's even worse than I thought.

"Marcia was shot?"

Harry shakes his head. "No. Not her."

"Then who? Who?"

"Mark. Mark was shot. He came home late, as he often does, if he comes home at all. As far as I know, she must have thought he was an intruder or something. When I came down, she was gone; Mark was lying on the floor of the living room, bleeding heavily."

I stop breathing. Everything inside of me is standing still. The words coming out of Harry's mouth are so unreal, so distant, so strange I can't take it.

"Marcia shot her son?" I ask.

"Yes. And then she just took off."

"How is he? Is he...?"

"He's alive. The bullet went into his shoulder. I called for an ambulance and he was taken to Holmes Regional. I stayed with the other children and sat with them till they fell asleep again. I called this morning, and he's still in intensive, but they expect him to make it. His dad came out here from Orlando and is with him now."

I stare at Harry, slowly shaking my head. Suddenly, I feel dizzy. It's overpowering me and I have no control of my body anymore. Harry grabs me just as I am about to fall and helps me get inside where I sit on a chair.

"Let me get you some water," he says.

I still feel like the world is spinning and I can't breathe. It's just too much right now. The whole thing.

"Here, drink this," he says, and hands me the glass. "It'll make you feel better."

I drink and close my eyes. It does make me feel better, but now I feel like I have to throw up. I bend down, but it doesn't happen. I raise my head again and look into Harry's eyes.

"Feeling better?"

"A little," I say. I finish the water.

"I'm glad that you were home," Harry says. "I had no idea who else to come to. I have only been in the house for a short while."

"The police," I say.

"They're looking for her. Mark told them she did it in self-defense. That he startled her and that she thought he was an intruder. I don't know what they'll do, but the kids were picked up by social services, and they're going to stay with their father in Orlando. It's bad, Mary. I am afraid you're all Marcia has right now."

36

January 2016

Tears are streaming across my face as I drive towards Sebastian Inlet. I chose not to tell Harry about the text from Marcia. I want to meet with her myself and hear what she has to say. He doesn't have to be involved.

Our old secret surf spot where we used to meet and surf is reached by a small trail through the bushes that leads to a desolated beach known among surfers as The Spanish House. We used to go there when waves were small at Cocoa Beach, especially in the summertime. Down here, they would always be breaking beautifully, and the water is so clear you could often see turtles and dolphins underneath you as you surfed.

It used to be my favorite place to go, but not today. Today, I walk across the trail feeling awful, feeling sick to my stomach.

What do I say to her? How do I deal with this? Do I tell her to turn herself in? Do I tell her to run away? God, please give me the strength and wisdom to say the right things, to do what is right.

When I reach the beach, I am all alone. I spot someone sitting in a chair about half a mile away, but that's not her, I think.

She's not here.

I growl, annoyed, and turn to walk back through the bushes, when I hear a small voice calling my name. I look to the side and spot Marcia. She is sitting underneath a bush, crumpled up, her legs under her chin. She is shaking. Her eyes are flickering from side to side.

"Marcia."

I walk closer and kneel in front of her. I try to make eye contact, but without success. "Marcia. Look at me."

But she doesn't. Her eyes are constantly moving, her head shaking. "They're coming, Mary. I know they are. I'm not going with them. I won't let them get me. I'd rather die."

"Who? The police?" I ask.

Finally, she looks at me. I don't recognize the Marcia I know in those eyes.

"All of them. They are all in on it, Mary. Especially that man."

"What man? Harry?"

"Yes. Yes. Him. I don't trust him. He keeps me awake when he walks around up there all night. I think…Mary, I think he killed that woman."

"What woman?"

"The one they pulled out of the river."

"Why do you think Harry had anything to do with that?" I ask.

"Because of the pictures, Mary. He has her picture and all the articles in his room. He thinks I didn't see it, but I did. I think he's a killer, and now he's coming after me. He's going to kill all of us."

I remove a lock of hair from Marcia's face. I don't smell alcohol on her breath. When I look into her eyes, she doesn't seem intoxicated. Just…just like she is very far away. Too far away for me to reach her. It frightens me.

"What's going on with you, Marcia?" I ask. "Do you even know what happened last night?"

"Last night, we went to Beef O' Brady's. Kids eat free on Tuesdays. I had a steak burrito."

I cup my mouth and press back tears. I have no idea what to say to her. "You need help," I whisper under my breath.

Marcia holds both her hands to her head and closes her eyes like she is in pain. "Stop it," she says. "Stop screaming!" Then she grabs my arm and pulls me closer. "Do you hear it too? Do you hear them screaming, Mary?"

"Who is screaming, Marcia? You're scaring me."

"The kids. They're crying. They're scared."

"What kids?"

"The kids!"

I get a terrifying thought. I don't want to think it, but I do. "Why are they scared, Marcia? Who is hurting them?" I ask, petrified of the answer.

And then it comes.

"I think…I think it is me."

37

January 2016

"WHO IS IT? WHO ARE THEY?" I ask. I don't want to hear this, I really don't, but I feel I have to ask. I have to know what is going on with her.

"Are they your children, Marcia?"

She shakes her head.

"There's a girl and a boy. They're on the floor. The boy had glasses on, now they are on the floor next to him. Broken. He's chubby. Has a birthmark on his cheek."

"And the girl?"

Marcia thinks about it for a little while before speaking. "She has long black hair. She's pretty. I think she is dead, but I'm not sure. She's wearing her PJs. They both are. *Twinkle, Twinkle Little Star*… there are stars on them. On hers. They're black. His say *Star Wars* on the front."

"And the grown-ups?" I ask, my voice shivering. "Where are the grown-ups?"

"They're right next to the children. On the floor too. The mother's eyes aren't closed. They don't blink. They don't move. The mother has a white shirt, but something is wrong with it. It's red in the front. There's a hole in it. There's a hole in her."

Marcia stops and looks up at me. "Did I do that? Did I, Mary?"

"I…I…don't know." I answer as honestly as I can. "But I think we need to find out."

She grabs my hand in hers and strokes it gently. "I love you, Mary."

I look into her eyes, and for one split second, I see her; I see the Marcia I used to know. I smile and touch her cheek. "I love you too,

Marcia. We'll get to the bottom of this. I promise you we will. Now, you need to come with me."

I help her get out of the bush. "Where are we going, Mary?"

"You need to turn yourself in to the police."

Marcia stops. I turn and look at her. She is shaking her head. "No, Mary. They'll kill me. They'll take away my kids!"

"They already have, sweetie."

She looks at me like she doesn't understand. I grab her by the shoulders. I force her to look into my eyes. I want to make sure she understands what I am about to tell her.

"Honey. You shot Mark last night. Now, I know you didn't mean to, that it was an accident, but he is in the hospital and the rest of your children are with their father."

Marcia's eyes widen. I see great fear in them. "I…I did what?"

I nod. "I'm afraid you shot Mark. He's going to be fine, though. Come."

Marcia shakes her head and pulls away from me. "No. No. I would never…not my son! It's not true. They're making this up. Someone is making all this up."

"You're not well, Marcia. I don't know what is going on with you, but you're not well. Come. We need to get you some help."

"No. They'll lock me away for the rest of my life. I bet it was Harry. He set me up, didn't he? You see, they're all linked with computers, Mary. And the phones. They have everything on us on the phones and computers. They spy on us and they know…everything. Harry is one of them. He did it."

"No!" I yell angrily. Where does she get these ideas? "You did this, Marcia. He took care of your kids. He's a good guy. He has tried to help you the best he could. Now, come with me."

"No. Something is wrong. I can feel it."

"You're not well, Marcia. That's what is wrong. You can't trust your own judgment. You're sick. Now come with me before someone else gets hurt."

She doesn't move. She stands still, looking at me, while shaking her head. I can feel I am losing her and it breaks my heart.

"Marcia, please. Just come. I'll do everything I can to help you, but you have to come with me. Now."

Marcia exhales deeply. She pulls out the gun that I am guessing is the same one she used when she shot Mark. I back off, knowing she might be capable of anything.

"I'm sorry. I can't," she says.

Marcia takes one last glance at me, then turns around and starts to run. I yell after her, but she disappears into the bushes, and in a few seconds, she is gone.

"Goddammit, Marcia," I moan. "How am I supposed to help you now?"

38

March 2006

A MONTH after the conference in California, Peter starts taking classes at UCF. Daniel takes him there and picks him up, while Kristin helps him write his papers. Meanwhile, their mother has become ill and is in bed most of the time, so Daniel has taken over Peter's care, much to his own family's regret. His wife complains that he is never home and his children tell him they miss him terribly. Daniel feels guilty, but he is also on a mission to give his brother a better life. Peter starting at the university is one huge step in that direction. With Kristin's help, it is possible.

"Your brother is truly amazing," the teacher tells him one Wednesday when Daniel drops Peter off for class. "You should see the last paper he wrote. Best in his class."

Daniel is amazed. He can't believe that the man they all thought had the mental capacity of a toddler could now dazzle the world with his knowledge.

Daniel decides to stay with Peter for the philosophy class, curious to know more about what his brother is interested in. Kristin sits next to him, helping Peter when he needs it. Daniel looks at her while she works, and can't help but find her spectacular.

To engage yourself so much in another human being is truly remarkable, he thinks to himself.

In his eyes, that makes her the most beautiful creature he has known. But he also can't help feeling a little jealous of her as well. She is now the person who is closest to his brother, and the only one who he'll write with. She has tried to teach Daniel the technique, but so far he has only failed. So have his siblings, and even his mother, that one time she gave in and tried. When anyone other than Kristin tries, Peter pulls his arm away and often scratches them.

After class is done, four of Peter's classmates walk up to him, books in their hands, backpacks on their backs. They ask him if he would like to go to lunch with them. He accepts by typing. Daniel goes with them. He goes in the line of the cafeteria to buy food for Peter. Kristin is right behind him, while Peter stays at the table.

"You know he usually buys his own food, right?" she says.

"Really?" Daniel asks.

"Yes."

Daniel grabs a pizza slice with pepperoni.

"Peter can't stand pepperoni," Kristin says. "He usually gets the ham."

Daniel wrinkles his forehead. "That's odd. He loves pepperoni pizza. It used to be the only thing we could get him to eat."

She shrugs. "Well, not anymore. Things change. People change, Daniel. Don't baby him. He's a grown man now with his own opinions, likes, and dislikes. And now he can express them as well."

With a feeling of defeat, Daniel puts back the slice and grabs one with ham instead. They walk to the table, where Peter's classmates have already sat down, and soon they're questioning Peter.

"How was it for you as a child when no one thought you could communicate?" a girl asks.

"Lonely," he types with the assistance of Kristin.

"So, how is it now?" another classmate asks.

"I am happy to be able to speak. I feel like I have finally come alive."

"What do you dream of? What do you want to accomplish in life?" the girl asks.

"I want to tell the world about us. I want to tell them people like me are more than just disabled. We can do more than just sit in a corner somewhere. We can do so many things."

The girl nods with a smile. Daniel is pleased to see how well they have taken Peter in. They seem curious, but not judgmental. It makes him feel good about his decision to let Peter take classes here. The girl especially seems genuinely interested in his story and who he is beyond what she can see. But then she asks a question Daniel had never thought would come, that he would never have thought of asking himself.

"Can you also fall in love?"

Daniel awaits Peter's answer with great curiosity. He has never thought of Peter in that way. That he could have feelings for anyone.

Peter types. Kristin reads his words out loud while assisting his arm.

"I can. I would love to be in a relationship more than anything in the world. But I don't know if someone like me can ever do that. I don't know if anyone would ever love me back."

39

January 2016

"I NEED YOUR HELP."

"Well come on in, then." Chloe steps aside and lets me into her house. She looks exhausted. Her hair is a mess and she is pale. "I was just napping," she says. "Stayed up all night working on that tip from Arizona. "It looks promising so far. What's up with you?"

"Marcia."

"What's with her?" I follow Chloe into the kitchen, where she pours each of us a cup of coffee. I go through her cabinets and find an old bottle of whiskey and pour a sip into my coffee.

"Uh-oh," she says. "You're making it Irish? Something is definitely up."

We sit down and I drink my coffee. I wait and let the alcohol do its job inside my body.

"So, what's with Marcia?"

"I don't know how to explain it," I say. "She is not well."

"Well she has been drinking a lot for a long time."

"That's not it. There is more. Did you hear what happened last night?" I ask.

"No."

"She shot Mark."

"That's awful! Is he okay?"

"Yes. He came home late, and according to Harry, she thought he was an intruder and shot him, but I have a feeling there is more to the story."

"How so?" Chloe asks.

"Don't tell anyone, but I saw her earlier today. She kept ranting on about how they were after her, out to get her, and how Harry was one of them, how he was a killer and she thought he had killed that woman who was found in the river recently. Then she had these flashbacks or visions or dreams; I don't know what to call them, but she saw things. She described something for me that was so terrifying I had goosebumps."

"What things?"

"Children that she believed she had hurt. And two adults. She kept asking me if she was the one who had hurt them. It was really creepy. I tell you I have never seen her like this before. And I am certain she wasn't drunk."

"What?" Chloe wrinkles her nose. "Well, maybe she took some pills."

"I couldn't smell any booze on her breath and she didn't seem intoxicated when I looked her in the eyes. She was all there, and yet she was so…far away."

"So, what happened to her? Where is she now? And what about Mark?" Chloe asks.

"Mark is going to be fine, they say. He was only hit in the shoulder. All the children are with their father. I tried to get Marcia to come with me, to turn herself in and get the help she needs, but she pulled a gun on me."

Chloe almost chokes on her coffee. "She did what?"

"She pointed it at me, then told me she couldn't come with me before she ran."

"Wow."

"I know." I sip my coffee. My hands are still shaking, and telling the story makes me feel terrible.

"Marcia? I can't believe it. She wouldn't hurt a fly."

"I know. But then I began to think. What if she has done awful things? She did shoot Mark. What if she is not well and has no idea what she is doing?"

"Hm. I'm guessing you want me to help you with that."

"Yes. I thought maybe you could help me look something up. Something she said. It requires that we get access to some old police files."

"I had a feeling that was where we were heading. All right. Anything for old Marcia."

40

January 2016

I STAY at Chloe's for a few hours, while she works on getting access to the police files. I walk up to her mom's room and sit down by her bedside. She is awake, but doesn't say anything. She reaches out her hand towards me and I grab it in mine. It feels so feeble, the skin paper-thin.

"How are you?" I ask.

"It hurts," she says with a whisper.

It makes me feel bad for her. I always loved Chloe's mom, Carolyn. She has been so good to me over the years when things were bad at home. I curse cancer while tears spring to my eyes.

"Is there anything I can get you?" I ask. "Water?"

"Yes, please."

I grab the glass on her side table and help her drink. The smell of death hits my nostrils. Carolyn grabs my hand again and holds it in hers. Then she looks me in the eyes. The way she looks at me frightens me slightly.

"Be careful, Mary. Things are not as they seem. Mark my words. The boy carries all the answers."

Carolyn stares at me intensely while I wonder what she is talking about. Her hands are both holding on to my arm. They are so cold on my skin. Chloe enters the room and Carolyn lets go of me, then slides back under the covers and closes her eyes.

"What's going on?" Chloe asks.

"I…I was just saying hello."

Chloe looks at the old woman in her bed. "She's still asleep."

"She wasn't a second ago. She looked at me and told me something about a boy carrying all the answers."

Chloe chuckles. We leave her mother and walk downstairs.

"She's been saying a lot of weird things lately. I have a feeling she might have a hard time distinguishing between dreams and reality. She is sleeping most of the day away. I'm afraid she doesn't have long. The doctors stopped the treatments six months ago. She's not supposed to be alive at all. They gave her four to six weeks."

"Wow. Guess she beat those odds, huh?"

"I know. I just try and make the most of the time I have left with her, you know? I try to cherish every waking moment with her."

I think about my own father as we walk back to Chloe's computers in the back of the house. I have no idea how he's going to get by. Will he ever get better? Will he be able to do anything on his own, and is it a life worth living if he won't?

"So, how's your dad doing?" Chloe asks, as if she has read my mind.

I sigh and sit in the chair next to hers. "He's not doing any better, but not worse either. But the house will be done soon, and then we'll all move in with him, I think."

"You will? That's wonderful, Mary," Chloe says. "I am so glad you and Joey are together. It was always you two. The world isn't right if you two are not together."

I shake my head. "No. I meant me, Salter, and Snowflake are moving in with him. Joey and me are a completely different story."

Chloe looks at me skeptically. "What's going on, Mary? I thought you were getting better. Trying to mend the broken pieces."

"Yeah. Well, so did I. But then he went out and slept with someone else."

"He did not!"

"She came to his house last night at midnight asking for him. She had no idea I was living with him."

"How embarrassing."

"Mostly for her," I say with a light chuckle. "Can you imagine?"

41

January 2016

"I HAVE THE FILE FOR YOU." Chloe clicks the mouse and opens a file. I pull my chair closer to better see.

"The Elingston case is a huge file," she says. "Contains hundreds of pages. Might take a while to find what we're looking for. By the way, what are we looking for?"

"Pictures," I say. "Descriptions of the victims and what they were wearing. Marcia described the children's clothing in detail. The way she described the kids reminded me of the pictures I have seen of them while still alive."

"That's going to be hard," Chloe says. "The house was on fire and the bodies severely burnt when they were recovered. The only reason they know it was murder was the footage from the neighbor's surveillance cameras and the fact that the body of the wife had been stabbed first, before the fire was started. That's what it says here. I can't believe they never found this guy."

"I know. I remember hearing about the case often. Back then, I was still working in Atlanta, and the story was all over. I was so afraid my editor would send me back, since it was so close to my old hometown, but luckily he didn't.

"It was huge. The town was crawling with journalists. Everyone was terrified. Can you imagine someone entering your house on a Saturday morning and holding you hostage only to get fifty-thousand dollars, and then, as you think it's all over because all they want is the money, they kill you and burn the house down with you inside of it. For what? Fifty-thousand dollars? It's so strange. Everything about this case puzzled us. People started locking their doors at night and even during the day. Not something we did a lot around here. Everyone became suspicious of each other, because the police believed the guy knew the family well enough to know their routines and know that they were capable of getting fifty-thousand dollars within a few hours without anyone thinking it was suspicious. Either they knew them or they had been observing them for a long time. People became suspicious of their lawn or pest guys or anyone that had access to their houses and lives."

"What's that?" I say, and point a paragraph in the forensic report. "It looks like the description of what was found on or next to the bodies, right?"

"Yes," Chloe says. "It says here that the only piece of clothing found was on the girl. A small piece of fabric."

"What did it look like?" I ask, and move closer to better see.

"There's a picture."

Chloe clicks the picture and it opens. I look at the small piece of fabric. Chloe is speaking, but I can't hear her anymore. Everything is drowned out by the sound of my heartbeat pumping in my ears. The piece of fabric is burnt on the edges, but in the middle, I can see the very clear picture of a star.

Twinkle, Twinkle Little Star.

"Mary?"

Chloe is waving a hand in front of my face. "You zoned out for a little there."

"It's the PJs," I say. "It's the girl's PJs. They had stars on them. Marcia told me the girl had stars on her PJs and the boy had *Star Wars* written on his."

Chloe freezes. She stares at me. "It does say in the report that the maid who usually worked for them said the girl usually wore PJs with stars on them, and therefore, they concluded that she was in her PJs when she died. How on earth could Marcia know that?"

"Was it mentioned in the news?" I ask.

"I don't remember hearing about it," Chloe says. "I can Google it quickly."

While Chloe googles it, I lean back in my chair. I rub my forehead, thinking about Marcia. I run through everything she told me in my mind, desperately trying to find an explanation, an answer to the question of how on earth she could know these kinds of details if she wasn't there.

"I can't find anything anywhere about it," Chloe says. She looks at me as she exhales. "What do you make of it? Do you really think...?"

"No." I say and get up from my chair. "I refuse to believe it."

42

January 2016

BLAKE FEELS SO alive he almost can't stand it. His heart pounds inside of his chest as he walks across the parking lot, his gloved hand inside of the pocket of his sweater, the knife clutched in it.

It's been awhile since he killed last, and the anticipation of the kill is overwhelming. It sends waves of chills through his body, making him feel like the most powerful creature on this planet right now.

Like a predator. Sneaking up on his prey.

It's a sensation no drug could ever give him, the thrill of taking a life, of holding the power of life or death in your hand.

He walks to the window and looks inside. He knows she is in there. He watched her from his car as she came back from the store, a bag of groceries in her hands. He watched her as she found the key in her pocket, then fumbled with the lock, almost dropping the bag. It left him with such a strong sensation in his body, knowing what he had decided to do with her, knowing that she has no idea.

She's not going to know what hit her.

He hopes she'll be screaming. He likes it when they scream and try to fight him. Gives him even more pleasure when he overpowers them, when he pins them down and they can't move. The struggle for their lives is what feeds him. Their will to survive at any cost is what he thirsts for.

He knows this one will be a struggle. She's a feisty one. He always chooses the spirited ones. It would be no fun if they just gave up, now would it?

In his mind, he goes through his previous killings, tasting every one of them again. He used to do mostly hookers that he would pick up on one of his nightly drives in the car his dad had given him. His first ever kill was a Puerto Rican woman. He picked her up in Cape Canaveral. She was beat up by some guy the night before and had bruises on her face already. He didn't really plan on killing her, he just wanted to get laid. But something about her made him want to hurt her. She was like a bruised animal, pathetic and weak. It was like she was screaming for it.

They had sex in his car, and when he came, everything inside of him just exploded in this unstoppable tsunami of anger. Some psychologists would probably argue that it was his anger towards his mother for not being there when he grew up, or maybe at his father for being just as absent, at least mentally.

Blake didn't care why, he just knew he had to do this, he had to hurt her in order to feel better himself. So he did. He grabbed her around the throat and simply held her while she tried to fight him. He is still amazed when he thinks about how calm he was, despite the rage filling him. It was like the act in itself finally calmed his inner demons, all the voices, all the emotions were finally quiet, drowned out.

When she wasn't breathing anymore, he dumped her in a garbage bin behind a restaurant. No one ever found the body. At least, he didn't think they did. He never heard anything. And he no longer cared. He knew now how to shut up the rage when it showed its ugly face, when it overwhelmed him with that itchy feeling.

But the thing is, it isn't working as well as it used to. He used to be able to wait for months, even a year in the beginning, between kills. But not lately. He needs to do it more and more often to get the calmness back.

Blake swings the door open and walks in. No one in sight. There is light coming from the bathroom. She has to be in there. Excitedly, he shuts the door quietly behind him and hurries towards the bathroom.

He hears her flush and can hear her humming. Then the water is turned on as she washes her hands.

Nice and clean.

He closes his eyes as he follows the sound of her every move. The water being turned off again, then the silence as she wipes her hands on the towel. She mumbles something at her own reflection, then turns and as she opens the door, he opens his eyes and stares at her with a wide smile.

For a quick moment, she looks startled, her eyes wide and open. When she sees the knife in his gloved hand, she gasps and runs for the door. He lets her get ahead, just for the fun of it, then storms after her, and just as her hands land on the door handle, he grabs her by her ponytail and yanks her backwards.

She shrieks and Blake clamps a hand tightly against her mouth and starts to pull her backwards. He throws her on the floor and she tries to kick him, but it hardly hurts. She is not a match for him at all. He slaps her across her face to let her know how strong he is. She screams. He closes his eyes for just a second and tastes her screams, her fear, her anxiety and terror. He feels like the Hulk, who grows bigger and stronger, then looks down at her and slaps her again.

He pins her to the ground, then places a hand on her mouth again. He doesn't want to alarm the neighbors. He doesn't want the police to arrive too early. Not until he's had his way with her, not until he has managed to shut up the unease inside of him.

"Please, don't," she begs behind his hand.

It only makes him smile even wider. The begging is the best part. He tries to imagine what it must be like being her at this moment. What is she thinking?

Will he stop if I beg? If only I can make him feel sorry for me? What if I cry? Will he know that what he is doing is wrong then?

It always amuses Blake that they try to beg. Do they really think he is someone they can reason with? That he is capable of feeling pity? Don't they know he has chosen them? That he has planned this and is determined to finish it? That if he doesn't finish it, he will explode? That there is no way back? No matter how much they plead and beg. There is no way out but death for them.

It's just the way it is.

"Don't do this," she tries again.

Blake laughs, and then slams a fist into the girl's face. It makes her shut up. But only for a few seconds. Then she starts to cry, mostly deep groans and sobs.

That's it, baby girl. Realize it is over. Let it sink in, then slowly give up the fight. I like to look into your eyes as you do.

It is his favorite moment of it all. When they finally give in, finally realize that no matter how much they fight, no matter how much they cry and plead for his mercy, there is no way out, there is nothing left for them but death.

"Why?" she asks in a daze.

He strokes her head gently with his glove, then leans over and whispers in her ear: "Because I can."

"Don't...don't..."

"Sh. There is nothing you can do. The sooner you realize it, the faster it will go," he says.

And that's when he sees it. The girl opens her eyes wide, but there is no more fight in them.

That's it. Let it go.

Blake then lifts the knife in the air above his head and the color drains from her face as he lets it sink into her body.

43

January 2016

MARCIA IS RUNNING up along the beach. She is panting heavily. It's hard to run in the sand. But she doesn't dare to go up on the street. She feels so confused. She can't get her thoughts straight. A thousand pictures are running through her mind, and she can't get them to go away, nor get the voices to shut up so she can think.

I need a drink.

Marcia stops and throws herself in the sand. Behind her, a row of big mansions are staring at her. She wonders if there are people in there, if they'll call the police if they see her. She also wonders if they have any alcohol.

Marcia closes her eyes.

"What am I even doing all the way out here?" she asks out loud. "How did I get here?"

She tries to remember, but she can't. All she knows is that she is in danger, that she can't trust anyone. She turns her head and looks at the houses again. She feels like she knows them, like she has been here before in this exact spot. She doesn't know why. Maybe they just look familiar, especially the big blue one.

Was it in a dream? It doesn't feel real.

Marcia shakes her head and turns away. She stares at the ocean. Nothing seems to make any sense anymore. She is sick and tired of remembering things, remembering her life in small bits and pieces.

Where do all these images come from? The ones of the children in their PJs and their parents, especially the one of the mother haunts her. The wound in her stomach, the blood on her shirt, the eyes staring at the ceiling. Marcia can't remember ever seeing anything like this. And then she remembers. Like a lightning strike, she sees him. In a ball of fire, he is thrown through the living room.

Mark!

"No!"

Marcia is panting and gasping for her breath. "Oh, my God," she whispers, clasping her mouth. "I shot him. I shot Mark!"

Marcia feels dizzy and has to lay her head down in the sand. She can't believe it. She can't believe it is true.

Did I shoot him? Did I shoot my own son?

She can't remember what happened afterwards. She just remembers firing the gun at him. She remembers thinking he was bad; she remembers the fear inside of her. Then what did she do? Did she call the police? Did she lean down and listen to his heart? Did she check his pulse?

No, you didn't. You ran, you coward. You ran away like the fugitive you are.

"I had to go," she says out loud, trying to get the voices to quiet down. "I had to get away before they got to me. I was so scared. Argh!"

Marcia gets up to her feet and yells at the voices. Then she falls to her knees, crying, sobbing.

What have I done?

You killed him. Just like you killed the others.

"No!"

Marcia bends over, crying even harder. She lies down in the sand and closes her eyes, trying to make it all go away. She wants to disappear, but doesn't know how to. Could she run? Just run? But where to?

She hides her face in her hands for a few minutes, then suddenly lifts her head up again. Now with a different look in her eyes, she raises her body to her feet and stares at the blue house, suddenly remembering it.

44

January 2016

I DRIVE to Holmes Regional in Melbourne. On my way there, I call Joey to ask him to be home when Salter gets back from school. He doesn't answer the first time, so I try again. I haven't spoken to him at all today, and have no idea where he spent the night. I fear that he went back to be with her. As I redial, I feel a knot in my stomach, thinking that I am the one who pushed him back to her.

I hope that I am wrong.

"Hello?"

Finally, he picks up.

"Mary?" he says.

"Yes, it's me."

"I am glad you call…"

"I am not calling to chat. I am going to Melbourne and I just need to make sure you are home when Salter gets there in half an hour."

There is nothing but silence on the other end. For a second, I wonder if he has hung up or if we have lost the connection somehow.

"Hello?" I say.

"Is that really why you called?" he asks.

"Yes. Can I count on you?"

"So, you don't want to talk about what happened?" he continues.

I exhale and take a turn. Some idiot almost crashes into me, and I honk the horn slightly more aggressively than needed. "No. I have a lot on my plate right now. I need time."

"I thought you had taken your time. I thought you had made

your decision. Wasn't that why you decided to stay here instead of going back to New York?"

"That was before Jackie. Listen, I really don't..."

"Jackie was before you came back, Mary. Don't you get it? I only saw her when I thought you didn't want me back."

I exhale. I pass the sign telling me I am entering the hospital area, and I drive into the parking lot. I stop the car and close my eyes as I put it in park. I feel so lost. I want to be with Joey, I really do. I want it for myself and for Salter. But I don't want to if it means I have to worry constantly about who he is with, if he is cheating on me again. I can't. I simply can't live like that.

"I don't," I say. "Not anymore."

"You don't what?"

"I don't want you back. Not anymore. Not like this. I can't." I touch the bridge of my nose and lean forward, taking off my seatbelt. I feel like crying. It hurts so badly inside of me I want to scream.

"But...but...Mary...it's me. It's us. It has always been us."

I can't hold the tears back anymore. I wipe them off and try to keep my cool. "I know, Joey, but I can't do this. I can't keep doing this anymore. It's just too hard. I love you, believe me, I do. And I love the idea of us together, especially for Salter's sake, but I can't. I can't take it anymore."

I can tell he is crying on the other end. This was not where or how I wanted to have this talk. But, what's done is done. I cry while holding the phone close to my ear. I feel so miserable, so devastated and destroyed.

"Mary...I...please," he is still crying on the other end. His voice is breaking; his sobs are loud. He is not even trying to hide it anymore. "Please, give me one more chance. I know I can do better. I know I can."

"Maybe you can, but I know I can't. Even if you never cheat on me again, I'll still never be able to trust you again. I am sorry."

To spare myself any more misery, I hang up. My body is shaking as I put the phone away. I sit for a few seconds and stare at the parking lot, biting my lip while tears rush across my cheeks.

45

January 2016

I HIDE my face in my hands as I finish crying, then wipe my eyes. I look at myself in the mirror and realize I look terrible. A full night of no sleep and now all the crying has messed up my face. I find my mascara and eyeliner and try to fix myself up a little, then decide there is nothing more I can do and leave the car.

Putting the conversation behind me, I walk to the hospital's entrance. I find Mark on the fifth floor. He is not alone in his room. Harry is standing next to his bed. He is talking with him, and they stop as I walk in.

"Hi," I say.

As I walk closer, I realize someone else is there. It's Jess, Marcia's sponsor. She is sitting in a chair, her back turned to me.

Mark smiles when he sees me. He doesn't look too good. Not just because of the wound in his shoulder. He is pale, his eyes are like deep black holes, and he is so skinny. I haven't seen him in weeks. He must have lost ten pounds since I last saw him. His hair looks strange.

"Mary!" Harry says and walks to me. He pulls me into his warm embrace. I am quite startled by this, but manage to hug him back awkwardly. I walk to Mark and grab his hand.

"How are you?"

"All right," he says. "The bullet only grazed me."

"He was very lucky," Harry says.

"I am so sorry for this," I say, pressing tears back. Seeing him like this breaks my heart.

"Don't be," Mark says. "You didn't do it."

"Well, I can't help feeling responsible. I should have known it was bad. I should have reacted earlier when realizing how bad her drinking had become," I say.

I feel Harry's hand on my shoulder. "You can't blame yourself."

"If anyone is to blame, it should be us," a voice says from the door. I turn and see Alex, Danny, Sandra, and Chloe as they walk inside holding balloons and flowers. I smile and shed a few tears that I wipe away.

"We knew way before you came back here that she wasn't doing well," Danny says and walks to the bedside. "Yet we didn't do anything."

"I guess we have all been too busy with our own lives and messes to realize how bad it really was," Sandra says, and walks up to him as well.

I am stunned to see her outside her house, in a place as public as a hospital, and she doesn't seem to be embarrassed at all by people seeing her. It's the first time since it happened that I have such strength and determination in her. It warms my heart.

"I could have done more as well," Jess says, and gets up from the chair. She walks around, introducing herself to everyone and shaking their hands.

"Me too," Harry says, and does the same.

"So, now we have all established that we didn't do enough," Chloe says. "How about we now figure out what to do about it? How to help Mark and his siblings and how to help Marcia."

"I met with her," I blurt out.

The surprise on my friend's faces is obvious. They're all speaking at the same time, so I have no idea who is saying what.

I continue. "She texted me this morning and had me come to our old surf spot in Sebastian."

"The Spanish House?" Alex says.

"Yes. I went there and met with her, thinking I could get her to turn herself in. Maybe talk sense in to her."

"Was she drunk?" Danny asks.

"No. At least I don't think so. She says she hasn't had a drink since Saturday night when I picked her up and took her home. Strangely enough, I believe her. She didn't smell like alcohol like she usually does; her speech wasn't slurred, and her eyes weren't glassy or red."

"She could have taken pills," Jess says.

"She seemed like she wasn't intoxicated or under the influence of anything, but still she was not the Marcia I know."

"What do you mean?" Jess says.

"It was like she...I don't know. Like something else was wrong... Like..."

"Like she was someone else," Mark says.

"You know what I'm talking about?"

Mark nods with a deep sigh.

"I think something is very wrong with her," I say. "Beyond the drinking. I think she is very sick."

46

January 2016

MARK IS EXHAUSTED, but feels comforted that his mother's friends are all here with him in the hospital. More than anything, he worries about his mother now.

"What do you mean sick?" Danny asks.

"I think she's suffering from a mental illness or something," Mary says. "She kept rambling about how everyone was in on a plot to get her or something. That's why she didn't want to turn herself in. She had no idea what had happened; she didn't even know that she had shot Mark."

"When did this start?" Jess asks, addressed to Mark.

He looks at her while his heart is pounding in his chest. For so long he has managed to keep his mother's condition a secret. He even thought he could get away with just telling everyone that his mother mistook him for being an intruder when she shot him. He is arguing within himself, while everyone in the room is looking at him. Can he confide in them? He knows they're all his mother's friends, that they're only trying to help. But what will happen to her if he tells everything? Will they lock her away for good? Will he have to live with his father, his abusive and violent father? He can't keep an eye on his siblings every hour of the day. He can't protect them if they send them all back there.

"Mark?" Jess asks and moves closer.

He looks her in the eyes. He knows her well. Back several months ago, when his mother had the DUI and was forced to go to the meetings, she was there for her. Jess took good care of his mother and things had gotten better for a little while. A lot better. He knew Jess played a big part in that. His mother had trusted her. So maybe he could too?

"I first knew something was wrong three years ago when she started to sound different."

"Three years ago?" Mary exclaims. Mark sees tears in her eyes. "You've been dealing with this for three years?"

"Yes. I don't know precisely when it started, but she was just different all of a sudden. She didn't drink that much back then. Not like she does now. But she never sounded happy. She didn't get excited about anything like she used to, and then there was this story about some people from her work. She worked at the fitness center on 520, the HealthPlex, in reception, and one day she told me that some of her colleagues were jealous of her and that she was certain they were planning something behind her back. Then later, she told me one day that she wasn't feeling well and that she believed that one of the scheming co-workers had stuck her with a needle with some drug to take her out of the competition for a top job. She kept complaining about feeling strange and said that she couldn't concentrate, and said it was all due to the drug. She was obsessing about it at home, constantly blaming her co-workers. I knew something was wrong, but I was eleven. What could I do? I had no idea what it could be. Later, she quit her job because she was afraid and she told me she didn't like to work on computers because the computers were bugged and they were trying to steal her many ideas. She believed she was going to invent something big and become a millionaire. All she needed was some peace and quiet to work on her ideas, and she couldn't get that when working all day."

"I bet she was so convincing you believed she would become a millionaire, right?" Jess says.

"We all did. She asked us to write lists of all the stuff we wanted to buy when we got all this money and places we would like to live. We were going to buy fifteen houses so we could live all over the world. She wanted so badly to take us to Spain. We started dreaming about all of it and couldn't wait."

"But it never happened. Instead, she got even worse, right?" Jess says taking his hand in hers. Mark feels like crying, thinking back on this, but he holds it back.

"Some days, I would come home from school and she would be sitting in the living room staring into thin air, completely zoned out for hours in a row. She would hardly blink or even change her expression. Then, after two hours like that, she would suddenly burst into laughter for no reason at all. Sometimes she would sit and stare at her hands for hours, when I would ask what was wrong with her hands, she would say they were different than they used to be. She would go from one job to another, but lose them as fast as she got them. One time when she worked at a restaurant, they called the house and told me she suddenly walked out of there and never came back. We didn't see her for days. When she finally came back, she had no idea she had been gone."

"Did she hear voices? Did she ever talk about that?" Jess asks.

"She did say that she talked to God sometimes and he told her the lottery numbers and that he was going to make us very rich. She would go into her bedroom and I could hear her talking to someone in there, even though she was alone. Sometimes she spoke in a language I didn't understand. She would scream that we were all going to die, that we couldn't drink the water because there was bacteria in it that was going to eat us up from the inside. She would tell me the walls had bugs in them. She told us we all looked different, my eyebrows were pointed upward and my ears had grown. She said things were moving when they were not. She stayed away more and more, and would come back thinking no time had passed, pretending like she hadn't been away, and then if I said something, I could tell she really had no idea. I started grocery shopping and making sure the little ones took showers. We would eat cereal mostly for all our meals, and then one day she would come home with her hands full of groceries and start to cook or take us out to eat because we had something to celebrate, but not be able to pay for it. The restaurants usually took pity on us and didn't call the police, but asked us to never come again. At the house, we never knew who would come in the door. Sweet and fun Mommy or weird Mommy or angry Mommy."

"And all this time, you had to protect your siblings and take care of them, huh?" Jess says and strokes Mark gently.

"I was always afraid. Some weeks ago, she started telling me she believed the government was controlling me. That I was part of a plot against her and that freaked me out. She would yell at me or wait behind the door and then attack me, and try to beat me when I entered the house. Sometimes I would wake up and she would be by my bed in the middle of the night, staring at me, holding a baseball bat in her hand. I became afraid to come home, and I figured me being there only made things worse. So I stayed away sometimes even at night."

While speaking, Mark had completely forgotten that the room was full of people, his mother's friends. He couldn't believe he told them everything just like that, but once he opened up, it felt like such a relief to finally tell, to finally talk to someone about this. Now he can feel the tears well up in his eyes and he can no longer hold them back. He lets them go and starts to cry.

"I am so sorry," he says. "I have failed. I should have done more. I could have helped her."

"No," Jess says. "Listen to me. Your mother is very ill. I have to say, I had no idea. She hides it well. But it sounds like she might be suffering from Schizophrenia. That is very serious. She might be out there doing stuff that she has no idea of. She might be a danger to others and herself. We need to find her. We need to find her fast."

47

January 2016

MONDAY IS ALWAYS a busy day for Kelly. She has to get up at six-thirty, make breakfast for all three of them, get Lindsey ready for school, make her lunch and drive her to school. Then she goes to Publix and gets everything for the coming week, planning every meal in detail, making sure it's organic and non-gluten. Today, she even has to go to the dry-cleaners and pick up Andrew's suit for his trip to Virginia. Then she goes back home, unpacks all the groceries, and has a quick cup of coffee before the cleaners arrive. Then she goes to the gym for an hour and a half, and grabs a sandwich when she returns to her newly cleaned house. After lunch, she does the laundry and calls the dentist to make an appointment for Lindsey, the half-yearly check-up that she always has in January. She drives to the library and picks up some books for her daughter to read before she goes back to the school and sits in the pick-up line.

The feeling of being observed seems to be gone today. Come to think of it, she hasn't seen the truck at all today. Maybe it did help that they talked to the police on Sunday. Maybe whoever has been watching her saw them go to the police station yesterday and got scared? Maybe.

"Hi sweetie, how was your day?" she asks Lindsey as she gets into the SUV and they drive off.

"Meh," the girl answers.

"Not good, huh?"

"Nicole is having a birthday party sleepover and I am not invited. She says her mom doesn't like me."

"I am sorry," Kelly says. She feels anger rise inside of her. She knows Nicole's mom well. Who does she think she is?

Kelly gets a flashback to her own childhood and all the times she wasn't invited to parties or kept out of the fun by mean girls in school. Being a teenager wasn't a fun time for her. She hates that her daughter soon has to go through that as well. It makes her want to homeschool her.

"Can we go get some ice cream?" Lindsey asks.

Kelly looks at the clock. There's a guy coming to look at the AC unit at four. It hasn't been working properly lately. She really doesn't have time for ice cream, but she can tell her daughter is really sad about the birthday-thing, and she wants to cheer her up a little.

"If we make it fast," she says.

"Yes!" her daughter exclaims.

Kelly chuckles and takes a turn towards their favorite ice cream place in Melbourne Beach, *Sundaes at the Beach*. She is in a good mood today. No brown truck and no weird people in hoodies staring at her or accidentally bumping into her makes her relieved beyond compare. She hasn't even received one phone call hang-up all day. She feels certain it is over. The small trip to the police station fixed it.

The sergeant there hadn't been much help. He basically told them he couldn't do much about it unless a crime had been committed, but he could tell his officers to drive past their house during the day, if that helped.

"That'll scare them away," Andrew told her afterwards, "Seeing a police car on the street. Don't worry. They're probably just waiting for us to go away so they can rob the house. But we're not going anywhere, and once they see the police car, they'll get lost."

Kelly didn't believe him when he told her, but now she has to admit, she was wrong. She is glad she was.

"I want a banana split!" Lindsey says, as they enter the shop.

The place is famous for its banana splits, so Kelly agrees to let her have one and she even orders one for herself. It's been many years since she last let herself indulge in such a feast, but today she feels like celebrating.

Bellies full of ice cream, whipped cream, chocolate, and bananas, they drive back to the house and park in the driveway. They barely make it inside before the AC guy arrives. Kelly calls Andrew to let him know the guy is here, and then tells him about her day.

"Not once did I see the truck, Andy. I am certain it's over."

"That's a relief," he says. "Now we can go back to living our lives normally again."

"I got your suit from the dry cleaners," she says, while Lindsey starts her homework.

"Perfect. I'll only be gone three days. You'll be fine while I'm gone, right?"

Kelly looks at her daughter, who looks up and smiles. "I think we will. I really do think we will."

"Great. Then I won't feel bad for going. You know I have to go. It's an important trip for the company."

"I know. We'll be just fine. Don't worry."

48

January 2016

I AM DEVASTATED. Completely torn apart. How could Mark have been going through all of this alone? How could he have lived like this for three years and no one knew?

Poor kid.

I can tell everyone is thinking the same as we say goodbye to Mark in the hospital and leave. No one talks in the elevator; we're all too torn up by guilt, and we can't help being a little angry with Marcia, even though we all know she can't help it.

Why didn't she ask for our help?

We have decided to all do what we can to find Marcia and get her back, so she can get help. Chloe and I have decided to go back to Sebastian, where I saw her last, and start looking for her in that area. I have no idea how she got down there in the first place. With her DUI, I didn't expect her to be driving a car, but again, with her, I really don't know what to expect anymore.

Jess decides to go with us and we all drive in my car. Meanwhile, Danny has to go back to the fire station, while Alex and Sandra told us they'll be looking for her in the Cocoa Beach area, in case she comes back. I look at the two walking close together, so close it's hard to tell if they're holding hands or not. I decide it's not my problem anymore. Angry as I am with them, especially now with what I am going through, I realize it's not my issue. If they want to make a mess, then they're on their own. I warned them; there really isn't more I can do.

"If she is, in fact, Schizophrenic, there really is no saying what she might do," Jess says as we hit A1A. "She could very well be suicidal."

134

"Do you think she might also be capable of killing someone?" I ask.

Chloe is sitting in the passenger seat. She looks at me. Our eyes meet. I can tell she doesn't want me to tell Jess what Marcia told me, but I feel like I have to.

"Anything is possible, really," she answers. "I mean, she shot at Mark, didn't she? Why?"

I shrug. "It was just something Marcia told me when I was alone with her earlier on the beach."

"You think she might have killed someone?" Jess asks, startled. "That is very serious."

"No. I don't think she did it, but…how do I explain this? She had these images, these visions that kept haunting her, she said. It might just be in her imagination. It didn't seem real at all."

"What kind of images?"

Chloe is signaling me to stop talking, but it's too late. Jess wants to know. I feel like it's a good idea to tell her, since Marcia told me she is a psychologist, so she should know about these things.

"I don't know. Some kids and their parents lying on the floor, the mother bleeding and the children, she believed, were dead. She kept asking me if I believed she had killed them. That's why I was wondering. Personally, I don't believe she is capable of killing anyone. Not Marcia."

"She did try to shoot her own son," Jess says.

"She thought he was an intruder," I say.

Chloe is being very quiet. I can sense that she doesn't like where this conversation is heading.

"According to what Mark told me, she knew it was him," Jess says. "She said to him that she believed he was working with the government in some conspiracy against her. But she was aware it was him when she pulled that trigger."

I can't say anything more to defend her. I haven't heard Mark's version of it, but I know in my heart that it is probably true, what Jess is saying. It just hurts so badly to know that my old childhood friend has lost it like this. The worst part is, I am starting to fear the worst. I am beginning to ask myself the question: Was Marcia there on the day the Elingston family was attacked in their own home and later killed? And if she was, then was she the one who brutally murdered that poor family? Could she commit such a horrendous act?

49

August 2006

"I don't trust her."

Daniel looks at his mother. She is better now and sitting by the fireplace of her house. She coughs between sentences, but has regained the color in her cheeks and the feistiness in her voice.

"She told me the other day that Peter doesn't like pop music, that he doesn't like to listen to it before bedtime. According to her, Peter told her so," she says. "Peter loves music. Especially Kelly Clarkson. It's not fine art, it's not classy, but it's what he enjoys listening to. And you know it, Daniel. Now she says he likes classical music instead."

Daniel doesn't speak. He looks at the wooden floors. He doesn't want to say it, but he knows she is right. Peter loves Kelly Clarkson and listens to her all the time. She's his favorite singer, and he even has his own little dance that he does, swinging his head from side to side when they put her on.

"No woman should tell me what my boy likes and what he doesn't like," their mother continues with an angry snort. "I cared for Daniel for twenty-five years. I already know what he likes."

Daniel can't blame her for being upset. His other siblings that are present in the living room are troubled as well.

"She told me he likes brandy and champagne," his older sister says. "Our brother never liked anything with alcohol in it. Remember when we let him taste wine? He spat it right out."

"Maybe his taste has changed," Daniel says. He is trying to defend Kristin, but he can see why they're upset. He has noticed it too. Kristin has been moving in on all areas of Peter's life. "It happens when you grow older. I didn't used to like wine either, but now I do."

"But she is changing everything," Daniel's older brother says. "Even the way Peter dresses. She told mother that what she bought for him was not what he liked to wear, then went out and bought all these suits for him, even shirts and ties. Why does Peter need to wear a tie?"

"I don't know," Daniel says with a deep exhale. He is tired of defending Kristin, but he feels like he has to. It was all his idea. He contacted her, he got her to care for Peter, and he was thrilled when she did. But now, he isn't so sure anymore. What he believed was an opening into Peter's world was starting to look more and more like a woman taking over his life. It was nothing like what Daniel had dreamt it would be.

"The reason I called you all to come today," their mother says. "Is that we need to stop this woman."

"What?" Daniel says. "But...but what about all the progress she has made with him? He goes to college now. He'll get a degree."

"To what use, Daniel? For what does he need this degree, exactly?" His brother asks. "It's not like someone is going to hire him. It's not like he can suddenly take care of himself. It's great if he enjoys it, but I'm not so sure he understands anything."

"That's not true. I've seen him in his classes. You should read the papers he writes," Daniel continues.

"That he writes? Are you even listening to yourself?" his brother says. "Peter has CP. He can't control his body. How is he supposed to write a paper?"

"Daniel. We no longer believe that he is writing them," his sister takes over.

"What?"

"We believe she might be assisting him a little too much," she continues, glancing at the other siblings, looking for backup. They're all nodding.

Daniel can't believe them. Yes, he knows it has all gone a little too far, and maybe the woman is taking over a little too much of Peter's life, but he still believes that Peter is communicating, that what he writes on that keyboard comes from him.

"The latest development is that she has told me Peter wants to move out. Apparently, he wants to move into an apartment on his own," their mother says. "There is no way he can do that. I refuse to let it happen."

50

January 2016

WE SEARCH the area around the Spanish House all afternoon, but with no luck. Marcia is nowhere to be found. Not on the beach, not in the park across the street, not in the inlet or around the pier. We talk to all the surfers and fishermen that we meet, but no one has seen her.

By nightfall, we are ready to give up.

"She could be anywhere," Chloe says, as we walk back towards the car. "There is no way we can find her once it gets dark."

The sun is setting over the land on the horizon and paints the sky pink. It is gorgeous. I stare at it for a little while, wondering if Marcia is all right. I keep seeing her face and those frightened eyes that I had seen earlier. I am afraid for her. Afraid of what she might do in her state of desperation. I know she is carrying a gun. I worry a police patrol will find her. That will never end well. She'll refuse to even talk to them, and then pull the gun. I just know she will.

"We can't give up," I say. "The police are looking for her for shooting Mark. If they find her before we do, there is no saying what will happen to her. I don't think she'll survive it."

Jess puts a hand on my shoulder. "Not everything in this world is your responsibility, Mary. Yes, Marcia is sick and a possible danger to both herself and others, but you can't help her if she doesn't want you to."

I look at her and think that it's a load of crap, probably the kind that psychologists tell themselves all the time, but this is not my patient we're talking about. This is my friend. I don't say anything, though. I am exhausted. And starving.

We get back in the car and drive home in silence. I can't believe we couldn't find Marcia. How hard can it be to find one person? I keep wondering where she could have gone to after she left me on the beach. She ran through the bushes, but where to? Where could she go? The sky is dark out now, and I have heard on the radio that a front is pushing through tonight. It is expected to cause heavy thunderstorms. The National Weather Service has issued a severe thunderstorm warning for our county from tonight until the morning, and there's a tornado watch. It's not as bad as a tornado warning, but still. It's not a night to be outdoors.

Will Marcia be able to find shelter?

I drop off Jess at the parking lot in front of her condominium in Cocoa Beach, and thank her for her help. "Anytime," she says with a smile and closes the door.

"You wanna grab a bite to eat?" I ask Chloe as we drive off.

"I can't. Gotta take care of my mom. I've been away almost all day. Sorry."

"That's okay," I say, and drive up in front of her old house on 7th Street. "By the way, did you get anything out of that tip from Arizona?" I ask, as she is about to leave the car. She nods. "It started to sound plausible. I checked with the newspapers and the police department. There's a couple up there that robbed a small liquor store recently, and they match the description. Could be them."

"Let me know if you find out more," I say with a yawn. I am so tired I can hardly see anything.

"Sure thing."

She slams the door to the car shut, and I drive off towards Joey's house. As I approach it, I am filled with an overwhelming sadness. I park outside in the driveway as it starts to rain. There is light coming from inside the house and I can see Joey in there walking into the kitchen. I am guessing he and Salter are watching a movie. I hope they have brought my dad into the living room with them. He needs the company. I sigh as I spot Salter and my dad in the living room. They seem engaged in some deep talk. Now they're laughing. They seem happy. Joey is joining them, holding a bowl of popcorn. I feel my eyes water. This is my family and I don't want to go in. I don't want to have to face Joey. I don't want to argue and ruin the atmosphere. They seem to be doing so well without me.

Instead, I take off.

51

January 2016

KNOWING I won't be able to rest or even stay still till I am sure I have been everywhere, I decide to drive around for a little, checking Marcia's usual places in Cocoa Beach. I go to the Sportsbar, the Beach Shack, and Coconuts on the Beach, even Sandbar. I check all the local places she might be, but no one has seen her for days. I walk the beach with my flashlight and look through the dunes. I talk to every drunk and homeless person I can find, but no one has seen her since Saturday.

Frustrated, I drive back. When I pass Marcia's place, I hit the brakes. The Seaview Suites is a row of small townhouses by 8th Street, across the street from the beach. It's a place where my parents never wanted me to go as a child. The rent is the cheapest on the beach, and therefore it attracts a lot of scum. There is almost always loud music coming from one of the houses and the sound of people partying.

There's light coming from Marcia's windows.

I park in front of her door and walk up. Someone is fighting loudly behind an open window somewhere. A dog is barking aggressively. I knock.

Harry smiles when he opens the door. "Mary?"

"She's not come home by any chance, has she?" I ask, thinking it's a long shot, but if she is as sick as I suspect her to be, she might as well be here as anywhere else.

He shakes his head. "I am sorry, no."

"I didn't think so. Just had to check," I say, and start to walk away.

"Wait. Don't you want to come in?"

"No. No, I couldn't."

"Please?" he asks. His eyes are pleading with me. "It's way too quiet in here without the kids."

I chuckle. "Don't tell me you miss them?"

He shrugs. "Guess I got used to the craziness around here, huh?" He looks at me. Our eyes lock. He is so handsome it almost hurts. I have to admit, I am tempted. I really want to go in. I want to be in his company.

"I just made a batch of chili. Do you want some? I have more than enough. I've gotten used to cooking for a lot of people, so I think I made way too much. You look like you could use a meal."

Really? Have you seen the extra chin I am growing?

I laugh. He is sweet. "Well, I am starving, and I have to say it smells heavenly."

He smiles again. "Come on in, then."

He rushes to the kitchen and finds a bowl for me. I sit at the table and let him serve me. I can sense that he is trying his best to make it good for me and it makes me laugh. I look at the huge pot of chili he has made.

"That is a lot of food," I say, as he pours some in my bowl.

"I know. I don't know what I would have done if you hadn't come along. I really don't like eating alone. Guess coming from a big family damaged me somehow."

"You come from a big family?" I ask, and taste the food. The chili is amazing. I feel the hunger now biting at me.

"Yes. Lots of brothers and sisters."

"Sounds nice," I say, and think about my own family. I shudder when thinking about my younger brother and who he turned out to be.

Talk about a dysfunctional family.

"And you?" Harry asks.

"I, well, it's a long story. I only have one brother, but I don't know him very well. He's a lot younger than me. As it turns out, I don't know him at all. I only really have my dad left, and he is paralyzed. That's a long story too. But back to you. Did you grow up around here?"

"Palm Beach Gardens."

"Ah, the rich area."

"It has its poor side too," he says.

"Of course. Is that where you're from? You don't look like the poor boy from the wrong side of the tracks."

"Guilty as charged. I guess you could say I was one of the rich kids. Seconds?"

I nod eagerly. I look around the room while he serves me another portion. I have never seen Marcia's house so neat, so tidy. Not that I have been there much since she moved in.

"So, what is a guy like you doing in a place like this?" I ask.

He shrugs. "Trying something new."

"Yeah, but come on. Why rent a room in this cheap place if you're rich? Why move to Cocoa Beach? Why is a guy like you not married with a bunch of children with your gorgeous athletic wife?"

He stares at me intensely. It makes me uncomfortable, but also warm inside. "Don't you just like to stick your nose in everything, huh?"

"Sorry."

His face eases up. "No, it's okay. I can't blame you for wondering; I just don't like to talk much about myself."

"Lots of baggage, huh?" I ask.

"You could say that."

52

January 2016

"So, what are your plans for your stay here in Cocoa Beach? How long are you planning on staying?" I ask, after a couple of minutes of silence. I am still eating. I can't stop. It's just that good.

"I don't really know yet," Harry says. He stopped eating long ago, and now it's just me. He is leaning in over the table, looking at me with a wide smile. "You really like it, don't you?"

I finish chewing and swallow. "I do," I say. I get embarrassed. I have eaten three portions now, and still I could eat more. "I am sorry."

"No. No. By all means. I like to watch you eat. It's so refreshing. So many women are scared of eating. I like it when they're alive, you know? When they don't hold back. I mean, if they're willing to indulge in a wonderful meal, what else would they be willing to indulge in, right? Women who don't hold back are often the most passionate."

I blush. Seriously blush at his words. "Then you won't mind if I take a little more?"

"Not at all," he says.

I scoop up another portion and eat it while he stares at me. I can't help laughing.

"What's so funny?"

"You are. You're just staring at me. It's kind of creepy," I say.

"I can't help myself. I enjoy watching you."

I finish my plate and push it to the center of the table. It's a habit I have always had. I don't know where it comes from. I like sitting here with Harry. He makes me feel good about myself. Joey is always on my case, teasing me about how much I eat. Here's a man who actually enjoys it. But, at the same time, I can't quite figure this guy out. Everything about him is a little strange. Why isn't he married? Why is he living here with Marcia? I haven't even been able to get out of him what he does for a living. It annoys me that he keeps avoiding my questions, but at the same time, I like him to stay a little mysterious. It's kind of sexy. It's been a long time since I have felt like this.

With Joey, it's different. We have known each other all of our lives, so there was never any mystery. There was no excitement or tickling sensation in my stomach, because—well, it was Joey. I loved him. I still love him, but I am starting to wonder if there needs to be more in a relationship, in a marriage? Were we just good friends who were married?

"You have to excuse me," Harry says, and leaves the table. He walks up the stairs to the restroom. I hear him lock the door. I sit at the table for a little while, but it's hard for me to stay still. I want to find out more about this guy so badly. Leaned up against the wall, I see a briefcase. I am guessing it's his and walk to it. I open it and look at the content. It's all news clippings. Pictures and articles. I pick it up and look at it.

What is this? It's all about that woman who was killed, the one they pulled out of the river!

So, Marcia was right when she told me he had pictures of her in his room? She told me she had seen them.

I pick up one of the photographs. I can see it's the same woman from the pictures in the newspaper, but in this picture, she is younger. Way younger. It looks like a school picture.

Why does he have this?

I look at one of the articles and notice that he has highlighted some of the names of witnesses that the police have talked to in the case. Why has he highlighted their names? The name of the woman was Shannon Ferguson. She was a third-grade teacher at Roosevelt Elementary School. I had no idea that she was one of the teachers at Salter's school.

I hear the door open, and hurry up and close the briefcase before Harry gets down the stairs. "So, do you think you'll have room for dessert?" he asks, smiling. My eyes glance quickly at the briefcase, while I wonder if I placed it the right way so he won't see I have opened it. Harry notices my glance and looks at the briefcase as well, then back at me.

"I have ice cream."

53

January 2016

I EAT the ice cream silently, wondering who this guy really is sitting across from me. Why is he so into the murder of this woman?

"You're so quiet all of a sudden?" he asks.

"Just enjoying the ice cream," I say. "And I'm really tired now. Been quite a long day."

Harry sighs and leans back in his chair. "I know what you mean. I'm beat too. What a night and day. I worry so much about Marcia. And the kids. They didn't seem very excited by seeing their dad today. I got the feeling it's not the best for them to live with him. Maybe you know more about that than me?"

I look into Harry's eyes. Scrutinizing them. I sense such an affection for the children in him. Children he hasn't known for very long. I have no idea how to read this guy. Is it real? Is he just acting?

"I never met Carl, but I know he used to beat them. That's why she moved away and took the kids with her. That's what she told me. But, then again, I don't know any more what is real and what she has been making up. I keep wondering if I know her at all. It's a little scary. I kind of went through the same thing with my younger brother. You think you know someone and then…well…" I shrug and finish my ice cream. "I don't know if you know what I mean."

Harry grabs my hand across the table. The gesture startles me. His hands are big and warm. Mine almost disappears inside of his.

"I know exactly what you mean."

Looking into his eyes, I get the feeling he does understand. His thumb is rubbing my hand. I begin to feel like I am cheating on Joey, even though we haven't done anything.

You're done with Joey, remember? It's okay. If he can do it, then you can too.

I pull my hand out of his grip. "I should go."

He looks disappointed. Then he smiles. "Of course. It's getting late."

"My son is waiting for me."

I get up and walk to the door. I hear him behind me, and seconds later, I feel his hand on my shoulder. It's heavy and warm. I turn and look directly into his face. He grabs me and pulls me close. His breath is on my face. Our lips are close.

"Why do I get the feeling you want this just as much as I do?" he whispers.

I close my eyes and enjoy his closeness. "Because I do."

"I thought you were taken. Marcia told me…"

"Shut up," I say, and place my lips on his.

He grabs my face between his hands while we kiss. I am so close to him I can feel his heartbeat. I look into his eyes as our lips depart from one another. He is moaning. "I want this too," he whispers. "I have wanted it since the first day I saw you. You're so beautiful, Mary."

Beautiful? Me?

He looks into my eyes. He is still holding my face between his hands, lifting it slightly to better study me. His eyes are staring into mine, devouring me.

"Your eyes are so…so deep and full of life," he says.

I look down and pull his hands away. "I…I hardly know you," I say.

He is shaking his head. "No. It doesn't matter, Mary."

I take a step backwards. I shake my head. "I should go."

"Please, don't go. Please stay."

I stare at his beautiful face. I can't believe I am about to walk away from this, but it's too early for me. I am not ready. I reach the door and I can feel the handle behind my back. I stare at him, then storm towards him again and kiss him one last time before I run out of the house.

54

January 2016

WHEN MARCIA WAKES UP, it's cold. She can hear loud noises. It sounds like thunder. It's raining heavily. She can hear it and starts to wonder where she is. She sits up in the complete darkness. She's lying on the floor, but it doesn't feel like she is inside. The wind is howling and blowing through something, it sounds like a door. Lightning strikes outside and lights up everything. She sees two cars next to her.

She is in a garage.

But whose garage is it and how did I get here?

Marcia tries to remember what happened the day before. All she can recall is going to Beef O' Brady's with the kids.

"Kids eat free on Tuesdays," she mumbles to herself, as she finds her way to the window and looks outside.

She must have found shelter here last night from the storm, but how did she get in? She doesn't remember. She looks outside at the storm raging. Puddles of water have gathered in the driveway as more is pouring down. She has got to get out of there, but this is not the time to be outside. Not with all those lightning strikes. It's too dangerous. She knows she has to wait it out. But how long will this storm last? She can't risk getting caught in here. People like these, rich people like this, own guns. They protect themselves. Marcia reaches down in the side of her pants and pulls out a gun. She doesn't remember where she got it, and startled, she drops it to the ground.

Marcia feels great unease spread as she tries to remember where she is and how she got there. But there is nothing but a big black gap in her mind. No matter how hard she tries, she simply can't put the puzzle pieces together.

She wonders where her bike is, since she usually never goes anywhere without it. Not since they took her driver's license.

When was that again? Last month?

Marcia shakes her head and sits back on the ground. Lightning strikes often outside now and keeps lighting up the room. She picks up the gun and feels how heavy it is in her hand. She knows how to shoot it. She remembers how her father taught her as a child. He would take her to the woods and help her shoot cans. The memory makes her smile. She loved her father. He was the best thing about her childhood. Until the day he vanished when Marcia was eleven. Her mom told her he was hit by a car, but later in life, she learned that he had jumped out of the top of a building, convinced he could fly like a bird. She had so many fond memories of him. Some days, they would dress up like ladies and skip to the grocery store, singing the song from *The Sound of Music*, "My Favorite Things," wearing wigs and hats, and then on other days he would sit in the corner of the living room in the darkness and stare at the wall for hours, mumbling. Marcia used to think it was her fault when he had those days. That she wasn't good enough. She still wondered if it was her fault that he jumped off that building. Maybe there was something she could have done differently.

Marcia puts the gun back in her pants, then looks around as the next lightning strikes outside and lights up the driveway. There is something awfully familiar about this driveway and the house. Has she been here before? Does she know who lives here? It doesn't look like the house of any of her friends. It's way too expensive, and the neighborhood is too nice. The cars are on the luxurious side as well. None of her friends live like this. Not even Sandra, who is the richest person she knows. Sandra is more the type that saves all her money. She doesn't spend it on big houses and cars. That's not her style.

Marcia sighs, while wondering where the heck she is and how to get back to her kids.

They must be worried. Poor babies. Maybe I can take a taxi back once the storm has passed?

She realizes she has no money as she goes through her wallet. She needs money to get home.

Maybe these people have some lying around the house? They'll probably not even notice it if it's gone.

55

January 2016

I WAKE UP WITH A START. I look to my side and see Salter in the bed next to me. He looks like an angel. Joey is sleeping on the couch in the living room for now. When I got back the night before, Salter was already in bed, and it was very awkward between Joey and me. I spoke as little as possible with him, basically just told him we hadn't found Marcia and that we would be looking again tomorrow, then went to the bedroom and climbed into bed, hoping that Joey would know that I didn't want him in the bedroom. I couldn't fall asleep lying all alone, so I ended up carrying Salter into my bed with me.

Outside the window, the storm is raging. I look at it while thinking about Marcia. I so hope she has managed to find shelter somewhere.

"Where are you, Marcia?" I mumble, while looking out at the storm. It's like Niagara Falls out there. I wonder if the roof of Joey's small house will hold through it. Then I wonder about the construction site where they're building my dad's house. I hope it'll make it through the storm as well.

I look at the clock. It's only five in the morning. I still have an hour and a half before I have to get up and get Salter to school. But I can't sleep anymore. I am too worried about Marcia being out there all alone.

Then I realize something.

I have a fan base. I have followers that read what I write. They helped me with my brother. Maybe they can help me with Marcia as well?

I jump out of bed and walk to the computer and turn it on. Then I start writing. I write a post about Marcia, about how much I love her, but also about how we believe she is very sick and in need of help. I tell them that she was last seen in Sebastian Inlet on the beach, but we have no idea how she got there, or where she could be now. Then I find a picture on my phone of Marcia that I attach to the post and press send.

I know it won't go viral, and I have no idea how many of my followers are from this area, but it's worth a shot.

As soon as it is done, I go back to bed, and close my eyes for what feels like just one second before the alarm goes off. Snowflake jumps up on the bed and starts to lick Salter on the face like he always does in the morning.

"Hey. Good morning," Salter says with sleep in his eyes, then pets the dog while laughing, because it tickles when the dog licks him.

I wonder when I should tell him that we won't be living with his dad once Grandpa's house is done. How do you tell your child that his parents messed up again? Even if I blame mostly Joey, I can't help feeling guilty myself.

While Salter gets dressed, I walk into the living room. Outside our door, Bonnie and Clyde are waiting, since I told them to stay with Joey for the night. I have a hard time coping with the pig's smell at night. They attack Snowflake and me as soon as I open the door. Well, mostly Snowflake, since he is by far their favorite. The animals run around sniffing each other like they haven't seen each other in months. Even Bonnie imitates the dogs and sniffs Snowflake's behind. It's quite the sight.

Joey is still asleep on the couch, so I take all the animals into the yard so they can do their business, then walk to the kitchen and make breakfast for my son. Joey wakes up and looks at me from the couch.

"You have no idea how much it kills my back to sleep on this thing," he says grumpily.

I shrug, but don't answer. I want to say a lot of things like *you should have thought about that before you slept with someone else, again*, or *that's what you get for cheating on me—again!*

But I don't. I don't want to fight anymore. And I especially don't want to fight in front of Salter.

"I have running club today," Salter says, as he shovels in his cereal. "Someone has to pick me up at four."

"We will," I say, without looking at Joey. I try to avoid him as much as possible, even though it is hard. I hand Salter his lunchbox. "Don't worry."

"What's wrong?" he asks, scrutinizing me.

"What do you mean?"

"Have you and Dad been fighting? Why is he sleeping on the couch again?" he asks. I hear great worry in his little voice.

I sigh. This is not the time to tell him, but I still don't feel comfortable lying to my son.

"We had a fight," I say. "Let's talk about it later today, all right? You'll be late for your bus."

"Tell me, Mom."

"It's a long story, Salter. We need to talk about it when we have more time to sit down and talk it over."

Salter's face goes pale. "That bad, huh?"

"I'm sorry, sweetie," I say.

"I knew you would blow it," he says, and looks at me disappointedly. I can hardly breathe. Seeing him like this hurts too much.

"Why can't you two just figure it out?"

"I...I..." I glance at Joey, who doesn't look back at me. I can't get myself to tell Salter what really happened. Not now. Not like this. I don't want him to resent his father, the most important male figure in his life. I look at the clock on the microwave. "Salter, you're late. You'll miss your bus."

Salter bites his lip. I want to pull him close and hug him, tell him everything is going to be fine, but I can't. I can't give him what he so desperately wants.

"Can I get a kiss?" I ask.

"I'm going to be late for the bus," he says, and leaves me hanging there while storming out the door.

"He's too old for that stuff," Joey says, and walks into the kitchen.

"Maybe," I say. "But I have to try."

"Why? You're babying him. All the other kids are going to laugh at him," Joey says angrily.

"Because his mother tries to kiss him? I think he'll survive."

Joey scoffs loudly. "You're smothering him. I'm sick of it. The boy needs to grow up and be a man."

He pours himself a cup of coffee.

"Yeah, because you're such a great role model," I say sarcastically.

He looks at me indignantly. "Why is it you get to make all the decisions, huh? You run all of our lives. You decide what he wears, what school he goes to, what he eats, and what activities he goes to. Heck, you even decide if we are to be a family or not. When is it my turn? When do I get to make decisions around here?"

I grab my cup and pour some coffee in it. I look at him. "When you start acting like a real man."

With that, I leave him and go back to the bedroom and my laptop. I feel like crying as I sit down, but I don't. I am too upset, too angry with him and his behavior. I open the lid of the laptop and check my emails. I have received one new one since this morning. I immediately forget all about Joey when I read it.

56

August 2006

DANIEL IS NERVOUS. He is looking at his siblings and his mother, who seems to be getting weaker and weaker every day that passes. They are waiting outside Kristin Martin's office. She is the one who called them up and asked them to come.

"This better not be about that moving out business again," their mother says. "I told her I am not going to allow it to happen."

"Maybe it's good news," Daniel says. "Maybe Peter learned something new and she wants to show us."

Daniel is afraid the whole family is starting to resent him for bringing Kristin into Peter's life. He's scared they'll take it all away and make Peter nothing but a vegetable again. So far, Daniel hasn't agreed to let Peter stop seeing Kristin, no matter how much his siblings and mother tell him they think it should stop. He is fighting for his brother. He still believes in this treatment. He still believes his brother speaks to them, even though it is with Kristin's help. He refuses to believe otherwise.

The door to the office opens and Kristin appears in the doorway. She looks stunning, Daniel thinks. Riveting even. Daniel refuses to believe she is as manipulative as his family does.

"Come on in," she says with a wide smile.

They get up and walk inside. Daniel helps his old mother, who struggles to walk these days. Inside the office, Peter is waiting for them. He is sitting in his wheelchair, his head bent to his chest, his hands knotted in fists. He groans when he sees all of them, making the chirping noises they have come to know as excitement.

"Sit down," Kristin says, and closes the door behind her.

Daniel sits next to his mother on the leather couch. His older sister is next to him; the other siblings find chairs to sit in. Their oldest brother decides to stand. Kristin walks up to Peter and sits next to him. She looks at all of them. Daniel can sense that she is nervous. It makes him uncomfortable.

"First of all, Peter and I would like to thank you all for taking the time to come in today. I know you all have busy lives and families to take care of."

"Why are we here?" their mother says.

"I am getting to that," Kristin says. "As you all know, Peter and I have been working together for almost a year now, and it has been quite fruitful. Within a short time of my treatment beginning, he was suddenly able to communicate with the outside world for the first time in twenty-five years. It is quite an accomplishment for someone like Peter. I realized quickly that he was a very smart young man, and he has a lot to tell the world. As you know, he has been taking classes at the university with me, and enjoyed it immensely. He has grown and become a man. It is time we start treating him like it."

"If this is about him moving into his own place again, then you can forget it," their oldest brother says. "There is no way he can handle that."

"I realize that it has been hard for you all to accept the fact that Peter now has wants and wishes for his own life, but be that as it may, we have chosen to respect your concerns. Together, we have found a solution we believe will be good for all parties," Kristin says.

"And what is that?" their sister asks.

Kristin clears her throat. "That he moves in with me."

"What?" their oldest brother yells.

"Never!" their mother says.

Daniel doesn't speak. He simply stares at Peter, who doesn't move a muscle. He doesn't even look at them while they're talking. He is biting his fingers, and Daniel knows it's going to leave sores that will need treatment.

"Now, now, hear me out!" Kristin says, and manages to calm them all down. "Before you rip my head off, I have something else to tell you." She glances at Peter, then reaches out to grab his hand in hers. It seems to Daniel that she is forcing it, holding on to it really tight so it will stay still. She looks back at them and looks their mother directly in the eyes when she says the words that are going to change everything.

"The thing is…we're in love."

57

January 2016

"I NEED YOUR HELP."

Harry looks at me with that mischievous smile of his. He is standing in the doorway of Marcia's house. He is wearing only shorts. No shirt. I try not to stare at the six-pack he has going on there. The storm has passed and it has stopped raining.

"I called Sandra, but she has a doctor's appointment today; Chloe has been up all night and needs to sleep; the boys are all at work, so that just leaves me with you. I don't want to go alone," I say, trying desperately to hide the fact that I really wanted to spend time with him.

"All right, then," he says and steps aside. "Come on in. I'll get dressed."

If you have to.

"Okay. I'll just wait here."

I sit on Marcia's couch, while Harry walks upstairs. As he is almost up, I turn and look at his behind. I know I am bad, but I can't help myself. He is really something. I am beginning to think I should just get it over with and sleep with him. But I don't know if the only reason I want to is because I want to hurt Joey back. That would make me a terrible person, I think. Maybe. Maybe I totally deserve it after what Joey has put me through. I don't know. Who decides these types of things? Who gets to say if someone is being a bitch or if it's completely okay since he did the same to you?

"Ready?" Harry is standing next to me. He has put on a T-shirt. It's Hugo Boss. Nice and tight over the six-pack.

He sees that I am looking at him and I blush when I realize it. I get up and stand next to him. He is a lot taller than me. I like that. Joey is small. We're about the same size. Makes me feel big when I am with him. Maybe it's about time I was with a taller man. Someone who'll make me feel small and delicate. Well, at least smaller.

"You know what?" I ask.

He chuckles. "Can't say that I do."

"I need to ask you something before we leave."

"Yes?"

"I know this is going to sound awful, but I need to know why you have pictures and articles of that woman they found in the river? Why are you so interested in her? You even have an older picture of her from when she was much younger, and I haven't seen that in the news or anywhere else?"

I just blurt it out. No use wrapping things up. I know he'll have to put two and two together and realize I have been going through his briefcase. That might make him angry with me or even make him resent me, but I can't hold it back anymore. I need to know what is going on before I can trust him.

He looks at me for a long time without saying anything. It makes me very uncomfortable. His eyes are on me, scrutinizing me. "You mean Shannon Ferguson?" he finally asks.

I swallow hard, wondering if I have made a mistake. No. I believe in honesty before anything else.

"Yes."

"How do you even know this?" he asks. I can tell by the tone of his voice that he is annoyed with me.

"Okay. I went through your briefcase, all right? You were in the bathroom last night, and I couldn't help myself."

"Ah, 'cause I thought maybe Marcia had told you, since I know she saw the clippings when she walked into my room one day."

Yeah, that would have made me look a lot better. Think, Mary, think!

"Well, she did. That's why I wanted to see for myself," I say, trying to save my dignity.

Harry looks away. I can tell he is angry. He sits down on the couch and exhales.

I blew it, didn't I? I totally blew it.

"Well, I can't blame you for not trusting me," he says. "But still. I thought we had something. I mean, last night was…"

"I know. I felt it too," I say. "I am sorry. But you are a stranger and I…well you could say I have trust issues."

Harry looks at me, then chuckles lightly. "All right. I'll let this one pass. Because I enjoy your company so much. But next time, just ask me, okay?"

"You kind of said you didn't want to talk about yourself," I say, "But let's not get stuck in the details. What's done is done."

"Okay," he says.

We look at each other in silence for what feels like forever. Then he gesticulates with his arms. "What are we waiting for?"

"You still haven't answered my question."

"Ah, that. Right. Well, if you must know," Harry exhales deeply and touches the bridge of his nose, "Shannon was my sister."

"Your sister? Oh, my God. I am so sorry," I say, and sit down next to him. "That explains everything. The old picture, the newspaper clippings."

"I came here to try and find out what happened to her. I didn't want anyone to know who I was, so I rented a room and tried to stay hidden. I've been trying to talk to all of her friends and colleagues up here, along with anyone who saw her in the last twenty-four hours before she was killed. I've asked them about her; since I lost contact with her many years ago, I didn't know much about her. But, so far, it hasn't led to anything. Her husband is the one who saw her last; they had a fight on the night she died. So far, he is the police's main suspect, but I know my brother-in-law, and he is no killer. I am trying to help him as well."

I look at Harry, feeling all of a sudden more attracted to him than ever. "I…I am sorry," I say. "I had no idea."

"How could you? I was trying to hide it." Harry starts to laugh all of a sudden. I look at him for an answer.

"What's so funny?"

"I bet you thought I killed her, right?"

"The thought crossed my mind," I say, feeling foolish.

"It never occurred to me that people would mistake me for the actual killer, but of course, it would look that way," he says. "That is so funny."

He sighs and looks at me. "Shall we go then?"

I get up from the couch, feeling all of a sudden relieved and happy. Now I don't feel bad for liking this guy.

"So, is Harry Hanson even your real name?" I ask, as we walk outside of Marcia's house.

"As a matter of fact, it isn't."

"It did sound like a cartoon character."

"So, I guess I'm not the secret spy I desperately wanted to be," he says with a smile. "My real name is Steven."

I grab his hand and shake it. "Nice to meet you, Steven."

We get into the car and I start the engine with a roar.

"So, where are we going?" Steven asks.

"Melbourne Beach." I am backing out of the driveway as I speak. "Long story short, I received an email this morning from a guy who gave Marcia a lift yesterday from Sebastian to Melbourne Beach."

58

January 2016

WHEN KELLY WAKES up in her bed, she feels rested for the first time in weeks. She opens her eyes as the alarm clock goes off, and then looks at Andrew, who opens his eyes as well. Today, he is leaving for his business trip, so they can't be late.

While he is getting ready, Kelly walks into Lindsey's room and wakes her up. Her dog, Max, is sleeping on the bed as she enters the room. Kelly sits on the edge of the bed and kisses her daughter's forehead.

"Rise and shine," she says cheerfully. Kelly feels good today. She is relaxed and not the least bit worried that her husband is leaving for three days. For the first time in a long time, she is not worried at all.

"Is it morning already?" Lindsey says, and rubs her eyes excessively. The light is bright in her eyes. Lindsey isn't much of a morning person.

"I'm making breakfast now," Kelly says. "Come down when you're ready."

"Can I have pancakes?"

"Not today, sweetie. It's a school day. There's no time."

Lindsey makes an annoyed sigh. "Aw, I thought it was Saturday."

Kelly chuckles and leaves her, knowing she will probably have to go up there again in five minutes to make sure she gets out of bed. But Kelly doesn't mind. Not today. Not now that everything seems to be so good.

Kelly turns on the radio in the kitchen and hums along to the music while pouring cereal into Lindsey's favorite bowl. She makes coffee for herself and her husband, and soon, Andrew comes trotting down the stairs.

"I'm late. I'm late," he says.

She hands him a cup of coffee. "Not too late to have some breakfast."

"You're right," he says and sits down. He looks at his watch. "I have five minutes if I don't run into traffic on the way to the airport."

Kelly serves him some of his fitness cereal that he has been eating lately. He wanted to lose weight, he told her, and he is beginning to look quite fit. Kelly worries about his desire to look good. Is it for her or for someone else?

Don't go there, Kelly. Don't start it.

She reassures herself that it's perfectly normal for a man his age to want to look good. And besides, it is for her benefit as well. She wants him to look good too. She likes to show him off when they go to charity dinners and auctions.

Kelly walks up the stairs to see how Lindsey is doing and finds her fast asleep on top of the covers. It looks like she got up and out, and then fell asleep again. It looks funny, and Kelly can't help laughing a little.

"Lindsey," she says and strokes her hair. "You have to get up, sweetie."

The girl opens her eyes. Kelly smiles. "Let me help you get dressed."

A few minutes later, they're all sitting in the kitchen. Andrew is typing aggressively on the phone, probably answering emails, Kelly thinks to herself. She pours coffee into his Tervis cup for him to take on the road.

"I don't want to go to school today," Lindsey complains when she sits down at the table.

"I know, but you have to," Kelly says, and serves her the bowl of cereal. "Don't you have music today? You love music."

"No. It's Art today. And you know how much I hate art."

"I'm sure the teacher will come up with something fun," Andrew says, and finishes his cup of coffee.

"You ready?" Kelly asks.

"I think so. I just need to run to the bathroom real quick."

Kelly nods. He always has to go right before he leaves. It's the thing that annoys her the most, because it's what makes them always run late. Andrew disappears into the toilet, and Kelly returns to finish packing Lindsey's lunchbox. She puts it in her backpack, then looks at her daughter, who has dropped her spoon and is staring at something with her eyes and mouth wide open.

Kelly turns her head to look at what it is and sees her husband standing in the middle of the living room, a gun to his head.

59

January 2016

I AM ENJOYING Steven's company. Steven. I like this new name for him. Suits him a lot better than Harry. He truly looks like a Steven.

"So, how much do you know?" he asks, as we cross the city sign to Melbourne Beach. "Do you know where she was dropped off?"

I shake my head. "The driver wrote in the email that he picked her up on A1A, where she was hitchhiking. She told him she was going to Cocoa Beach. He was going to Cape Canaveral, so he said he could drop her off on the way, and she got in. But then, as they drove along, she suddenly freaked out. She started to scream for him to stop and said that she was armed in case he tried anything. He stopped the car at a park by the beach in Melbourne Beach, where she opened the door and jumped out. He watched her run towards the beach, cross over, and disappear down the stairs. He was in a hurry, so he took off."

"That's odd," Steven says.

"Seems like everything with Marcia is quite strange these days," I say.

I go silent for a little while and think about my meeting with her the day before. I still can't get that look in her eyes out of my mind. It wasn't Marcia. It was like it was someone else, someone completely different. It scared me senseless, and still does when I think about it. I have no idea what she is capable of. What she might do when she is in that state of mind. I can't stop thinking about those things she told me and how it all fits with the police files from the Elingston murders in 2010.

"What's the name of it?"

"Sorry, name of what?"

"The park?"

"Ah. It's Spessard Holland. The south end. It's actually right here."

I turn into the parking lot and stop the car. I grab my phone, and for just a second, I look at the display, wishing Joey had called. But he hasn't. It makes me sad. I miss him, even though I am still so angry with him.

Will I ever be able to let him go?

"So, what's the plan here?" Steven asks. He looks out at the heavy clouds above us. The front that is supposed to pass us isn't over yet. They've promised more thunderstorms all day today. The beach probably isn't the safest place to be. I open my weather app and look at the radar.

"All the storms are still way inland," I say. "It'll be at least an hour before the next one comes out here. So I say we search the beach area now. She could have found shelter from the storms under the boardwalk. She might still be there."

"Let's do this, then," Steven says, and opens his door.

We both get out of the car. I have this nervous uneasy feeling inside of me as we walk across the boardwalk and onto the beach. I push it away, thinking it's just because I am worried about Marcia. The dark—almost black clouds on the horizon look threatening. I always thought it would be easy to shoot an end-of-the world apocalypse movie here in Florida on a day with thunderstorms. It looks like it is the end of everything. Like, in that movie, my favorite from my childhood, *The Neverending Story*. When *The Nothing* arrives to destroy them all.

"Marcia?" I call.

Steven crawls in under the boardwalk. I keep walking along it. It has been raining and blowing like crazy, so there are no footprints in the sand. I stare at the deserted beach. The wind is coming from the south and is nice and warm on my skin.

"She's not under here or the other boardwalk on the north end. It doesn't look like anyone has been sleeping under there."

"Where is she then?" I look at Steven, feeling desperate and lost.

He shrugs. "I don't know. Maybe the restrooms or somewhere else in the park?"

"I think they lock the restrooms at night, and there isn't much else up there besides parking lots and bushes. But let's go check just to be sure."

60

January 2016

"WHAT ARE YOU DOING?"

Kelly's voice is shaking as she stares into the intruder's eyes. She realizes she knows those eyes. She has seen them many times before. Outside the library or Publix. Walking past her in a crowd or on the street when walking the dog.

"I know you," she says. "You helped me the other day. I had forgotten my purse when eating lunch. You came running out from the restaurant and gave it to me. I thought it was the nicest thing. Why…what…?"

"Shut up," the intruder says. The gun is unsteady in their hand. The eyes looking at Kelly are those of a madman.

"Mom?" Lindsey says.

"Sh, baby. Just stay calm and do whatever you're told to, alright?"

"We'll do anything. Just don't hurt us," Andrew says.

Kelly can hear the terror in his voice. It freaks her out.

"Everyone in the living room, now!" the intruder says. "Hurry up!"

Kelly grabs Lindsey by the hand and, trembling, they walk into the living room. Lindsey is whimpering and Kelly tries to hold her.

"Get down on your knees. All of you!" the intruder yells. There is an inconsistency to the tone of the voice.

"What do you want from us?" Andrew says, when he is on his knees, the gun pointed at the back of his head.

"What do you want from us?" the intruder repeats, mocking him.

When they're all on their knees, the intruder walks in front of them. The intruder pulls down the hoodie on the sweater and kneels in front of Andrew. Kelly hears him gasp.

"You?"

The intruder smiles. "Yes. Me, Andrew."

"But…but I thought…"

"That you had gotten rid of me?" the intruder bursts into loud laughter.

"Who is this?" Kelly asks, feeling a stitch of anger going through her body. Is this someone Andrew has been involved with somehow? Is this some sort of revenge? To hurt his family? Is that why the intruder has been stalking them? Watching their every move? Is that why?

"Shut up, bitch," the intruder says. The gun slams into Kelly's face. Hard. Kelly gasps in pain, then tumbles to the floor. In the darkness, she can hear Lindsey scream.

It'll be okay, baby. Mommy's fine.

Kelly is out. She doesn't know how long…it might have been an hour. When she wakes up, she is still lying on the floor in the living room. Her daughter is next to her, face flat against the tiles. She is crying helplessly. Kelly blinks her eyes and returns to reality, only to realize her husband is right next to her on the other side. His face is also flat against the tiles. His eyes aren't moving. His body is limp; blood is running from a wound in his forehead. As the realization sinks in, Kelly tries to scream, but the impact of the shock is so deep she cannot get any sound across her lips.

Andrew!!

The gun is now placed to the back of Kelly's head. "Please," she finally manages to mutter through sobs of despair. "Please, don't hurt us. I'll give you anything you want. Anything."

"I need fifty-thousand dollars. Can you get me that?"

"Yes! Just don't hurt us."

"Good. And pizza. I am in the mood for a pizza."

61

August 2006

"YOU'RE WHAT?"

Daniel stares at Kristin. She is still holding Peter's hand in hers, holding onto it firmly and stroking it gently. Daniel feels like he is in a movie or a strange, surreal dream. Did she really just tell them that she and Peter were in love? Peter, who until recently had the mind of a toddler; Peter, who can't get out of his chair, who depends helplessly on the care of others; Peter, who drools and bites his fingers to blood, who can't control a muscle in his body? Peter, who is almost fifteen years younger than she is? Him? His brother?

"Excuse me?" their mother says.

She seems as baffled as the rest of them, but somehow she manages to turn it into anger. Daniel can feel it from where he is sitting. Her fragile body is twitching in fury.

"I do realize it must be hard for you all to take in, and I want you to know that I completely understand, but it doesn't take away the fact that we're in love and have been for quite some time."

"That's ridiculous," their mother says, snorting while she speaks. "Peter doesn't know what love is. He is not capable of having that kind of emotion. This has got to stop."

"I realize how strange this must sound to your ears, but it is, nevertheless, the truth," Kristin says. She lets go of Peter's hand and pulls out something from the table next to her.

"Here. This is the transcript of one of our conversations we had six months ago, when we first realized we had feelings for one another."

She hands the transcript to Daniel, who looks at it, his heart throbbing in his chest. He reads how they have talked about kissing and Peter asking Kristin if she could *ever love someone like him* and her answering *yes, I have loved you for a long time.* Then he answered that so had he, *now what do we do?*

Daniel can't stand reading this; it makes him feel sick to his stomach, and he hands the transcripts to their mother.

"This is preposterous," their mother says, holding the papers in her hand. "This doesn't prove anything. Anyone could have written this. You're manipulating him and you have been from the beginning."

Kristin looks disappointed. "I had really hoped you'd under-stand," she says. "We love each other. Love knows no boundaries."

"But…" Daniel starts, then stops. He has so many questions, so many things he can't comprehend. "How? How do you know it's him talking and not you? You are, after all, supporting his elbow when he writes this. How can we be sure that it comes from him and not from you, because you wished it to be so?"

Kristin stares at him. "Do you think this is my dream scenario? You think I wanted to fall in love with a man in a wheelchair? I love him for what he is inside, behind all this, and because I love him, love his wonderful sparkling personality, I love everything he is too. Even if it means he can't do a lot of things." Kristin looks at Peter again and smiles. "Yet, not everything is impossible for him. I might as well tell you right away." She clears her throat.

"I am pregnant, and it is Peter's."

Daniel stares at her, eyes wide open. He's at a loss for words. So are the others. Only their oldest brother manages to say something.

"How?! How on earth is that even possible?"

"It was Peter's greatest concern," she says. "That I wouldn't be attracted to him physically, even though I kept telling him I loved everything about him. He has CP, but that is not all he is. He is a wonderful, charming, warm intelligent person, and that is who I fell in love with. The first time we had sex was in my house one day after classes. How did it work, physically, you might wonder? Well, it wasn't easy. We lay on the bed and kissed. We took our time; Peter was overwhelmed and needed extra time. I told him we could just lie close if he wanted to. I got naked and took off his clothes…"

"Enough!"

Their mother rises to her feet. "I don't want to hear any more of…" she stops midsentence, then touches her chest. It happens so fast, Daniel hardly has a chance to react. Her face turns pale and she falls to the floor. All the siblings run to her.

"She's not breathing," Daniel's sister says. "Call 911!"

While Daniel is dialing on his phone, he watches his oldest brother approach Kristin Martin, his fist in the air in a threatening posture.

"You'll never come anywhere near this family again. You hear me? Not any of us. Not me. Not my brothers and sister, and certainly not Peter. Do you hear me?! NEVER!"

January 2016

WE DON'T FIND her in the restrooms or the park area either. We search the bushes and the area around the benches, but nothing. I refuse to give up and I convince Steven to go down to the beach again. I know Marcia loves the beach, and I have a feeling she will seek the beach and the ocean, even if she is sick. This is where she grew up, this is where she felt safe as a child when her father went nuts at the house. She often slept on the beach when it was really bad.

"I think we should walk a little," I say.

Steven looks at the sky. The big black darkness is getting closer. "We don't have long before that hits us," he says.

"It's long enough," I say.

"As you wish."

We start walking. I think about the kiss we shared the night before and wonder if he thinks about it too. Our hands are very close to each other when we walk, our arms rubbing against each other. I fight the urge to grab his hand in mine. I don't know if I only want him to be close to me because I am sad and wounded, if I want to hurt Joey, or if it's really because I like Steven. 'Cause I do. I really like him, but I can't stop thinking that he is not my type at all. I am usually more into the surfing lazy bad boy types. Steven is too perfect. But maybe I've changed my type? Maybe I am done with those good-for-nothing types? I know he is the type that I would like to fall in love with. I know he would treat me well. I know he would take care of me. And I would enjoy that six-pack of his.

While I think too much, as usual, he grabs my hand in his. The gesture startles me and I twitch. He looks at me, as if wanting my approval, and I smile.

"We'll find her," he says and kisses the top of my hand like a gentleman. "I am certain we will."

"I sure hope so."

We walk out of the beach park area and into a residential area, where the big beachfront mansions are lined up one after another overlooking the Atlantic. Each has its own boardwalk to the beach, and the yards are covered in sea grapes. The houses are a lot bigger than the ones you see in Cocoa Beach, even on the beach. These are three-to-four-million dollar mansions. I have heard that most of the people living here are doctors. I can't blame them. It's a little too far from a city for my taste. I like having a downtown to walk or bike to, but other than that, it's gorgeous out here. A little desolate, though.

"You think she walked all the way down here?" Steven asks.

I shrug. "She might. But, then again, she could have walked north as well."

"There's nothing here but houses."

"I know. It's a dead end," I say with an exhale and look at the sky above us. The storm is getting dangerously close now. We can hear the thunder now and see the lightning strikes in the distance.

"We need to get back to the car," Steven says, "If you don't want to be caught down here during that thing."

Disappointed as I might be that we haven't found even a trace of Marcia, I know he is right.

Being the lightning capital of the world, Florida is not a place to be outside in a thunderstorm. Every year, some tourist from up north refuses to leave the beach in time and gets struck by lightning. A guy we grew up with, Jared, was struck three times during child-hood. It's one of those stories you only believe because you know him, but it's true. He survived all three times, but that is the exception to the rule. I, for one, don't want to try and see if I can do the same.

Just as we're about to turn and walk back, I spot something.

"What's that?"

"What's what?" he asks.

I walk to the boardwalk leading to one of the mansions.

"I really don't think we have time for this," he says.

"Just give me one sec."

I walk up on the boardwalk.

"That's private," he says.

"I know. I just have to…" On the boardwalk, they have a small bench where you can sit and watch the ocean. I stop and pick something up.

"Bingo." I look at Steven with a smile, just as the sky cracks above us with loud thunder. "She was here. This is her scarf. She always wears this. Even when it's ninety out. It was a present from her father before he died. She has been here. Marcia was here."

63

January 2016

KELLY'S HANDS are shaking as they press the numbers on the phone.

"Not a word, you hear me?" the intruder says, the gun pointed at Kelly's temple. "Just act normal."

"Papa's Pizza."

"Yes, hello. I would like to order a pizza," she says, her voice about to crack as her eyes, once again, glance at her husband, who is on the floor in a pool of his own blood. Lindsey is sobbing, hiding her face in her hands, while lying flat on the floor.

"Delivery or carryout? Hello? Ma'am? Are you still there?"

Kelly feels the gun being pressed harder towards her temple. She catches her breath. "Yes. I'm still here. Sorry. Delivery, please."

"Alright. What's the order?"

Kelly stares at the body of her husband. She can't take her eyes off of him. Such despair overwhelms her and she can't move. It went all right when she called the bank and asked them to bring the money. She managed to keep her cool and not lose it, but she simply doesn't have the strength to do so now. Not anymore.

What's the use anyway?

Kelly stares at the intruder, thinking there really is no use, that they'll both be killed anyway, no matter what. As soon as the intruder gets the money. The intruder certainly seems mad enough to do it.

"Ma'am? What's the order? Ma'am?"

But I'll have to sign for the money when John from the bank arrives. The intruder can't do that alone. I am still needed. I can't be killed yet.

"Ma'am? Is anything wrong, ma'am?"

"Yes," she says, her heart throbbing wildly in her chest.

"Yes, what?"

Kelly glances at her husband, then back at the intruder, who is breaking a sweat. Their eyes meet and lock.

I'll show you. I've got a few tricks up my sleeve as well. I am not down yet. I refuse to let you get away with this.

The gun in the intruder's hand is shaking heavily now. The intruder's breath comes in ragged bursts. The intruder might be playing tough, but Kelly sees right through all that. The intruder is nervous. Anxious.

You messed with the wrong woman, my friend.

"Ma'am?"

Kelly is still staring into the eyes of the intruder as she opens her mouth and finally speaks.

"Help. I am being held hostage. Me and my …"

She doesn't get to say anymore before the phone is pulled out of her hand. The intruder shuts it off, frantically fumbling with it.

This is it. This is your chance.

Knowing she'll not get another chance, Kelly acts fast. She leaps through the air and lands on top of the intruder, pinning the intruder's body to the floor. The person beneath her screams and the gun is knocked out of their hand. It slides across the tiles. The intruder groans and whines, while Kelly throws in a punch, hitting right on the nose. The intruder screams again and Kelly is surprised at her own strength. But the intruder is stronger. The intruder grabs Kelly around the throat and manages to get a good tight grip on her. Seconds later, Kelly is gasping for air and no longer able to throw any punches. The intruder presses Kelly off. Kelly is struggling to breathe, trying to fight the intruder off her, grabbing their wrists, trying to pull away, but the intruder is a lot stronger than her, and soon she is pressed to the ground, the intruder tightening the grip on Kelly's throat. Kelly is only making gurgling sounds now. In the distance, she can hear her daughter whimpering and crying. Her vision is getting blurry, and soon there is nothing but darkness.

This is it. This is how I go. Please take good care of my daughter, God. Please take care of her.

As she drifts off and gives in to the daze, she can feel how the grip is being loosened on her throat, just before the sound of the gun going off rips through the air. After that, there is nothing but silence. Silence and darkness.

64

January 2016

"DID YOU HEAR THAT?"

Steven looks at me, his eyes wide. He turns his head and looks at the house behind us.

"Was that…?" I ask anxiously. "It wasn't thunder, was it?"

"It sounded more like a gunshot," Steven says, then pauses. "I think I know this place. This house…" Steven freezes, then looks at me. "My brother lives here."

"Your what?" I ask.

"I have only seen the place in pictures, on his Christmas cards that his wife sends out of the family. I lost connection with him many years ago. It's a long story. But I have a bad feeling about this, Mary. I have to go check."

I look at the scarf in my hand and think about Marcia. A terrifying thought hits me. What if she fired that shot? What do I do? Do I call the police?

"Let's go," I say, and pull his sleeve.

He follows me up the boardwalk leading to the house. We run as the rain starts to pour down on us. We approach the windows leading to the beach and look inside. In there, in the living room, I see Marcia. She is bent over what looks like the body of a woman on the floor. She has a gun in her hand. Not far from her lies a man in a pool of blood.

"Oh, my God," I say, and clasp my mouth.

"That's my brother!" Steven says. His voice is breaking.

"Marcia. What have you done?" I mumble under my breath. I feel devastated. I can't believe what I am seeing. It truly is heartbreaking.

Marcia moves away from the body on the floor and walks to a

little girl lying on the floor further away. The girl is moving, worming around on the ground.

She is trying to get away! She's trying to get to the door. And now, Marcia is going to stop her. She's going to kill her like she killed the two others!

"Don't!!" I scream, and start hammering on the window. "Stooop, Marcia!"

The sound startles Marcia, and she turns to look at us. She doesn't seem to recognize us. She simply stares and doesn't move. Her head is tilted slightly, like she is wondering about something.

Steven is at the sliding door now and pulls it open. We storm inside and he throws himself at Marcia, knocking her to the tiles. Marcia goes down, screaming and yelling loudly.

"Help! Help!"

Steven manages to get the gun out of her hand, while I run to the daughter and grab her in my arms. She is crying helplessly, screaming in terror. I sit on the floor, pull her into my arms, and hold her tight. Her body is shivering in horror while I try to get her to calm down.

"Sh. Sh. We're here to help you."

Seconds later, I hear sirens outside. I look at Steven and our eyes meet. Marcia is still screaming underneath him, kicking him, telling him she will never give in to the government's repression; she'll never tell them anything, that aliens will come for her soon, take her back to their ship and make her pregnant, that the government wants her for her knowledge. I can't stop crying when looking at the scene and the two bodies. I realize there is no more I can do to help her.

I close my eyes as the realization sinks in. Seconds later, the house is filled with boots, loud voices, and yelling men with guns pointed at us.

65

January 2016

THE BODY IS STARTING to smell bad. Blake realizes he has to get rid of it. The last few days he has kept her in the bed, kept coming back to see her and enjoy the work of his hands. This one was special to him. It was different. She is different.

But there is a time for everything, and now it is time for him to leave her. The smell will soon be a problem, and the body will be discovered.

Blake plans to be long gone by the time it is found. He has orchestrated everything down to the smallest detail.

He lifts the body up, and puts her gently on the ground, the smell tormenting his nostrils. Blake then grabs his knife, cuts open the cheap mattress, and starts pulling out the filling.

He thinks about his sister as he prepares for his next move. Blake remembers her only vaguely from their childhood. He was only three when she left town and never looked back, so they don't have that many memories together. All he knows is that he hated her when growing up. He loathed Mary and how proud their father was of her, always bragging about her accomplishments as a journalist, her career on CNN and later at the *New York Times*.

Look at her now, Daddy dear. Oh, how the mighty have fallen.

Doing a blog. Like that is anything to be proud of. Blake knows she has a lot of followers. He is one of them, constantly keeping an eye on what she is up to, what she posts. He even comments on it using his alias, Nightrider123. But he is not impressed with what she is doing, not at all. The small piece she did on him and Olivia actually had him laughing out loud.

Like that is ever going to lead to anything.

Blake laughs again while thinking about how he has written

several emails, from different accounts, using different aliases to lead them away from where he is really hiding. Using local stories of criminals robbing stores or whose description matches his and Olivia's. In that way when they check up on it, they sound plausible. The one in Arizona is his masterpiece. He just knows they'll be falling for that one. He hopes in his quiet mind that they'll all go there to look for him. It would amuse him greatly. His only regret is that he'll not be there when they find out they've been fooled. He'll be far away doing what he always does, getting himself in trouble, but never paying the price for it. It is amazing how easy it is to get away with a crime. It makes him feel invincible. It's like they can't even get close. It's too easy.

And so much fun.

Blake looks at her picture that he keeps in his pocket. A picture taken from one of the newspaper clippings that his father kept of her articles in the scrapbook. The big blue book that he had in his office and showed to his friends and colleagues, while Blake was never mentioned. Not even the time he got an A in math. His father didn't even listen when he told him. He just handed him some cash and told him to go get himself something proper to wear and to get a haircut.

"Lord knows you can afford it, boy. No need to look like a bum. Your sister always dresses nicely."

Blake destroyed the scrapbook when he was twelve, in a fit of rage, yelling at their father for his attention. He ripped it to pieces, but kept the picture.

You'll never find me, dear sis. Never. But I will find you. When you're least expecting it, I'll come for you.

66

February 2007

It is raining on the day the trial begins. Daniel sits with Peter in the courtroom. Peter doesn't seem to understand what is going on. At least, Daniel doesn't think he does. He is biting his hands, as he usually does when he's upset. He has been doing that excessively lately, and it worries Daniel. Peter's hands are filled with deep sores that won't heal. As long as he keeps biting them, they won't, the doctor says.

They're surrounded by their siblings, and Daniel suddenly misses his mother tremendously. He can still see the expression on her face as she fell to the ground in Kristin Martin's office that day six months ago, a hand pressed against her chest. She was dead when the ambulance arrived. Everyone in the family blames Kristin Martin for her death. Now, they want her put away.

"She completely ruined our family," their oldest brother argued when they held the first meeting about it. "She deserves to be locked up. She's a pervert and has abused all of us. Especially Peter."

The door to the courtroom is opened and Kristin is brought in, accompanied by two officers with strict looks on their faces. She has lost a lot of weight, even though she is pregnant. Her clothes are dangling on her shoulders. Her face seems longer, her cheeks are sunken in, and her eyes seem bigger than before. She is still beautiful, but not in the way she used to be. She looks like a beaten animal. The only thing thriving seems to be her growing stomach. Three months till she is due with Daniel's niece or nephew.

Daniel doesn't like to think about what will happen to the child, where it will grow up if she is convicted. No one else seems to care about it. They almost postponed the trial because of it being so close to her due date, but the family insisted on having it done before. They intend to show her no mercy for what she did.

There is no excuse. Nothing to justify her actions.

Peter groans and makes a lot of noises, and Daniel turns his head to look at him. He looks into his eyes.

Is he looking at Kristin?

One of his older brothers sees it as well and leans over to Daniel's ear. "It's only natural that he reacts to seeing her again after all she did to him."

Daniel nods. She is, after all, charged with sexual abuse of their poor defenseless brother. Living out her sick fantasies, getting pregnant with someone who has no idea what love is, who has no way of saying no.

"We were in love," Kristin says, when the trial begins and she is called to the stand. She is asked about her relationship with Peter. She turns and looks at him. "We are still in love. We're just not allowed to be, because the world doesn't acknowledge that people like Peter are capable of something as simple yet fundamental in life as to love someone."

"But the man has the mental capacity of a toddler. He has gone through many tests and they have all shown the same. How do you explain that? The man has never said a word. He can't even control his own movements. How do you know that he loves you back? He suffers from profound mental disabilities. How can you tell me he gave you consent to have sex with you?" the prosecutor asks.

"He might not be able to speak or even hold a spoon on his own, but those are motor skills. It says nothing about who he is, what he knows, or how intelligent he is," she answers.

"But the tests and assessments do, right? I mean, that is why we have the tests. To determine people's intelligence and capabilities, am I right? They're designed for that very purpose."

"That's what I used to believe, yes," Kristin says. "Until I started to work with these patients, with Peter. I realized he was smarter than we thought, and started to believe he had a private chamber in his mind, a place where all his adult thoughts were trapped behind his sickness, behind the palsy. So, it makes a lot of sense that he would fail the tests, since the tests are made for people who can answer verbally, read and write. What I found was a way for Peter to share his intelligence. I found a way to reach that chamber of his, and you will be amazed at what I discovered."

"And what, exactly, is that?"

"That Peter has a beautiful mind. A mind with a wonderful personality, who is more than capable of feeling and giving love. I fell for that mind. Not the body or the sickness. I fell in love with who he was. But the world, his family, won't accept it. They want to keep him in his prison, so the world will never hear what he has to say again. He is once again being treated like a severely impaired person and has lost all control over his life. They have taken away his freedom. They're silencing him and keeping him from becoming who he can be. Worst of all, is that he'll never be with the one he loves. If I am convicted and sent away, then he'll never get to be with his child either. Who is abusing whom here?"

As Kristin speaks she stares directly into Peter's eyes. Daniel realizes it and is truly amazed. Never in his lifetime has Peter been able to keep eye contact with anyone. Kristin smiles and tilts her head while looking at him. Her eyes water as she speaks. Much to his surprise, Daniel sees a tear leave his brother's eye as well. He watches it as it rolls across Peter's face and lands on his upper lip, where it stops.

Daniel looks at it, not knowing what to say. Meanwhile, Kristin is being grilled in the chair.

"Isn't it true that the type of treatment you used on Peter has been subject to lots of controversy?" she is asked.

"Yes," Kristin answers.

"Isn't it true that many tests made with people like Peter undergoing the same treatment and supported writing on a keyboard, have been widely criticized? Isn't it true that in one test, where the typers were asked to name objects their facilitators couldn't see or know of, that in nineteen studies of facilitated communication performed, that they found zero validation through one-hundred and eighty-three tests?"

"That was the conclusion, yes," she says, her head bent.

"So, how can you claim that it works?"

"I just know that it does. I know that he speaks to me. I'll swear on the Bible; I'll sign anything to make you believe what I say is true. I know that he loves me. I know that he wants to marry me."

A wave of shock goes through the spectators in the courtroom. The judge asks for silence. Daniel can't stop looking at his brother, as a second tear leaves the corner of his eye.

Am I making a mistake? Could it be? What if?

Daniel writes a note and passes it to the prosecutor, who reads it, then looks back at Daniel. Daniel nods.

"Your honor," the prosecutor says. "The family requests that Kristin Martin does those tests with Peter. The same tests used in the experiments where all one-hundred and eighty-three failed."

January 2016

THEY TAKE MY STORY. A detective writes everything I say down, and asks me a thousand questions. He has introduced himself as Deputy Brown. He's from the Brevard County Sheriff's office.

Even though it kills me, I tell him everything. I tell him I believe Marcia entered the house and killed the husband. He tells me it looks like the woman is still alive, and I watch as the paramedics take her out of the house. I tell him we entered the house because we believed Marcia was about to kill the daughter. He tells me they found the family's dog dead in the hallway when they entered.

We stay in the house for hours, going over the questions again and again. I call Joey and ask him to pick up Salter from running club at the school. While talking to the deputy, I can see Steven doing the same, while a female detective is trying to take care of the young girl. Marcia is taken away. Kicking and screaming, they have to carry her out of the house, handcuffed, while the gun is secured.

Then I tell the deputy the rest. I tell him I believe Marcia might have been the one who killed the Elingston family on Merritt Island six years ago, that she told me she remembered things about them, like what clothes they were wearing. I don't tell him about Chloe or the police files I have seen. There is no need to. He can connect the dots himself. Or someone else will do it for him.

"She is not well," I say. "She shot at her own son two nights ago. She thought he was part of a conspiracy against her. She is very sick, I think."

"So, what you're saying is, you believe she has done this before?" Deputy Brown says.

"Yes. I am afraid so."

"And to another part of the Elingston family?"

"Another?"

"Yes. Andrew Elingston is the name of the man who was killed here today."

"That's odd," I say. I look at Steven, who is still talking to a deputy as well. His eyes meet mine for a few seconds.

Wasn't he his brother? Does that mean…?"

"It could look like she was targeting them. Do you know if she had any grudges against the family? Any unresolved disputes?"

I shake my head. "No. I really don't."

"All right," he says. "I'll let you go for now, but we'll probably have to take you in for more questioning later."

"Okay."

The deputy leaves, and I wait for Steven to finish up as well. Seconds later, he approaches me and we're asked to leave the house. The team from forensics is coming. I take one last glance at the man lying on the floor, in the pool of blood. Someone covers the body with a white blanket.

Steven stares at his brother. I grab his hand in mine.

"I'm sorry," I say.

Steven's body is shaking. "I can't believe it."

We continue outside, and then we stop. Steven bends forward. He is gasping for breath. I put my arms around him and pull him closer. I try to comfort him, while he cries in my arms.

"I can't believe he is gone too," he mumbles and pulls away. He looks at me with terror. He clasps his face with both hands and bends forward again like he is trying to catch his breath after a long run.

"I can't believe it," he says again.

I help him get to the car, and we drive off. He cries most of the way, while I try to keep myself together enough to be the strong one. But seeing a man like Steven lose it like this makes it hard not to get emotionally carried away also. I struggle to hold back the tears.

I keep wondering about Marcia and why she would target Steven's family. Could they have done something to her years ago that I didn't know about? And what are the odds that Steven would move in with her, renting a room from the woman he was looking for? 'Cause she killed Shannon Ferguson as well, didn't she?

I can only assume so. The gruesomeness of her actions leaves me speechless. I can't believe that twice someone I love dearly has tricked me. It makes me seriously doubt my own judgment of character. Am I really that stupid? That easily manipulated?

I look at Steven. How about him? Can I really trust him?

"You knew it was Marcia, didn't you?" I ask, as we get closer to Cocoa Beach. "You knew she had killed your sister, right?"

He doesn't look at me.

"How did you know?" I ask.

"I didn't. But I knew the police had been looking at her when investigating my sister's murder. They had her in for questioning."

"What were their grounds for questioning Marcia?" I ask.

"Apparently, she told someone that she believed she had done it. That someone went to the police to report it. They questioned her and, according to the detective taking care of my sister's case, Marcia admitted that she believed she might have done it, but then withdrew the confession a few hours later, telling them she never admitted to anything. They said they still looked into her, but that they didn't have enough evidence to build a case against her."

"So, you stalked her?" I ask.

"You might call it that. I found out who she was and started to keep an eye on her. When I realized she was renting out a room, I thought it would be the perfect possibility for me to get really close to her and maybe find evidence."

"But you liked her, didn't you?"

He scoffs. "I did. Mostly, I felt bad for the children. I realized there was a person behind the coldblooded killer that I took her for. Now I think I understand better. She's sick. She's not herself. But she still killed my siblings. I don't know if I can forgive her for that, no matter how sick you tell me she is."

I exhale and drive up in front of Marcia's townhouse. We sit in the driveway in silence for a few minutes.

"I don't think I can live here anymore," he says. "I'll grab my things and go back tonight."

"I can't blame you," I say. "So, where is home to you?"

"Winter Park," he says.

I smile. It's not that far away. About an hour's drive. Maybe I could see him again. I don't know if he wants to, though. Maybe I am connected to too many bad memories. I can't blame him if he wants to just forget everything about me.

"Can I see you again?" he asks. "I know it's odd. I know I should be thinking about getting as far away as possible and putting all this behind me, but there is something about you that makes me feel peaceful. At ease. You make me happy. I hate to turn my back on that."

I smile, lean over, and kiss him. "You have my number," I whisper.

Part III

THE BOY CARRIES THE ANSWER

68

February 2016

"CLOSE YOUR EYES."

I roll my dad in his wheelchair down 7th Street towards the beach. I have found a chair for him that fits his needs, and even supports his head when he gets tired of holding it himself. It has extra big wheels, so it can go through sand. It cost a fortune, but is so worth it. The past few weeks, I have been walking with him on the beach every morning, letting him finally get outside. It has changed everything for him to feel the ocean breeze on his face again.

Today is a special day. Today we're not going to the beach.

"Keep them closed, Dad. No peeking."

"I'm not," he argues.

"Good."

I push him towards the driveway of my childhood home and into the lot. The tiles are brand new and make it look stunning.

"Now you can open them," I say, and stop.

I watch his face as he sees the house for the first time. He is visibly moved.

"It's done," I say. "The workers finished yesterday, and today we can move in."

"Wow," he mutters. "It's even better than the old house."

"It has a lot of new features," I say. "To make it easier for you to get around. It has everything. A lift on the stairs to elevate you in your chair to the second floor. A lift in the bedroom to help you get into bed. Everything you'll need to make this your home again. And mine."

"So, you're coming with me?" he asks.

"Of course I am. Someone has to make sure you don't get yourself into trouble, right? Salter and I will be there."

"And Snowflake?"

"Snowflake too."

"Good. I've really grown to like that dog. He keeps me company when I feel alone."

"That's what he does," I say. "Do you want to see the inside?"

"Sure. But tell me first. What about Joey?"

"Joey has his own place. You know we haven't been doing very well lately. Besides, I am seeing someone else now."

"I don't care much for that Steven guy," my dad says. "Forgive Joey and have him...move in with us. It's best for...Salter and...for the dog. Snowflake will be miserable...without Bonnie and Clyde. Mostly...Bonnie, I believe."

"We'll visit," I say, closing the discussion.

I take my dad through the house and show him how everything works. He is truly impressed and very moved. But something is off. He is not as happy as I had expected him to be.

I roll him outside in the backyard leading to the ocean. I stop his chair on the big wooden porch and he closes his eyes and breathes in the air.

"Now you can get the air you love so much every day," I say. "Isn't it wonderful? Aren't you pleased?"

He opens his eyes and looks at me. I detect a deep sadness in them, and I wonder if all this reminds him too much about his former life with Laura here or about the fire that left him paralyzed.

"It is all very, very nice...and perfect," he says.

"But...?"

"But I...really like living...at Joey's. I like...the life with all the animals...and having my family...close to me. I am afraid...I'll be lonely here...in this big house."

"You're kidding me, right?"

"I'm sorry," he says and looks away. "I am being...ungrateful."

I sigh. "No. No of course not, but living at Joey's house was temporary. You knew that. It's too small for all of us. We have kind of overstayed our welcome there. It's time we all move on."

He nods. "I know. I know. It's just...well I liked living...this close. We'll be fine here...too. I am sure...we will."

He sends me a reassuring smile, but I am not convinced.

69

February 2016

MARK LOOKS at the ceiling in his room. He thinks about the many nights he has lain here worrying about his mother, wondering where she is and when she'll come home. The house is quiet. It's odd, when it has been so filled with noise for so long. Even at night there would be noises coming from all his siblings, snoring or talking in their sleep. It was never quiet.

Not like it is now. Right now, it's eerily quiet.

All three of his siblings are at their father's in Orlando. They live there now. They wanted him to move there as well, when he was allowed to leave the hospital. A nice social worker told him that it was best for all of them if he lived with his father, since his mother was in prison, charged with murder. She also told him there would be a trial and that he might be asked to testify against her, if he would agree to that?

No, he wouldn't, he told her. But she said a court might tell him he had to. Unless they believed he would suffer emotional trauma for doing so. It was up to the court to decide.

His dad came to pick him up and drove him to Orlando, where his siblings greeted him. It was when looking into their eyes he knew he had to leave again as soon as possible. Especially Tim, the youngest, had changed a lot already. In their room, later at night, he showed him his back, and Rose and Tammy both told him how their father had beat them as well. Mark could feel the anger rise in him as they told him everything, and at night, he decided to leave. Not that he felt good about his decision, no he didn't. He hated having to leave them there with that monster, but if he stayed, he knew his dad would eventually break him as he had done to the others, and then he would be of no help to his siblings. It was his job to protect them, and he would do a better job if he were on the outside of it.

He just hasn't figured out how, yet.

Mark hitched back to Cocoa Beach. Hoping to find Harry in the house and ask for his help. He was disappointed—yet not surprised—to find it empty. He moved in and started going from door to door asking for work. He could do anything, he told them. Yard work, repairing garage doors, tree trimming, plucking mangoes, anything they needed. So far, it has kept him fed.

Twice the lady from DCF has been at the door to the house and knocked, flanked by officers from Cocoa Beach Police, probably looking for him, but he has managed to hide when they came inside. No one knows the house like Mark. He has his hiding spots in the small attic where they would never think of looking for him.

Today, Mark is planning to go down to the beach and ask tourists if they want a surf lesson. It's been the easiest way to make a little extra lately. Using his mother's surfboard, he gets thirty dollars an hour for pushing in the little children and teaching them to get up on the board. It's, by far, his favorite way of making a living.

Every now and then, he runs into some of his friends from school, but he doesn't tell them where he is living. He just tells them that he moved to another school. Sometimes, he can tell in their eyes that they know his story, that they have heard about his murderous crazy mother, who killed all those people and shot him as well. He loathes those pitiful looks.

They have shut off the water and electricity to the house, but Mark manages without. He goes in the ocean every morning and showers at the beach. There's even a restroom he can use when he needs to do more than pee. Electricity, he doesn't need much of yet. He eats mostly bread or dry cereal straight out of the box. It isn't very hot out yet, so he doesn't need AC either, but he knows it won't be long before he will.

He often wonders how long he can stay where he is and hopes desperately to soon be able to find a way out. He keeps thinking about his mother. He hasn't been able to go visit her in prison. He doesn't dare to. He knows she is waiting for her trial, that they're certain she killed a lot of people. He doesn't believe them. Yes, she shot at him that night when he came home, but that was in self-defense.

Mark can't stop thinking about her and how bad she must be feeling, trapped in an awful place like that. She is so fragile. Being in there is bound to kill her.

You have to do something, Mark. And you know what it is. You have to do it. Even though it is painful. There is no way back now.

70

February 2007

KRISTIN MARTIN's hand is shaking as she grabs onto Peter's elbow. She has done it a thousand times before, but this time, the outcome is going to determine the course of the rest of her life.

Daniel can see on her face that she is afraid. Everyone in the courtroom is watching her, holding their breaths, as Daniel steps forward. He approaches Peter in the wheelchair and his eyes meet Kristin's shortly before he stops and looks at his brother. The plan is for him to ask a series of questions about a subject that Kristin has no knowledge of, something only Peter will know the answer to, if he is, in fact, as smart as Kristin claims him to be. The answer will hopefully help the jury determine if he is able to communicate, if he was able to give his consent to having sex with Kristin or not.

Daniel takes in a deep breath. He looks at her as he collects himself. He doesn't really know if he wants her to succeed or not. He is unsure what he hopes will come out of this. Does he want her to go to jail? Maybe. He has been lying awake so many nights cursing her for what she did, how she tricked all of them, especially him, how she manipulated him into believing what he so desperately wanted to believe. But seeing what he saw in Peter's eyes the day before in court when he looked at Kristin, he is torn. What if? What if she is right? Would he be willing to send his brother's only love, his only voice to the world to jail? Does he have the heart to doom their baby to a life without parents?

No one will take the child. You know they won't. Heck, you've already decided not to. Jill will kill you if you do. The rest of the family will disown you.

Daniel blinks. He is the one who suggested this test. Now, he must perform it. He is unsure of why he suggested it. Was it because he thought it would save her or condemn her?

It's out of your hands, Daniel. She has to prove herself.

"Alright," the prosecutor says. "Daniel. You can ask your first question."

"Okay," Daniel says, and clears his throat. He looks at his piece of paper, at the questions that he and his siblings have made together. He is struggling to keep the paper still.

"So, tell me, Peter. When we were younger, we had a dog, a golden retriever. What was his name?"

Daniel bites his lip while waiting for the reply. He avoids looking directly at Kristin as she assists Peter when he starts to type. Instead, he focuses on Peter's fingers while he types his answers slowly, one letter at a time. The answer is read out loud by someone the court has appointed. Daniel is holding his breath.

"Charlie," the woman yells. "It says Charlie."

Daniel lets out a breath of relief. "The answer is correct," he says.

"You may ask your next question now," the prosecutor says.

Daniel looks down at his paper again, then back up at Peter, whose eyes are on the ground. All this commotion is a lot for him to take.

"So, Peter, tell me, how old was Charlie when he died?"

They wait a shorter time for the answer this time.

"Five," the lady yells.

Another correct answer.

"Tell me, who is Jimmy?"

The answer comes even quicker this time.

"My favorite uncle."

Yet another correct answer.

"Who is Sigetty?"

There's a long pause before Peter writes his answer. It is read out loud. The court-lady's voice is shrill.

"My nephew."

Daniel looks at Kristin and freezes.

"Is the answer correct, Daniel?" The prosecutor asks.

Daniel shakes his head. "No."

"Let the court know that the answer is wrong," the prosecutor says. "Sigetty is another name for Peter's uncle; it's his middle name."

Maybe Peter didn't know? Daniel asks himself and gets himself ready for the next question.

"What is the frog?"

The answer arrives quickly and is read out loud.

"Our old car."

Daniel finally dares to look at Kristin. There is no way she could have known that. It is the name they gave the car when they were children because it was green like a frog. The fact that the answer is correct fills him with joy. Daniel realizes he wants Kristin to succeed. He wants them to be in love. He wants her to be right when she says she didn't do anything to Peter that he didn't agree to himself. But he is afraid that he is the only one in his family thinking this way.

"The answer is correct," he says.

The sound of surprise goes through the rows of spectators that have grown day by day as the trial has been going on. Most are journalists covering the bizarre case, but a lot of activists are occupying the seats as well, yelling every now and then for Kristin Martin to hang in there.

"Alright. Last question," the prosecutor says.

Daniel's palms are sweating and he wipes them on his trousers. The next question is the hardest one to answer. This next one, she has no way of knowing.

"I showed Peter something in the waiting room this morning before we came in here. What was it?"

The silence is devastating. Daniel looks at Kristin; their eyes meet, and he can tell she is scared. Even more than earlier.

Please be the correct answer. Please be correct for all of us. For Peter's sake. Please be correct.

The answer comes slowly, a lot slower than the others. It seems as if Peter is struggling to find the keys to press. Daniel wonders if he is too tired, if it's all a little too much for him.

The answer finally arrives and is read out loud.

"An old photo of our grandfather."

The judge looks at Daniel. "Is that correct?"

Daniel drops the paper to the ground. No one was in the waiting room with them when he showed the picture. There is no way Kristin Martin could have fabricated that.

"Yes. Yes, Your Honor. It's correct."

February 2016

I INVITE the entire crew over for a barbecue as soon as we're settled in the house. They all arrive late in the afternoon, and we hang out on the porch, eating burgers and drinking beer. It's a nice warm night out, and we decide to have a bonfire and make S'mores for the kids.

Sandra is there with Ryan, and I observe her and am not surprised to notice how she constantly looks at Alex. He glances at her constantly as well, even though he sits with his wife, Maria. Their daughter Ava hangs out with Salter down by the beach. They seem to have become quite good friends. I feel like we're walking on a volcano about to erupt with this. I am afraid what it might do to the group once their affair is found out. I am still angry with them for acting like this, for their betrayal, but what can I do? I have told them how I feel about it, still they do it anyway. I tell myself they're grown-ups and make their own choices. Even if I don't believe they're being very mature about their decisions.

It has seemed to help Sandra get back some of her confidence, though. She seems happier and stronger, even though Ryan doesn't pay any attention to her at all. He is deeply engaged in talking to Chloe. He is visibly flirting with her, and it makes me feel sick. Chloe seems to mostly think of him as very annoying. She has to be the pickiest person I have met when it comes to guys. Come to think of it, she hasn't had many boyfriends over the years. I know she was into my brother for a little while, until he showed his true colors, but that is all I have heard of. I wonder if she is ever lonely or sad with the way her life has turned out. She never shows me if she is.

"So, is Joey coming later?" Danny asks me. He is wearing a T-shirt that says *Cocoa Beach Fire Department*. I don't know anyone who is as proud of his job as Danny. It's kind of sweet.

"I don't know," I say. "I invited him, but I don't think he really wants to hang out with me lately."

"What happened with you two anyway? I thought you had figured things out? It seemed like you were doing good again."

I sip my beer and look at him. "It didn't work out. You know how it is. Sometimes it lasts, sometimes it hurts instead."

"That sounds like an Adele song," he says.

"I think it actually is a line from one of her songs," I say, laughing.

He shrugs. "I guess we just have to accept the fact that you're not getting back together, then. I am sad for you two, though. It's hard to understand. You always were so perfect together."

"Apparently, not perfect enough."

Danny nods and drinks his beer.

"What about you?" I ask. "Are you soon ready to move on?"

"I guess. It's been four months since she died. Maybe I should get back out there? I just really don't want to get onto that train, you know, going on internet-dates and all that. It has all changed so much since we were young. I don't think I can be a part of that. I tried that Tinder-thing but...it's just not me. It makes me feel so old."

"Maybe there is another way," I say.

"I heard you were seeing someone? That guy that lived at Marcia's house?"

"Yeah. We've been on a couple of dates. We've been down to Heidi's Jazz house a couple of nights and heard some great music. It's kind of become our favorite place to go together. But it's still very new."

"But, you like this guy?"

I sip the beer and nod. "Yeah. I think I do. It's just hard with Salter and Joey and everything. It's kind of hard for me to let go of the feeling that we're not going to be the happy family that I always believed in."

I look at my dad, who is sitting on the other side of Sandra. They're both laughing. I smile, thinking how great it is for my dad to be able to be with people again, to get out of his room. His physical therapy is going well, his trainer says, and he has now regained some movement in several of his fingers. That is great news, since the trainer says that if he can get some parts of his body back, then there might be a chance he can get others as well. It gives us hope.

"I miss Marcia," Danny says, and puts his feet up on the chair next to him. "You can say a lot of things about Marcia, but she sure knew how to get a party going." He chuckles lightly, then his eyes turn sad.

I know how he feels. I miss her too. Now that we're all gathered —well almost all of us—she is kind of missing. Her loud laughter, her inappropriate remarks, her getting too drunk after a few hours, her dancing and telling us we're getting old and boring. I even miss her loud music that she always somehow puts on when we reach a certain point in the evening.

"How is she, by the way?" he asks.

"I don't know."

"Have you visited her?"

I am ashamed to say I haven't. I shake my head.

"You?"

"Nope. I don't think any of us have. I feel awful. What kind of friends are we anyway?"

"I don't know," I say. "It's not that easy. I wouldn't know what to say to her. I mean, she killed a lot of people. I saw the look in her eyes when she was walking towards that girl, a young girl about Salter's age. I can't…I don't know if I can forgive and forget that easy. Especially now that I'm with Steven. I know she is sick and all, but what do you say to her? I will never be able to understand."

"Maybe we don't have to forgive and forget," Danny says. "Maybe we should just show her compassion. Show her we still love her."

I nod. He is right. Not a day goes by without me thinking about her almost every hour of the day. I feel awful that she is sitting in that prison waiting for her trial to start. I just hope she gets the help she needs. "I think you're right," I say. "Maybe you and I should go visit her someday soon?"

"I think I would like that."

"Is this supposed to be a party?!"

I turn and look at Joey, who is stepping onto the porch. I feel a pinch in my heart. I am so glad to see him. I really wanted him to come. I smile, but in the next second my smile completely freezes, when someone else steps onto the porch as well, holding Joey's hand.

"I want you to meet someone," he says. "Everyone, this is Jackie. Jackie, this is the Crew."

72

February 2016

DANNY GETS UP IMMEDIATELY and walks to Joey.

"Come on, man," he says. "You bring her to your ex's party?" he asks. "Not cool, Joey. Not cool."

Joey stares me down, his tongue rolling inside of his cheek. "What are you talking about? She's my girlfriend. I can't bring my girlfriend to a party now?"

"Come on, man," Danny says. "You two barely just split up. Your son is here too. Do you really want him to see this?"

"Well, she's seeing someone; why can't I?"

"She didn't bring him here, today, did she?" Danny asks.

Joey shrugs. "So what?"

Danny sighs. "You're drunk, Joey. Go home."

"No way! I'm here to be with my friends and hang out with my girlfriend; now, if you'll excuse me, I want to go mingle. Come, Jackie."

Joey walks and his shoulder pushes Danny's as he passes him. My stomach is in a knot. I walk over to Danny.

"Idiot," he mumbles.

"It's okay," I say. "But, hey. Thanks for standing up for me like that. That was very gentlemanly."

"I can't believe he would bring a date," he says.

"I can't believe he would bring *her*," I say.

"What do you mean?" Danny asks, and looks into my eyes.

"It's nothing." I shake my head and try to avoid looking at him. I don't want to tell them the story. Joey is their friend too, and I don't want to sew bad blood. It's the same with Salter. I haven't told him what happened, since I don't want him to hate his father. Instead, he hates me for leaving his dad, but I'd rather have that. His father is important for him. He's the role model.

"I know that look. It's not nothing. I know he cheated on you in New York…oh no, he cheated on you with her, down here? Ah, that makes so much sense. That's why you broke up again."

"I really can't hide anything from you, huh?"

"You shouldn't have to," Danny says. "That's what friends are for, right? If you can't tell me stuff like this, then where are we?"

Wow. I knew Danny was a good friend, but I had no idea he would back me up like this.

"Thanks," I say, and finish my beer. I glance at Joey, who is talking very loud and entertaining the others with how fast he can drink a beer. He suddenly seems like he is a teenager again.

"You want to see, huh? I bet Jackie would like to see it, wouldn't you, Jackie?" he says and grabs a new beer. "Now, time me."

He places the beer to his lips and starts to drink. I've had enough. I walk to my dad and look at him. "You ready for bed?"

"Yes," he says with a deep groan. It has become easier for him to speak. He doesn't have to stop as much to catch his breath or to focus on the words as he did earlier, but it still tires him. "It was very nice…talking to you, Sandra, but now…I'll leave. The night belongs to the young.Goodnight, my…dear."

"Goodnight Mr. Mills," Sandra says with a chuckle.

I help my dad get back to his room and into bed. I cover him up and brush his teeth, then kiss his forehead. "Thank you…for a wonderful evening," he says. "Don't let Joey get to you. He just… misses you."

"I won't, Dad. It only makes me realize it really is time to move on."

73

February 2016

"We'll need you to testify against her."

It's Monday and Detective Brown has asked me to come in to the Sherriff's office in Rockledge. I have been there several times since the incident in Melbourne. It hasn't stopped being painful yet.

"You're kidding me, right?" I say. "You have everything I told you in your files; can't you just use that?"

He shakes his head. "The thing is, we can't get a valid testimony from Marcia Little. She says one thing one day then something completely different on another. One day she tells us she is guilty, then she withdraws it the next. I need your statement."

"How about the woman?" I asked.

"She hasn't woken up yet," he says.

I suck in my breath. "Still?"

He shakes his head. "They don't know if she ever will. Her brain was deprived of oxygen for a very long time."

"So she was strangled and not shot?"

"We believe there was a fight between the two of them. Then Marcia Little tried to strangle her."

"What about the girl?" I ask, thinking it's odd that they would fight when Marcia had a gun and could easily have shot her. She had the gun in her hand when I saw her through the window. Why would she try to strangle the woman?

He shakes his head again. I can tell he is troubled by this case as well. "She hasn't spoken to anyone since it happened. She is in such deep shock that she refuses to speak. We've tried everything. Every time we approach her with our questions, she breaks down in a severe asthma attack and needs medical attention. Her child psychologist tells us it might take a very long time before she'll be able to talk again. So far, she stays in the hospital as close to her mother as possible. They can't get her to leave her mother's bedside."

"I can't say I blame her," I say.

"But now, you might also be able to understand that, so far, all we have are yours and Steven Elingston's testimonies. You both saw Marcia there."

I stare into the eyes of Detective Brown. I don't know what to say to him. I really, really don't want to have to testify against my friend. At the same time, I want justice to be served for Steven and his family, especially the poor kid sitting in the hospital right now by her mother's bedside. It breaks my heart.

"We know her attorney will plead for insanity, so with your testimony, she will be committed to a psychiatric facility for an indeterminate period."

"So, you'll basically lock her away in a mental institution for the rest of her life," I say, swallowing hard.

"She did kill a lot of people, Mary."

I rub my forehead. I feel awful. This entire thing makes me feel like the worst person on the planet. But what are my choices? Either I say no to testifying and Steven gets no closure and he'll hate my guts, or I say yes and I am the reason my friend will be locked up for life. I know it's the right thing to say yes, but I don't feel good doing it.

"Alright," I say. "I'll testify."

"Perfect. We'll be in touch with the details." He gets up and reaches out his hand. "Thank you."

I shake my head and press back my tears. "Please don't thank me."

74

February 2007

ON THE MORNING of the verdict, they all hold their breaths in the courtroom as they wait for the jury to decide. Daniel can't stop looking at Kristin, while she is sitting at the table with her attorney waiting for her fate to be decided. Peter is still there as well, sitting in his wheelchair next to Daniel, seemingly indifferent to what is going on around him.

Suddenly, the red light flickers in the courtroom, signaling a verdict has been reached. Daniel looks at Kristin, who lifts her head and looks at the light as well. He wonders what is going on inside of her right now. He can't imagine how scared she must be.

Daniel sees her as she glances into the crowd and finds her mother's eyes; Kristen's mother is holding hands with Kristin's father. They have been present for all the days of the trial, supporting their daughter through it all.

During the past many weeks, they heard testimonies from expert after expert witnessing about the keyboard treatment and whether it worked or not. They heard as many opinions as there were experts. It painted the clear picture that there still is a lot of controversy about the type of treatment, the judge concluded.

The jury enters the room, one after another in a long line. Daniel looks at their faces, wondering if he can somehow read their verdict from their facial expressions. But he can't. They wear the same emotionless expression they have throughout the entire trial.

"Has the jury reached a verdict?" the judge asks.

"We have, Your Honor."

Daniel's heart is pounding loudly in his chest as they read it out loud. He can barely hear the words as they fall. The room starts to spin; his beating heart drowns the voices out.

Guilty? Did they say guilty? It can't be!

A roar of chaos goes through the courtroom. Voices, some are clapping others disagreeing. Daniel stares at Kristin, who collapses onto the defense table in loud convulsive sobs.

Daniel feels the panic spread in his body as another loud roar fills the air. Daniel turns to look at Peter, who yells at the top of his lungs. The sounds are strange and make no sense; his arms are in severe spasms, hitting his face again and again, causing his nose to start bleeding.

Daniel and his siblings jump to help Peter and hold down his hands. "We have to get him out of here," his older brother Jack says. "Before he hurts himself."

Andrew jumps for help as well, and together, they get their younger brother out of the courtroom.

"What the heck happened in there?" Daniel asks, when they get outside. Peter is still groaning loudly and they have to strap his hands down when they put him in the minivan.

"What do you mean?" Andrew asks, and shuts the door on the screaming Peter. "We won."

"Won? But…but the test. She passed the test. She got all the questions right," he says. "Peter knew about the photo. Only he could have known."

"That might be," Jack says, as Shannon joins them outside. She lights up a cigarette. The only one in the family that smokes.

"I'd say she was lucky," he continues. "She guessed it somehow."

"Plus there was the one question she didn't answer," Shannon says, blowing out smoke. As usual, Daniel's older brother by seven years, Steven, keeps his distance. He hasn't talked much to them during the trial.

"But that was one Peter could easily not have known. The rest she passed," Daniel continues. "The rest were correct. Even the one with the photo. How can they say she is guilty?"

Jack places a hand on Daniel's shoulder.

"There is nothing we can do, Daniel. The jury has spoken. She got what she deserved. This is what we wanted, remember? Now, let it go."

"What about the baby? What's going to happen to the baby?" Daniel asks, while Jack and Andrew get in the car. Andrew stops halfway and looks at him.

"You take it, if you're so eager to save it."

75

February 2016

STEVEN and I go to Heidi's Friday night and listens to some jazz singer from upstate. She is wonderful and I buy her CD afterwards, even though I don't have a CD player. I just feel so bad for her, since she is so talented, and I know they don't make any money in that business.

We walk home along A1A, holding hands, enjoying the nice evening air. I like February in Florida. Well, I guess I love every month here, since the weather is always so nice.

"That was a great performance tonight," Steven says. "I'm beginning to see why you love this place so much."

"It is my favorite," I say. "What's not to like? The food is great, the music awesome, and the company enjoyable."

Steven chuckles. "So, how's Dad doing?"

Steven has met my father twice and knows all about his story, but so far, my dad hasn't been very welcoming to him. He seems to still be quite hung up on Joey and wants us to figure out our differences. I try to explain to him that it is definitely over, now that he showed up with that bimbo to my house. He kind of put the nails in that coffin himself. But my dad won't accept it. I tell Steven he'll come around in time.

"Better," I say. "He's regained the use of four fingers in total now, so that gives us some hope."

"That's amazing."

"I know."

We walk in silence the rest of the way and stop in front of my dad's new house. We've reached that awkward point we always do when we have to either say goodbye or move to the next level. I know I want to, but I don't know if it's too early still. Will I ever be ready? Will he grow tired of me before I do get ready?

"So…this is me," I say. I feel bad for not inviting him inside, since he has to go all the way back to Winter Park.

"I know it's you," he says, as he leans over and kisses me. He looks me in the eyes when our lips part. He has gorgeous eyes. Just looking him at me makes my heart race. I realize I really want to be with him. I really want to go all the way with him.

"So…" he says.

"Do you want to come in?" I ask. "Salter is at his dad's."

"I thought you'd never ask."

I laugh and kiss him back. His lips are tender. I like that about him. There really isn't anything I don't like about him.

"Then come."

He follows me towards the front door, and I look for my keys, when suddenly I see something. A figure in the darkness, moving. My first thought is that it's an animal, but as it approaches, I realize it's not. It's human. It's a young boy.

It's Mark.

I walk towards him. "Mark? What are you doing here?"

He looks awful. He has always been on the skinny side, but this is ridiculous. "Who is it, Mary?" Steven asks.

"It's…it's Mark." I say, fearing his anger, knowing how much he hates Marcia right now. Mark doesn't seem to notice Steven. He is staring only at me.

"Mary," he says. "I need your help."

76

February 2016

"WHAT'S GOING ON, MARK?"

I put a cup of hot chocolate on the table in front of him. I spray some whipped cream in both his cup and mine.

Mark smiles with caution as he looks at the cup. This was what he wanted when I asked him what I could make for him. I was thinking more in terms of a meal or something, but if this is what he needs right now, than that is what he is getting.

"Don't think I've had hot chocolate since I was a kid," he says, with longing in his voice.

"You're still a kid," I say.

"Been awhile since I felt like one."

I sit next to him and sip my hot chocolate. I am glad that Steven decided to go back to Winter Park when I told him I had to help the boy. He seemed a little annoyed, but he'll have to live with it, I think. Right now, Mark is more important.

I exhale and look at the boy. "I know. Things must have been really bad for you, huh?"

He shrugs and looks away. "I'm fine."

"So, tell me, why aren't you at your dad's in Orlando like the rest of your brothers and your sister?"

"I ran away," he says.

"I kind of figured that part out. But why? Is it that bad there?"

Mark looks into my eyes. He reminds me of a scared bird. He doesn't answer my question. He doesn't have to. I put my hand on top of his and we drink our chocolate in silence for a little while. I know he is eager to talk to me, but it seems like he needs a little more time to get the words right. I wait patiently, even though it's getting late.

"I have to get her out of there," he says.

"Who are we talking about now? Your sister?"

He shakes his head. "Mom."

I take in a deep breath, thinking about Marcia. I know how he must feel. At least I think I do. "There really isn't much we can do," I say.

Mark slams his fist on the table. I jump.

"Yes, there is."

"What do you mean? I saw her, Mark. She was there. She shot that poor man. She told me she killed those people back six years ago. She told me she remembered what they wore, what they looked like when they were killed. I am sorry, Mark, but she is ill, and if she is convicted, then hopefully she'll get help."

"No. They'll just lock her away for life. I know how these things work," he says intensely. "She'll never get out of there again."

"But, sweetie. Maybe that's for the best. That way, she won't hurt anyone else. Out here, she is a danger to people. I know it must be hard to understand and difficult to accept that your own mother…"

He slams his fist onto the table once again. "No!"

I lean over and place my hand on his shoulder. "Mark…"

He pulls away from me and stands to his feet. He points at me and looks into my eyes while he speaks. "My mother is no killer. She might have shot at me, but that was in self-defense. She is not a ruthless killer. I know she isn't."

I stare at the young man in front of me. He suddenly seems so adult, so grown; I can no longer see him as just a child.

"You know something, don't you?" I ask.

He freezes, and then sits in his chair again. He looks down, then up at me before he finally nods.

I lean back, and then drink another sip of the chocolate, thinking I need to listen to what he has to say. I can tell by the look in his eyes that he is not just making this up. This is serious and it is eating at him.

"Tell me everything," I say. "You can trust me. You know that, right?"

It takes a while before he answers.

"I know my mom trusted you. So, I guess I can as well."

77

February 2016

"I HAVE NEVER TOLD this to anyone."

I find some Oreos and marshmallows to go with the hot choco-late, while Mark finds the strength to tell me what he knows. I can tell it is very difficult for him.

"I won't tell anyone either unless I have your permission," I say. "That's my promise to you. Cross my heart."

Mark nods. His eyes hit the edge of the table. I am bracing myself for what is about to come.

"I saw something," he says and looks at me again.

"What did you see?"

"On the night the woman was murdered, that teacher."

"Shannon Ferguson?"

"Yes. I saw her. Down by the river."

"You saw her?"

"Yes. I was actually looking for my sister."

"Rose?"

He nods. "I had realized she had started sneaking out at night, so I wanted to follow her and see what she was up to. I spotted her walking down Minutemen Causeway wearing a miniskirt, and I followed her on my bike. I wanted to stop her and tell her to go back, tell her it was a school night and no twelve-year-old should be out on a school night. But before I could get to her, a car stopped and she was picked up. Terrified, I followed them to the other side of the river bank, where the car stopped."

Mark stops and looks down. He shakes his head.

I grab the pack of Oreos and eat three in a row. "What did you see, Mark? Tell me."

"I saw her get dropped from the bridge. It was a full moon, so it was easy to see. I spotted the truck stop on top of the bridge, then someone got out, pulled out the body, and let it fall from the bridge I still remember the plump sound when it landed in the water."

"And you're certain it was Shannon Ferguson's body?" I ask.

"Yes. I was close to the bridge and it soon drifted towards me. I could see her face in the water. I know her."

"How do you know her, Mark?"

He looks me in the eyes. "She used to be my teacher in third grade. Her hair was shorter now, but she still looks the same."

I grab yet another Oreo, while digesting this news. "Oh, my God, Mark. Did you see who dropped her off the bridge then?"

He nods. "Yes. I didn't see the face, but it wasn't my mother. I would recognize my mother anywhere. Besides, this person drove away in a car, a dark pick-up truck. My mom doesn't even have a car. She has no license, remember?"

"She could have stolen one," I argue. "But you're certain it wasn't her?"

He nods again. "This person was tall. My mom isn't tall."

"But it was a woman?"

"I couldn't tell."

"Did you call the police?"

Mark looks into my eyes, then down at the table.

"I'm guessing you didn't," I say.

"How could I?" Mark is crying now. "My sister...Rose was in that awful car...with that awful man who was...doing things to her...and I was just standing there. If I told the police, they would take her away from me. They would ask me what I was doing there and they would know that she was selling herself to men like that. Her life would be ruined. They would know...they would know that things weren't the way they're supposed to be with my mother, with us."

"But this information might have helped your mother?" I say. "I mean, when she was arrested? She is being charged with the murder of Shannon Ferguson."

"I know she would rather go to jail herself than have her daughter taken away. Besides, who would ever believe me? She's my mom. I am supposed to try and protect her."

The kid was right. As an eyewitness, he wouldn't stand in court. But it gave me a new perspective on things. This news forced me to re-think everything I thought I knew about Marcia's case.

78

February 2016

I MAKE the bed in the guestroom and let Mark sleep there while I pace up and down the kitchen floor. I feel awful, confused, estranged even. What the heck is going on here? If Marcia didn't dump the body of Shannon Ferguson, then who did? And did that person also kill her? Could Mark have seen wrong? Wouldn't he be able to recognize his own mother? You'd think so.

Could he be lying?

While eating Oreos straight from the box, I sit by the computer and start researching whatever has been written about the case in the media. Scrolling through one story after another, I soon learn everything about this Shannon Ferguson that is known to the public. Nowhere does it say if she was thrown from a bridge or not. Only that she was found by someone fishing at the river one morning, a tourist hoping to catch some early fish before the sun came up. He had seen her floating towards him and wondered at first if it was a manatee.

How does Mark know the body was dumped from the bridge? Could he be speculating? Making things up? But why would he? To protect his mother? Wouldn't he have gone to the police with his information then? And why add the story about his sister to it? It didn't sound like something a fourteen-year-old would come up with.

What if he is right? What if Marcia didn't do it?

I shake my head slowly and walk to the kitchen to find a bag of chips that I bring back to the computer. I wonder if I should call Steven and tell him this. I feel like I need to share this with someone, but I am not sure Steven will take this well. He is so convinced Marcia killed her and his other siblings. But no one ever managed to answer the question why? Why would she target his family and kill them like this? They haven't even managed to establish any connection between them; they have no idea how she even knows them.

Who is that person on the bridge?

I keep imagining the figure standing up there, looking down, as the body plunges into the water beneath. It was a tall person, Mark said. It's not much to go on.

I stare at the screen, where a picture of a younger Shannon Ferguson, taken from when she was hired at Roosevelt Elementary School, fills the screen. The article speculates about who would hold a grudge against a very loved teacher in our local community. It also tells that she was stabbed thirteen times in her chest before she was dumped in the water. Forensics reports show she was still alive. Water in her lungs proves she was still breathing, and the cause of death was, therefore, drowning.

A chill goes through my body and I lean back with a sigh when my phone suddenly rings. I look at the display and realize it can only be the only other person awake at this hour around here.

Chloe.

"There is something we need to talk about," she says.

I chuckle, noticing that she brings no excuses for the late call. She never does. To her, this is the normal time to be awake.

"Sure. I'm up anyway," I say.

"I'm coming over."

Less than a minute later, she is in the kitchen of my dad's house. I make some coffee for the both of us. It's almost three o'clock anyway, and I have realized I'm not going to get any sleep tonight anyway, so I might as well stay up.

"So, what's up?" I ask, and serve her the coffee.

She has a very serious look in her eyes as she speaks. "Something is wrong. Something is very wrong."

"Okay? What are we talking about here?"

"Marcia. I took another look at her case. I simply can't believe she would do such terrible acts. I went through her case file and found this." Chloe puts a piece of paper in front of me.

"It's from the forensics report," she says. "Ballistics. From the Elingston house. The second one. Look at the results."

I look down at the paper, then back up at Chloe.

"They don't match," she says. "The bullet that killed Andrew Elingston didn't belong to the gun they found in the house. It didn't belong to Marcia's gun."

79

April 2007

"HE'S IN HERE."

The nurse walking ahead of Daniel stops in front of a closed door and turns to look at him. "I have to admit, he has not been the easiest among our patients. He has caused us quite a lot of trouble."

"Peter? He's the easiest in the world," Daniel says, startled. "He's the gentlest human being on this planet."

The nurse snorts. "Well, we haven't seen much of that since he got here."

Daniel can't believe what he is hearing. It was Shannon who called the day before and told him that they had called—again— from the home where Peter lived since their mother died and since the trial ended, and told her that Peter was causing trouble there, asking them to come and visit him.

Daniel has been there a couple of times before, but work and family have been taking up a lot of time lately, and the visits have been further apart than when he lived at the house.

Maybe it is just a bad excuse for not coming because Daniel can't stand the place, can't stand to see his brother in a place like this.

But his siblings all think it is a great idea. They found the most expensive home with the best care, they say.

"He's going to love it there," Jack argued when Daniel objected and asked if there really wasn't any of them who could take Peter in. "There's going to be a lot of other people who are just like him. He's going to have a blast."

A blast is very far from what Daniel is looking at now that the nurse is opening the door to the room with the words:

"We had to strap him down."

Daniel stares at his brother lying motionless, arms and legs strapped to the bed. He has to calm himself down to not say something he might regret later on.

"Strap him down? But…why?"

"He was hurting himself and everyone else trying to help him. He smacked one of the nurses in the face and gave her a bruise. We really can't have that. It was for the good of everybody."

Daniel takes a couple of angry steps towards his brother. His wrists are bruised from trying to get loose. He is lying completely still now. Doesn't even react when Daniel approaches him. Usually, he chirps when he sees Daniel. Chirps with excitement. But not today. He is not even screaming like he usually does when he is upset or angry.

Daniel waves a hand in front of his face, but his eyes don't even blink. Daniel is shocked by this lethargy from his usually so lively brother.

"What happened to him?"

"We had to give him something to calm him down," the nurse says.

"Drugs? You gave my brother drugs?"

"He was hurting himself. And constantly gnawing at his hands. Look at them. Those sores won't heal if he continues to chew them."

"He only chews them when he is upset."

"That might be, but he has been doing it excessively since he got here. We had to do something. The wild movements with his arms are so uncontrolled we never know when he'll hit someone."

"But that's his disease, for crying out loud," Daniel says. "He can't control his muscles and movements."

The nurse sighs. "I know. But what do you want us to do? We have to wash him. We have to feed him. We can't do that if he is constantly moving. The doctor recommended it."

"I would like to be alone with him, if I may," Daniel says, struggling hard to keep his cool.

"Very well. I have places to be too," the nurse says and leaves the room.

Daniel sits next to the bed. He reaches out and grabs Peter's hand in his, something he can usually never do, since he rarely stays still. Daniel tries to get eye contact with his brother, but Peter's eyes stare eerily into the ceiling; they don't move, they hardly blink.

It's like he's not even alive anymore.

Daniel strokes his brother's hand several times, while tears leave his eyes, thinking about how alive Peter used to be when he was at the university or when debating with his classmates after class. How vibrant he used to be when working with Kristin and discovering new things with her. Daniel tries not to, but he feels so guilty for having deprived his brother of that world. No matter if she manipulated his words, it was still better than this. Wasn't it?

Now Kristin was in jail, and so was Peter.

"I am sorry, brother. You have no idea how sorry I am," he whispers.

80

February 2016

"They never told you this, did they?"

Chloe leans back in her chair and looks at me, her arms crossed over her chest. "The police never told you that the bullets didn't match the gun."

I shake my head pensively. "No."

"They conveniently left that out," Chloe says.

"What do you mean?" I swallow another Oreo and wonder if I'll get sick if I eat any more. Probably. They do a great job of keeping me awake, though.

"They didn't tell you because then maybe you wouldn't agree to be a witness for them. But that is also why they so desperately need you. Without yours and Steven's testimony, they have nothing. If they can't match the murder weapon with her, they don't have much to go on."

"More like *nothing* to go on," I say.

This puts me in a very difficult position for sure. I don't want to be the one to put the last nail in Marcia's coffin. I don't want to be the sole reason she is locked away for life. Especially not now that there is doubt about her guilt. I, for one, am not convinced anymore.

"There is something else," I say. I look at the door to the guestroom, where Mark is sleeping. At least I hope he is. He looked like he needed it badly.

"What's that?"

"Mark came here tonight. He's sleeping in the guest bedroom. He told me something that shook me deeply."

"Really?" Chloe sips her coffee and grabs some chips from the bag. I know she is used to eating at night as well. Well, to be frank, she does everything at night. She never eats much if she's awake during the day. Me, I eat both night and day if I can get away with it.

"I promised I would only tell if he agreed to it, but I think he knows he can trust you as well. He saw the body be dumped."

"What body?" Chloe asks.

"Shannon Ferguson. The teacher. He saw someone dump her from the bridge. He says it wasn't his mother, that this was someone taller."

"Why hasn't he said anything?"

"That's the thing. I can't tell you that because it'll break his heart; just trust me that he has thought about it every minute since, but he couldn't."

"Why? It could have helped his mother? At least in the case of Shannon Ferguson. I don't understand this."

I sigh. I can't betray Mark's trust and tell her everything. "He is afraid to get someone else in trouble, okay? Ask him yourself when he wakes up. I just can't tell you unless he agrees to. He trusts me."

"Okay. So you're telling me he saw someone else dump the body, not his mother? Am I getting that right?"

"Yes."

"So that is two deep inconsistencies in the case against Marcia," Chloe says. "We have to do something. We can't let them put her away with such light evidence."

"I couldn't agree more," I say. "But what? What do we do?"

Chloe looks pensive. She is biting the inside of her cheek.

"We could go to the detective with everything we know. Maybe they'll look into it," I say.

"You know as well as I do, they won't," Chloe says. "They have their killer. They believe she is guilty. Heck, she has even admitted to being guilty."

"But also pulled it back again," I say. "They can never use her testimony in court. She has no idea what she is saying."

"I know that and so do you, but they don't. I mean, who's to say when Marcia is clear minded and when she isn't. When she's confessing or when she's pulling it all back again? The bottom line is, they'll do anything to prove her guilt. They won't listen to loose allegations like these. So what if the gun wasn't a match? Maybe she had another one that she used and disposed of somehow?"

"Maybe she didn't act alone?" I say.

"What do you mean?"

"Maybe there was someone else in the house? The one who had the right gun, the same person who dumped the body from the bridge?"

Chloe looks pensive.

"But where does that leave Marcia? As an accomplice?" I continue.

"Maybe. Or just in the wrong place at the wrong time."

I exhale with a deep breath. "How do we find out?"

Chloe stands to her feet.

"I may have an idea."

81

February 2016

SHE IS SLEEPING when we enter the room at the hospital. No one notices us as we walk through the hallways. Everything is in night mode. There are no guards outside the door either. I wonder why. They were, after all, victims of an attempted murder. But, apparently, that didn't give you any extra protection. Probably because they believed they had their killer.

We walk slowly towards her. I remember her name is Lindsey from the police files. She is sitting in a chair next to her mother's bed, her head lying on top of her mother's stomach, her eyes closed. She is snoring lightly.

I put a hand on her shoulder while Chloe makes sure to close the door silently behind us. The girl gasps and looks up at me. Her eyes are still in the daze that is sleep and blinking as she looks at me. She gets agitated and starts wheezing.

"Don't be scared," I say. "I'm not here to hurt you."

She doesn't look like she believes me. The wheezing is getting worse. I can't blame her for being afraid. She doesn't say anything. I know she hasn't spoken at all since the attack in her home. I don't expect her to now, especially not to me, a complete stranger, who is trying to prove the innocence of the woman everyone believes killed her father and left her mother in a coma.

"I'm Mary. This is Chloe. We're just here to talk to you a little bit," I say. I smile and look at Chloe, who smiles as well. Her smile is far from comforting. I know I have to be quick before anyone finds us here.

"We're here to talk to you about the woman in your house, the one who was arrested in your house. I know it must be hard for you to talk about, and we won't ask you to. Just help us a little, okay?"

Lindsey stares at me. Her eyes are frightened. Again, I can't blame her. But then the unforeseen happens. The wheezing calms down and Lindsey nods. She doesn't speak, but just nods, agrees to us being there, while catching her breath. We find her inhalator on the end table by her mother's bed, and she takes a few deep breaths till the wheezing stops completely.

I grab my phone and find a photo of Marcia in it. I zoom it with my fingers so she can see her face up close. "This is her, right? She was in your house, right?"

Lindsey stares at it for quite a while, then up at me. I expect her to start wheezing again, but she doesn't. Instead she nods. Then she lifts her finger and points at me.

"Yes, yes I was there too. I didn't think you'd remember me. I came in just before the police arrived."

I am glad she remembers me and understand that is why she trusts me. I wonder if she trusts me enough. "I realize this must be very difficult for you, Lindsey. But we need to know what happened. We fear the police are about to make a mistake, one that will cost our friend to be locked up for life."

I show her the picture again. She smiles when she sees it and a warm feeling overwhelms me.

"Did this woman shoot your father?" I ask. "Was it her?"

Lindsey's wrinkles her forehead. Her eyes are torn in confusion. Determined, she shakes her head.

I look at Chloe behind me. "I knew it," she says. "I bet they never asked you."

I look at Lindsey again. "Then, who did shoot your dad?" I say, knowing very well she can't answer me.

Once again, Lindsey stares at me, then points at the phone in my hand. She opens her mouth and says the words I know will never leave me again.

"S-s-save."

She is struggling to get the word across her lips, and she speaks while pointing at Marcia. She starts to wheeze again and grabs her inhalator.

"Save? Marcia...Marcia saved you?" I say with cheer in my voice. She nods eagerly, while breathing through her inhalator.

"Marcia didn't hurt anyone, she tried to save you!"

Lindsey nods with big eyes.

Chloe grabs my arm. "Ballistics," she says. "Ballistics showed that Marcia's gun had been fired. She had residue on her hands. It just didn't match the bullet that killed the father."

"She fired to stop the intruder, who had probably already killed Andrew Elingston. The question is if the intruder was hurt."

"Not enough for her to not be able to escape," Chloe says.

I look at the little girl in front of me. I get so emotional looking into her eyes. I can't believe this much bad can happen to one little girl. It's devastating. I lean over and kiss her forehead. She grabs me around the waist and holds me tight. It's the best hug I've had in many years.

82

February 2016

MARK IS awake when we get back to my dad's house. So is my father. While Chloe goes home to sleep and take care of her mother, I throw together some pancakes and serve them for my father and Mark. I miss Salter when I watch Mark eat. Salter is spending the entire weekend with his father. I realize I haven't thought about Steven once since last night.

While the others eat, I call him up.

"So, what was so urgent last night?" he asks.

I sigh. I don't feel like I can tell him everything, but I want to talk to him about it anyway.

"It's…we believe Marcia might be innocent," I say.

"What?" His tone is angry. Rightfully so. He doesn't know the entire story. I can't tell him what Mark has told me or what Lindsey told me. At least not yet, so I go with the evidence.

"Ballistics show that it wasn't her gun that killed your brother, Andrew. It was another gun."

"So what? She could have used two guns or something. Maybe ballistics is wrong. I know she did it, Mary. I saw her, she went for my niece with that gun. She would have shot her if we hadn't interfered. You know I am right. You saw it yourself."

I sigh. I don't expect him to understand. But I want him to trust me on this. "What if she was trying to save them instead?" I ask. "What if her gun was fired, but at the intruder instead?"

"What the heck? Are you kidding me?"

"I'm very serious, Steven. The evidence doesn't add up. I am telling you. Marcia could be innocent."

"But she's not. I know she isn't," he says. "She did it. She hasn't even tried to defend herself. If she saved them instead of killing them, then why doesn't she tell that to the police?"

"I don't know," I say. "She is sick. Maybe she doesn't remember."

"She has admitted her guilt."

"But also pulled it back."

"That doesn't make her innocent."

"Doesn't make her guilty either."

"But she is…she is guilty, Mary, and she'll be locked away. I promise you she will. I won't sit here and watch while she gets away with killing most of my family. I simply refuse to. Leave it alone, Mary. This is my battle to fight. We're finally about to get closure. Do you have any idea what it is like to not know what happened to your family? No, you don't. Because it was my family."

"I understand why you are upset but…"

"No buts. You leave this alone; you hear me?"

"Hey. Marcia is my friend," I say a lot harsher than intended. He's got me angry now. "I am not about to stand here and watch as they convict her when she is innocent. She has a life too; she has children too."

"Then I guess we don't have anything more to say to each other," he says.

Really? Wow!

"I guess not."

I hang up and realize I have burnt the last pancake beyond recognition. Mark looks at me from the table.

"Was that Harry?" he asks.

I nod and remove the burnt pancake.

"His real name is Steven," my dad says. "Apparently…he lied about it."

"Steven?" Mark asks.

"Yes," my dad says. "Doesn't sound like…he's going to come around here…again."

"That's too bad. I liked Harry, or Steven," Mark says.

I grab a pancake from the stack for myself.

"So did I."

83

February 2016

I MANAGE to get half an hour of sleep before the doorbell wakes me up. Outside is Danny. He is wearing another T-shirt with his department's logo on it, and it makes me chuckle. I try to hide it to not hurt him. He looks very muscular in this one.

"Are you ready?" he asks.

"For what?" I say sleepily.

"Remember?"

"No."

"We are going to see Marcia!" he says. "Don't tell me you've made other plans. I pulled some strings, you know how us guys in uniform like to help one another…"

"No, but I do love the way you always manage to remind me."

He looks at me, then shakes his head. "Anyway, I got us on the list for visiting her today. Normally, you have to apply first and all that, but…"

I smile. "You know someone who fixed that, am I right?"

"Sure did."

"That's perfect," I say, and lean over and kiss his cheek. "You have no idea how perfect it is."

Danny touches his cheek while I storm back in the house to get myself ready. I throw on a dress and brush my hair. I stop as I pass Mark on my way out. "Have you even seen her?" I ask. "Have you visited her?"

He shakes his head. "I can't. DCF is looking for me. They want me to go back to my dad's."

I nod. "Maybe we should wait a little before we take you, then," I say. "I'll make sure to give her a kiss from you. You're welcome to stay here in this house until we find a more suitable situation for you, all right? Be here when I get back."

He smiles. "Are you kidding me? You have an Xbox. I am never leaving this house again."

"That's Salter's. Be careful, it's a time consumer. Don't spend all day playing, okay?"

"No, ma'am."

I laugh and run for the door. Danny is standing in the doorway, waiting for me. "Shall we?" I say, and walk past him.

I tell him everything on the drive there. Except the part about Rose. I leave that out for Mark's sake. But Danny needs to know the details as well. He needs to know I believe Marcia could be innocent.

"I never believed she was guilty," he says. "Just couldn't get it to fit in."

"I know. You're a better man than I," I say.

"I sure hope so," he says with a laugh. "Since you're a woman and all…"

"You know what I mean. I feel so guilty for having believed she did it, for agreeing to testify against her."

"It's different for you," he says. "You were there. You saw her in that house, bent over the lifeless body of that woman."

"But you can't tell your little police-friends or anyone else in uniform," I say. "I don't trust them."

Danny looks at me like I am crazy, then shakes his head. "Nah, who am I kidding. I know you're right. This is a high-profile case and solving it is important. They won't back down now. Not when they feel like they're this close. I do know the guys at the Sherriff's office that well."

I sigh, content that Danny understands, as he drives up in front of the maximum security prison in the middle of nowhere on the road to Orlando. I remember it from just four months ago when I visited my brother in here. I swore I was never coming back to this place.

Guess that didn't work out very well for me.

84

February 2016

THEY BRING MARCIA IN. My heart drops as I see her on the other side of the glass. She looks confused, her eyes clouded. I feel the walls closing in on me, thinking about her being in here, thinking about how I was part of putting her here. How I believed she had done those awful things.

"Hey, Mary. And Danny. What a surprise," she says, sounding almost normal. But then she adds, while looking at me, "I thought you were in New York?"

I smile, but not because I am happy. Mostly because I feel so terrible for her. She needs help, not to be in jail. Being in here can't be helping her. It can't be good.

"How are you, Marcia?" Danny asks.

"I'm great, Danny. Thanks." Her voice is shrill. She leans over and whispers with great emphasis. "They're trying to kill me."

I chuckle, although I am not amused. I try to lock eyes with her. "Marcia. We need to talk to you. We need your help."

She looks at Danny, then back at me. "Of course. Anything for the crew. Just keep your voices down. You don't want *them* to hear."

"Of course not," I say, playing along. "We need you to remember something for us. Do you think you can do that?"

"Sure," she says, like it is the easiest thing in the world for her. I brace myself because I know her memories are all over the place.

"All right. So, we are trying to help you. Remember that, okay?"

She nods. "Okay."

"We don't believe you killed all those people."

She tilts her head slightly. "Oh. I hate to disappoint you, but I do believe I did. It was my lawyer…what's his name again? …Anyway, he told me to pull back my confession, but I did it. I am pretty sure I did."

I lean over and look into her eyes. "Why? Why are you so certain?"

Marcia is surprised by the question. "Because I remember it. I still hear them scream sometimes."

"What are they screaming, Marcia? What exactly are they screaming?" I ask.

"Well they're screaming: *You did it, Marcia. You killed us!* Most of the time. Other times, they're just screaming for help."

"When they scream, are there many different voices?"

Marcia looks at me, then at Danny. "I don't understand."

"Are the voices those of children? Of men or just a woman?"

"Usually a woman, why?"

"Tell me something, Marcia, what happened to Shannon Ferguson?" I ask.

"I killed her, why?"

"How did you kill her?"

"I stabbed her and dumped her in the river, why?"

"How many times did you stab her?"

"Thirteen times," she says. The answer comes swiftly. The tone is the same as if I had asked her how many children she had. There is no emotion, no regret, and no sadness of having to relive this once again.

"And then what did you do with the body?"

"I dumped it in the river, I just told you."

"How did you transport it?" I ask.

Marcia stops. She leans back in her chair. "I…I don't really remember. I guess I must have stolen a car and taken it there. It's really very blurry."

"Try and remember. For me, Marcia. How did you dump the body?"

She shrugs. "I don't know. I just threw it in the water. I can't remember, Mary."

"Then how are you so certain you even killed her?"

Marcia sits up straight with an exhale. "Because I remember what she looked like. Not alive. When she was dead. I remember the blood. I remember the yellow shirt she was wearing. I remember the flowers of blood that had spread on it. When they showed me the pictures of the body, I recognized her. I remembered her from when she was on the couch, the one with the flowers, where she was stabbed, where I stabbed her."

"Do you remember doing it?" I ask. "Do you remember taking the knife and stabbing it into her?"

"Mary, maybe we should…" Danny tries to stop me, but I signal that he needs to back down.

Marcia looks even more confused. Her eyes are flickering.

"Do you recall what it felt like?"

Marcia shakes her head. "No."

"Where did you do it?"

"At her house."

"Did you knock her out first, or did you stab her first?"

"I don't remember."

"So, you're telling me all you remember is standing in front of a dead body, the body of Shannon Ferguson, who was lying on a couch in her house? You don't remember stabbing her; you don't remember dumping her."

Marcia is shaking her head violently now.

"Mary, I don't think this is good for her," Danny says.

"I know. I just need to get answers while she is still there mentally," I tell him, and look back at Marcia. "Tell me about what happened at the Elingston house," I say.

She nods. "I entered the house and shot the husband, then tried to strangle the woman…" Marcia looks into my eyes. I detect deep confusion in them now. "It was thundering outside. I was in the garage…I was sleeping…When I heard something…No, that wasn't then…that was something else, maybe a dream, I don't…" Her eyes go blank and she looks away. "I don't remember. The police tell me I black out when I do the bad things. When I kill. That's why I don't remember doing it. My mind isn't right, they say."

"Marcia I need you to help me, so I can help you," I say. "I know it's in there somewhere in your mind. There was someone else with you in the house that day when Andrew Elingston was killed wasn't there?"

"No. The police say I was there alone, that I acted alone."

"It doesn't matter what the police say," I say. "I am interested in what you say. What you remember."

Marcia looks like she is scrutinizing her brain. She looks at me, and then tilts her head again. "Mary? Why aren't you in New York?"

I sigh and give up. I look at Danny. "I don't think we're getting any more out of her."

"It was great to see you again, Marcia," Danny says.

"I'll get you out of here," I say, just before I get to my feet, heart-broken, crushed. "Trust me."

Her face lights up. "Great! Then maybe we can go to Beef O' Brady's. Kids eat free on Tuesdays."

85

November 2010

DANIEL DOESN'T LIKE daytime TV. Yet he still watches it excessively every day while waiting for the phone to ring and someone to offer him a new job. Well, maybe it isn't entirely true that he doesn't like it. He does enjoy some parts of it, like the parts when other people tell their stories and make him feel better about his own. When Jerry Springer has them jump each other in desperation to blame someone else for their lives going wrong, Daniel feels a little better about himself. Not because his life is any better than theirs are, 'cause it really isn't. No, he feels relieved because at least he knows who to blame. Himself. No one else can take credit for screwing up his life, like he can himself.

Daniel has lost everything. His job, his wife, his family. He has moved away, as far away from Florida as he could, and now he is sitting in a small condo in Upstate New York, in a small snowy town called Accord, numbering around five hundred citizens, wondering if life will ever be good again.

He can't blame Jill for leaving. Daniel started drinking and didn't care for his family in the way he was supposed to. To be frank, he hadn't for many years before then. Taking care of his brother Peter and the work with Kristin took too much of his time. He missed out on everything. He neglected them. The guilt following what happened to Peter after the trial ate him alive, and that was when he started to drink for real. Then everything else slid out of his hands. Soon he was fired, and his wife told him she'd had enough.

Coming from a wealthy family, Daniel has enough money to last him a lifetime, and for his family as well. So, he gave them a huge sum and told them not to miss him because he wasn't worth it, then left without telling them where he went.

Daniel looks at Jerry Springer as he watches the two young women fight on the stage. He is smiling and shaking his head. Daniel knows very well why Jerry is smiling. The fighting is what keeps people tuning in to his show.

A true moneymaker.

Daniel sighs and gets up from his chair. He walks to the kitchen to get another beer. He can't remember when he last ate. Maybe it doesn't matter. Daniel has played with the thought of drinking himself to death. No one would miss him. His body could rot away in the apartment until it started to smell and some neighbor called the cops. They'd find him between beer and vodka bottles. Maybe so many the door would be blocked. The place would smell so bad they'd have to wear masks to not throw up.

Except that just isn't quite Daniel's style.

The women in the TV are screaming and pulling each other's hair over some guy who watches with a sly smile, like he thinks he's the king of the world to have two women fighting over him.

Daniel watches it from the kitchen while he opens the refrigerator. The big muscular guys are now splitting them apart and the fighting part is over. As the show goes to commercials, Daniel bends down and pulls out a beer. When he looks back at the TV, it's been turned off.

What the …?

Daniel looks around to locate the remote. He spots it on the kitchen counter.

Did I put it there?

No. Daniel always puts the remote in the same spot. He likes things to have their place and always keep them there. Thinking he's probably more drunk than he thought, Daniel grabs it and turns the TV back on. With the beer to his lips, he walks back to the recliner, sits down, and puts his feet up. He sighs, satisfied, and drinks some more of the beer, hoping he'll pass out soon and sleep the rest of the day.

No need to be awake anyway.

His eyes stare at the screen as the show returns and the two women once again plunge at each other. Daniel chuckles.

"Every freaking day it's the same. Every freaking day."

It's in the reflection of the TV screen that he realizes he is no longer alone in the apartment. Someone is standing behind his chair.

"What the…?"

He jumps out of his seat and faces the person.

"What are you doing here?"

The voice answering is calm and collected. Not at all as filled with anger or revenge as he has expected. Nothing like those people on TV. It's not remorseful either.

"You know why I am here."

86

February 2016

I HARDLY SPEAK a word on our way back. Danny is very quiet as well. It's not until we reach the bridge leading to the barrier island that Danny finally says something.

"So, what did you make of all that she said?"

I shrug. "All I know is that I don't believe she killed any of them. She doesn't remember anything about it. Don't you think you'd remember at least a little bit?"

He shrugs as well. "I don't know. If she's as sick as we believe, then I'm not sure we can believe anything she says. She could have blocked it out somehow. If she is really mentally ill, then I believe the brain can do that."

"True. I do suspect that she suffers from Schizophrenia. But what she does remember strikes me as odd."

"I'll give you that much," he says, and drives up in front of my dad's house. We hug goodbye and I walk inside. I yell to my dad that I am home, then grab my phone. I walk outside and sit in the sun, while wondering if I should do it or not, debating, arguing back and forth, then decide to do it anyway.

"Hello?"

"It's Mary. Now before you get mad at me again, I am not calling to say anything about what happened yesterday. I understand why you're mad at me. I am calling because I have a question for you."

Steven exhales. "All right. What is it?"

"I know it's going to sound strange, but bear with me."

"Depends on the question," he says.

"Did your sister have a couch with flowered-fabric on it in her house?"

"What?"

"I know it's odd, just answer me, please."

"Well then, the answer is no," he says. "She had two beige couches, leather, as far as I remember."

"Ah, okay," I say. "That is all. Thank you."

"That's it?" he asks. He sounds so disappointed.

I pause. "That depends," I say.

"Depends on what?"

"On you. If you're still angry with me."

Steven chuckles lightly. "I am sorry. I didn't mean to be so angry with you. Of course you're trying to protect your friend. It was wrong of me."

I smile and spot Mark as he walks up from the beach with a board under his arm. He is wearing board shorts and he is wet. He places the surfboard on the grass and showers. I am glad to see that he is not just cooped up inside. He is so skinny it hurts looking at him, and I decide I will make him a big lunch today, once I hang up with Steven.

"Apology accepted," I say.

"Great. So I get a chance to see you again?"

"Yes."

"I am glad. Maybe next weekend? We could go to Heidi's. I'll call you, okay?"

"Sounds good."

I hang up and look at Mark, who now approaches me. "Was it any good?" I ask, referring to the waves. They look small.

"A lot more fun than expected," he says. He stops in front of me. "So. How'd it go? How was she?"

"I'll be honest with you. She didn't make much sense. She seems okay, given the circumstances, though," I add, to not give him more to worry about. "Tell me one thing, did you go to Beef O' Brady's a lot?"

He grabs a towel from behind a chair and starts to dry himself. "Yeah," he says. "We went there every Tuesday. At least, we used to until she got worse. It sort of became this tradition because, you know…kids eat free. That way mom could take us out without spending a lot of money."

It makes sense. Marcia never had much to spend, and with four kids, it was probably always tight for her. It also explains why she always mentioned it when I talked to her. It was a big thing in her life to be able to take the kids out every Tuesday. It was the one thing she could hold on to, the one thing…*wait, how did she manage to remember it every Tuesday?*

"Say, Mark. Did anyone else eat with you on Tuesdays?"

"Yeah, sure. Mom's sponsor was there too."

"Jess?"

"Yes. She's the one who always knew how to find mom and make sure she came home. She would drive us all there in her truck. She would also take us home."

"Did she spend a lot of time with your mom?"

Mark shrugs. "I think so. She helped her a lot."

"Was she with you the last time you went to the restaurant?"

"Sure."

"When was that?"

"I don't know. In January some time. Five-six weeks ago. Why the sudden interest in her?"

I shake my head. "No reason. Just got me thinking. That's all."

87

February 2016

When Mark is inside the house, I pick up my phone again. I call Chloe.

"Just the person I wanted to talk to," she says. "I have something important I need to talk to you about."

"Me too," I say. "Back in the beginning of the investigation of the murder of Shannon Ferguson, the police looked at Marcia because someone had told them that Marcia herself believed she had done it. I need you to tell me who the person was. I need a name."

"I can tell you right away," she says. "I have the files right here. I printed all of them out, just in case they somehow managed to lock me out of their system."

I can hear her flip the pages. My heart is beating fast now. An idea is shaping in my mind, but it's still vague. I can't see the details yet.

"Here it is. Yes. Someone came to the station and told the police that Marcia Little had told her she believed she might have killed Shannon Ferguson."

"And the name?"

"It says here her name is Kristin Martin."

"That's odd," I say. "I was certain it would be Jess, Marcia's sponsor. Well, thanks anyway."

"Wait, I have something…"

"Not now, Chloe. Later, okay?"

I hang up, frustrated. No, that's putting it too mildly. I am aggravated. I am good old-fashioned pissed. I was so sure of my theory, whatever it was. I didn't have the details, but somehow I believed Jess had framed Marcia.

Something is off about her and her relationship with Marcia. She told me she hadn't seen Marcia in three months when we arrived at that AA meeting. Why did she say that if she had seen her only a few weeks ago? Why did Mark say that she always knew where to find Marcia when no one else could?

There could easily be a very ordinary explanation for all these questions, but I have this feeling, this itch, that there isn't. I sit down in front of my computer with another deep sigh, wondering how the heck I am supposed to solve this. How I am to prove Marcia's innocence? I will never be able to live with myself if she is convicted of this.

Not knowing what else to do, I decide we need food to think. In the kitchen, I start lunch, and soon Mark comes out and helps me. I am making a big portion of spaghetti and meatballs. I have a feeling Mark will like it because it has always been Marcia's favorite dish. So much about him reminds me of her when she was that age.

"Smells divine," he says.

He sets the table, and I get my dad out of bed, using the lift and help him get into the wheelchair. I bring him to the table, where he smiles when he sees Mark. He seems to enjoy having the boy here.

I feed him a spoonful of spaghetti and meatballs. "Oh, this is good," he says.

Mark digs in as well.

"So, tell me, Mark, what else do you know about Jess?" I ask. I am not ready to let go of this angle just yet.

"Not much," he says.

"Do you know her last name?"

"No."

"Do you know if she has any family? Any kids?"

"I don't think so."

"Did your mom spend a lot of time at her place?"

He shrugs. "Maybe. I never knew where she was."

We finish the meal, and I clean up, while my dad is enjoying the sun on the porch. I look at my laptop from the kitchen and an urge overwhelms me. I walk to it and sit down. I Google Jess and try to guess her last name. Then I try to search for Jess and Cocoa Beach, but only a lot of useless stuff comes up. I try something else. There is something about that name, Kristin Martin, that rings a bell. I've heard about her somewhere before. I Google her name and…

Bingo!

I lean back with a deep sigh, as I open the first picture that Google found.

"Well, hello there…*Jess*."

88

February 2016

"SHE FELL IN LOVE WITH HIM."

I am almost yelling in the phone.

"Who fell in love with who?" Chloe asks.

"Kristin Martin. She was a therapist or a professor of some sort. I knew I had heard that name before. She was that lady who fell in love with a disabled man, and was sent to jail for three years and nine months because she couldn't prove that the guy had given his consent to have sex with her."

"Ah. Now I remember. That was a long time ago, right?"

"She was convicted nine years ago."

"So, she's out now?"

"Exactly. And, get this. The disabled man was the youngest in the Elingston clan. And she is also Marcia's sponsor," I say. "Calls herself Jess. The two of them have been spending a lot of time together, I believe."

"Ah."

"I need you to find her address. It must be in the police file somewhere," I say. "I dropped her off the other day outside her condominiums, the Palmas De Majorca by 3rd Street North, but I don't know which number she lives in."

"I'll check." Chloe disappears for just a second, then returns. "Here. Apartment number 329."

"Great, thanks."

"By the way, there is something I have been meaning to talk to you about...Joey asked me to..."

"Not now, Chloe. I don't want to hear about him. I'm not ready yet. Besides, I need to find this woman."

"Don't go alone!"

"I'll be fine," I say, and hang up. Thinking about what she said, I go to my dad's room and grab his gun from his safe to bring with me, just in case.

I look at Mark who is playing Xbox in the living room and wonder if I should tell him anything, but decide not to. There is no reason to alarm him further. He's been through so much.

"I'm going out for a little while," I say to both my dad and Mark, then walk to the car. I drive to the Palmas De Majorca, where I park and walk towards the condos. I want to call the police, but I don't have enough evidence to prove anything. They'll only think I'm crazy. I need to look into her eyes while I ask her about it.

My plan is to pretend I am here to talk about Marcia, and if that doesn't work, then talk about my own addiction to food and how to get out of it. How I am going to get her to talk about the Elingston family and the murders, I haven't figured out yet. But somehow, I will.

It's one of those condominiums where the stairs and hallways are all outside. They are very common in Florida, because it is always so warm out. I walk up to the third floor, find her condo, and ring the doorbell. There is no answer. I ring again, then look in the window, covering my eyes from the light with my hands. I have to stand on my tippy-toes to reach. Inside, I immediately spot something that makes me shiver.

A couch.

Not just any couch. A couch with pink flower-covered fabric.

I swallow hard and pull back. Maybe I am in over my head here. Maybe I should get the police involved instead, but how? How am I to make them believe me? The couch was in Marcia's head, not in any evidence material. Besides, why should they believe me? Because of what Mark said? Because the woman has been in jail before? Because of a stupid couch? Still doesn't prove anything.

"Can I help you?"

An elderly woman approaches me.

"I was just visiting someone."

"I live right next door. She's not here anymore," she says and points at Jess's door. "She rented the place a year ago, fully furnished and everything. Guess she knew she wouldn't stay long. A nice woman, though. She'll be missed around here."

"Do you know where she went?" I ask, feeling my heart drop with the prospect of yet another murderer getting away on my watch.

"Yes. I spoke to her this morning when she left. She told me she was going to Winter Park. A lovely place this time of year."

I stare at the old lady, while everything inside of me is screaming.

Winter Park? She's going for the last Elingston. The only one left.

Oh, my God. She's going to kill Steven!

November 2010

THE GUN IS POINTED at him as they drive. They're in his car and he is behind the wheel. It's a long drive. Eighteen hours, and they only stop for coffee and food. Daniel is exhausted, but feels kind of uplifted as well. For the first time in a long time, he is actually doing something.

"Take me to see him," Kristin said, back at the condo.

Of course that is what she wants. To see Peter after spending almost four years in prison. Daniel can't blame her, and to be honest, he is really excited to give Peter the chance to see her again. The past years have been terrible for him, and in the end, Daniel simply stopped visiting Peter because he couldn't stand it anymore. He couldn't take seeing him lying there, strapped to his bed with dead eyes like some vegetable. He couldn't stand the guilt.

Daniel fought for years to get him out of the home. He drove his siblings crazy, constantly bugging them about it, telling them they had to do something. Anything. But they refused.

"He's fine, Daniel," Jack would say, over and over again. "He's safe. He's being taken care of."

But what did they know? They never visited Peter. They didn't even care enough to listen to what Daniel told them. They were just happy to have Peter locked away somewhere, so they no longer had to care. So they could move on with their lives and put it all behind them.

Daniel even suggested that he take care of Peter himself. He told them he could take him to his home, he and his wife would care for him, maybe hire a nurse to be there all day long. Jill protested wildly, but he told her he had to do this. That he couldn't live with himself anymore. He would do anything to get Peter out of that awful place.

Even if it meant losing Jill. Daniel was desperate, the guilt was eating him so badly he couldn't sleep or eat, and that was when he started drinking, like seriously drinking. But, no matter how much he begged his siblings to let him ease Peter's pain, to give him back his life, they never would agree to it. And they had to. According to the law, they all had to agree since they had joint custody over Peter after their mother died.

"He's still in there," he kept telling them, using all the same arguments he had when they were much younger. "I know he is. What if he understands everything? What if he is a normal man with normal intelligence in there behind the disease, a man who just can't communicate because his body refuses to cooperate?"

In the end, he gave up. Gave up as everything slowly slipped out of his hands. But the guilt wouldn't leave him alone. In the end, after Jill had taken the kids and left, moving far away seemed like the only reasonable thing left to do.

"You really don't have to point that thing at me," Daniel says, as they approach the home in Rockledge.

Kristin looks down at the gun, but doesn't remove it.

"I'll take you there anyway," he continues.

She smiles cautiously. He still thinks her smile is beautiful. The years in prison have been hard on her, and she looks at least fifteen years older. Her hair is cut short and it makes her look like a boy. But she still has that quality about her.

"All right," she says, and puts the gun back in her purse. "But it's right here, in case you don't behave."

Daniel parks the car and they walk up to the entrance. He can sense Kristin is nervous. She is not allowed to be anywhere near Peter. They both know that. She could go back to prison for this.

"It'll be fine," Daniel says.

She nods with a nervous sigh. "I hope so."

Daniel presents Kristin as his wife at the counter, and soon they're both shown to Peter's room. As the nurse opens the door, and they both enter, they see Peter in his bed. Kristin cups her mouth when she sees him. Daniel feels like someone punched him in the stomach.

"Oh, my God," Kristin says, addressed to the nurse. "What have you done to him?" She walks to his bed and touches his straps. Daniel feels sick to his stomach. He can't believe how small and skinny Peter has become. It's like there is almost nothing left of him. Not a single muscle, nothing but skin on bones. He hardly recognizes his face. Peter looks more dead than alive.

"We have to keep him strapped down," the nurse explains. "It's the only way we can keep him calm, the only way he doesn't hurt himself or others, for that matter. It's for his own good, really."

She sounds just like Daniel's daughter when explaining that she only hit her younger brother because *he started it!*

"You monsters!" Kristin says.

"As I said. It's for his own good. We have tried to contact the family and tell them—well, tell *you*, that he refuses to cooperate with us, but no one seems to react to our inquiries. Don't blame this on us," the nurse snorts angrily, then leaves the room.

"What have they done?" Kristin says, after the nurse is gone. Her voice is breaking and she is fighting to breathe between the sobs. "What have *you* done?"

She walks to Peter and unleashes the straps on his arms and legs. He doesn't move. Kristin waves a hand in front of his eyes.

"He's not reacting?"

"They probably sedated him," Daniel says, condemned by the responsibility. "I think they do that."

"Sedated? But how...why...why Daniel? Why would they do such a terrible thing? How could you let this happen?"

Daniel shrugs. "I...I've tried everything."

Kristin helps Peter to sit up by putting pillows underneath him. She sits in front of him and looks into his eyes. His head keeps turning away from her.

"He's completely lethargic," she says, startled. "Peter never used to be like this. He was in constant movement, never would settle down, weren't you, Peter?" She strokes his cheek gently while she speaks. "Dear gentle sweet Peter. You were so full of life. What have they done to you? They took everything from you. They took your beautiful voice."

When she speaks, something seems to happen to Peter. His eyes are looking at her. Kristin is crying heavily while yelling, agitated. "Did you see that, Daniel? He looked at me. He is still in there. I know you are, baby. I know you are still there. Can you see me? It's me, Kristin. Hi."

Peter's eyes are staring at her now. Daniel's heart is thumping. Next, Peter lets out a small vague sound.

"He chirped!" Daniel says, tears in his voice. "Peter just chirped again. Just like he used to when he was happy, like he always did when we were kids. Did you hear it, Kristin, did you?"

Kristin wipes away a tear and nods with a sniffle and a light laugh. "Yes. Yes. I heard it. I told you he's still in there." Kristin points to her bag on the floor. "Could you grab that for me?"

Daniel hands it to her. "I brought something for you, darling, she says, and pulls out a keyboard. Let's see if you can remember how to use one of these. I'll help you. Just like we used to. Do you remember that?"

Peter chirps again. Daniel is struggling to hold back tears. To see life in Peter's eyes again is like seeing sunlight after years of darkness. It's such a relief, such a deep hopeful sound.

Kristin grabs Peter's elbow and holds it in her hand. Daniel moves closer to see what Peter is typing. It takes a few minutes before his arm moves and the first letter is typed. Soon the rest arrive like pearls on a string.

"He does remember how to do it," Kristin says. "I knew he would. I knew I could get him to speak again. I'll give you your voice back, Peter. What is he writing, Daniel?"

Daniel writes down each letter, then when Peter is done, he reads it. He looks at Kristin.

"Don't look at me like that. Tell me. What does it say?"

Daniel can hardly get the words across his lips.

"Please kill me."

90

February 2016

I drive like the wind towards Orlando and Winter Park. Meanwhile, I am on the phone trying to get ahold of Steven, but he doesn't answer.

"Pick up. Pick up!"

But of course, he doesn't. I have only been to his house once, a couple of weeks ago when we went to a concert at the Amway Center in Orlando and I picked him up. So, I know where to go.

It takes me about an hour to get there. He lives in one of those nice cookie-cutter neighborhoods where all the houses are big and expensive, but they all look the same. I park in the driveway next to a brown truck, that I am afraid might be hers.

I try and call his cell one last time, and when he doesn't pick up, I storm to the front door. Not knowing what else to do, I ring the doorbell, one hand on my father's gun inside my purse.

Seconds later, Steven comes to the door. He looks surprised. "Mary?"

"Are you alright?" I ask, thinking of how Jess or Kristin held those families hostage before killing them. Maybe she is doing the same to Steven right now, maybe she is hiding somewhere behind the door, pointing her gun at him, waiting for him to say something to me, to alert me, and then shoot him. I have to be careful right now. I have to be very careful.

"Sure? Why wouldn't I be? A little startled to see you here, but…"

"Can I come in?"

He looks confused. "You know what? Now is not a very good time. The house is a mess…and well…I wasn't expecting you."

I scrutinize his eyes to see if I can detect anything, any signal, any small sign that he is, in reality, fearing for his life. I remember the many documentaries I've seen about the killing of the Elingston family in their home, and how both the accountant and the pizza deliveryman never noticed the fear in the father's eyes when he opened the door. I don't want that to happen to me.

"I think I am coming in anyway," I say, and push my way in.

I am armed and not afraid to use it.

"Mary…don't."

But it's too late. I am already inside the hallway. My phone rings and I look at the display. It's Chloe.

"I can't talk right now," I say. "I'm at Steven's. I'll call you back."

"But…"

I hang up and silence the phone before I put it in my pocket, while looking around me. No sign of her anywhere.

"Mary…I am kind of in the middle of something."

"Moom?"

The voice breaks through the air.

The voice of a child.

I turn and look into the face of a boy, about the same age as Salter. "Who are you?" he asks.

"Phillip, your mother is in the back smoking a cigarette. I am in the middle of something here," Steven says.

The boy sighs and turns away. I stare at Steven.

What the heck is going on here?

"What is this, Steven?" I ask. "Who is the boy? And who is his mother? Are you married or something?"

Steven laughs. "Divorced. You know that."

"Is the kid your son? He looks a lot like you."

The boy carries all the answers.

Steven walks to me and grabs my shoulders. "Mary. I only want the best for you. I really like you, I do. But if you keep asking all these questions, you'll get yourself in a lot of trouble, do you understand me? I say you leave now and forget you ever met me, all right?"

That's got to be the weirdest way anyone ever broke up with someone.

"But…Steven…I'm here to warn you. I know who killed your brothers and sister. And I am afraid she's coming for you."

Steven looks at me, and stares into my eyes.

"Your hands are kind of hurting my shoulders, Steven," I say.

My phone vibrates in my pocket, and I pull it out. It's a text from Chloe. Steven's hands are still holding on to my shoulders while I read it.

STEVEN ELINGSTON WAS KILLED IN 2010. GET OUT NOW!

91

February 2016

I TRY TO ACT CASUAL, but Steven sees it in my eyes, sees the shift from confident, to fearful. I can't hide it. He lets go of my shoulders, then shuts the front door behind him and locks it. My hand is on the gun in my purse, but I am shaking. I have no idea what is going on.

The boy carries all the answers.

Another voice approaches. It is her. It's Kristin Martin.

"What's going on in here?"

"Mary knows," Steven—or whatever his name really is—says.

Kristin looks at me. "Ah, that's too bad. I had hoped we could keep you out of this. I really liked you, Mary." As she speaks, she lifts a gun and points it at me. I pull mine and point it at her.

Kristin laughs. "Do you even know how to shoot one of these?"

"I'm a Florida girl; you figure it out."

It's a lie; I am not the type of Florida girl whose dad taught her to shoot. But I can tell it works.

Kristin's smile stiffens. "All right, but I really don't have time for this. Would you, Daniel?"

Daniel?

Daniel walks towards me and reaches out to grab the gun, when I fire it at him and hit his arm.

"What the hell?"

"Don't be a wimp," I say. "It's only a scratch. I told you I know how to shoot one of these. As a matter of fact, I have spent a lot of time on the shooting range the past three months, since I had another run-in with a murderer. Now, you two tell me what the heck is going on here before I get really mad. Who is the boy?"

The boy carries all the answers. That's what Chloe's mother told me. I have no idea how she would know, but I am going with it.

"He's mine," Kristin says. "Phillip is mine and…Peter's. Daniel's younger brother."

"The disabled one?" I ask, suddenly remembering reading that she was pregnant at the time of the trial. "You had the child in prison?"

"Yes. Well, I was taken to the hospital, and that's when they took him away from me. I didn't get to see him for four years. I never saw him learn how to crawl or even walk. They even took away my rights to be with him when I got out."

"My brother took him in," Daniel says. "My brother Steven took him in. But when Kristin got out, he didn't want her to see him. He kept her away from her own son."

"So, you killed him?" I ask.

Kristin looks at Daniel, then chuckles. "Daniel shot him in his own home. In anger."

I look at Daniel with disgust. "Your own brother? You shot him in cold blood?"

"He only got what was coming to him. It was the only way I could get custody of Phillip and Kristin could be with him again. But that wasn't all. We wanted justice for both Phillip and Peter. Peter had been suffering in the most inhumane way at the home my siblings put him in, and when Kristin and I visited him after she was released, he was so sick, so miserable that all he wanted was to die. As a matter of fact, he asked us to kill him."

"So, you killed him?" I ask.

Kristin makes a flipping sound with her lips that's barely a rasp-berry. "No. I love him. We love him. No, we decided to help him. To give him what he deserved, what he should have had many years ago."

"Freedom," Daniel says. "We wanted him to be free, and not only that. We wanted him to be able to have a family, to be with his son and the woman he loves."

I nod as the pieces suddenly fit. "So, you killed the other siblings so that you'd be the only one with custody of your brother, so you could decide where he lives and who he lives with, am I right?"

"It's as simple as that," Daniel says. "We're actually on our way to go and get him now. He is being discharged at my request at three o'clock today. Then we'll get as far away from here as possible. No one will look for us, since they've already caught the killer."

"Marcia," I say. "You framed her."

"If it helps anything, then I am really sorry for her, that it had to end this way. But, yes, she was perfect for our plan," Kristin says. "After getting rid of Steven in 2010, we almost got caught. The police in Denver where he lived kept asking us questions, and we realized we had to be a lot more careful. Daniel was even arrested, but luckily they didn't have enough evidence for a trial. We knew we had to find another way to make sure we wouldn't be suspects. Being a professor in psychology, I know more than anyone how fragile people with mental illnesses are, and I got the idea to find someone to take the fall for us. We took the next six years planning this, looking for the right person in all the places that you'd expect to find someone that unstable, like AA. And along came Marcia. She was perfect. I became her sponsor, and soon realized she had no idea what was reality and what was in her head. She drank way too much and had many black holes in her memory. It was perfect. So I became close with her and she stayed the night at my place a lot of times, and that's when I started showing her the pictures."

"You kept pictures?"

"Of all of them. How else would I show Peter what I have done for him, what I have done for our love? I showed them to Marcia again and again. Starting with the ones of Jack Elingston and his family. I told her how they screamed for help, how scared they were, and then told her she had done it. I told her details about them, and soon she believed she had done it. It was…"

"Perfect, I think we have established that, thank you," I say. "I can't believe you'd exploit her like this."

"Oh, it was so easy. Steven killed Shannon Fergusson in my condo. She had been fighting with her husband and called Daniel. She was crying and asking him if he would come. Since Daniel had moved back here to Winter Park, after Steven died, the two of them had gotten close."

"That explains why you knew what kind of couch she had in her home," I say. "I was wondering about that. You told me you weren't very close with her."

"We didn't used to be," he says. "I was just getting her to trust me. The fight with her husband made it perfect. He wasn't there. He had taken off, probably to be with the woman they were fighting over, the secretary. I told her I was going to visit a friend and asked her if she wanted to come with us, get something to eat. I took her to Kristin's place. I sat her on the couch and started to explain to her what was going to happen. I told her we would kill her and the rest of our siblings, so that Peter could be freed. I showed her pictures of our poor brother, so she would understand what she had done to him. Then I showed her the knife. She didn't even try and fight me. I guess we took her by surprise. I stabbed her thirteen times. Kristin took her to the bridge and dumped her. We needed to make sure they would look for a woman."

I have a bad taste in my mouth. I feel like throwing up. How could anyone be this calculated, this coldblooded?

"Wait. How did you get her to be in the house in Melbourne Beach, in Andrew Elingston's house?" I ask.

"That's the beauty of it. I had no idea she was there. I had shown her pictures of the house and of the family to prepare her to take the blame for what happened, but I had never imagined she would actually be there when I entered the house. It cost me a shot to the shoulder, but it was so worth it. I couldn't have orchestrated it better myself. When she jumped out from behind the door as I was trying to strangle the mother, I knew for the first time that we were going to get away with this. I ran out of there as fast as I could and left her there, then called for the police. She was trying to save them, but instead she incriminated herself. I knew they would never believe her, even if she were capable of telling the truth. Nothing she says makes any sense. I knew she would be sentenced to undergo psychiatric treatment, and to be frank, she is better off there than out here in the world. She is sick, Mary."

I am so mad now I want to shoot her right here, but I can't. I need her to stay alive to tell all this to the police. Instead, I lower the gun so fast she doesn't react, and I shoot her in the foot. She screams and blood gushes out onto the wooden floor.

"You're the one who is sick here," I say.

Kristin lifts her gun swiftly and angrily, while humping on one leg towards me. When the shot is fired, it drowns out everything in my mind. I lose my sense of direction and have no idea what is up or down. It feels like I am falling until all I see is darkness.

February 2016

"MARY? MARY? GODDAMMIT, MARY, WAKE UP!"

The voice yelling is distant, but insisting. I am floating in a sea of stars when I realize it's me it's calling for. I blink my eyes and make the darkness go away. Then I smile.

"Joey?"

"Oh, thank God, Mary. You're alright!"

"Where am I?"

Another face is above me now, looking down. "Hey, Chloe. What are you doing here?"

"I came to check on you and see what you were up to this time," she says. "Are you all right?"

"I don't know. Am I?"

"You look fine," Joey says. "No holes in your body, no blood."

"But I heard a shot. Right before I passed out," I say. "I thought I had been hit."

"Well, Joey kicked the door in, and when we entered, Kristin over there was about to shoot you, so Joey shot her and we believe you slipped and hit your head on the tiles."

I feel my head and find the bump. I look at Joey while trying to sit up. I am still very dizzy.

"You saved me?" I ask.

He nods. I can tell he feels pretty good about himself. "It was nothing. Just glad I always have a gun in my truck."

"You have a gun in your truck? That's not very safe when you drive around with a nine-year-old kid."

"Maybe it's not the time or the place to discuss this," Chloe says. "We need to have a paramedic look at your head and see if they need you to go in for observation." Chloe signals one of the uniformed men, and I realize the place is swarming with them.

"What happened to Kristin Martin and Daniel Elingston?" I ask with a groan. My head is starting to really hurt now.

"They have both been taken away. Kristin in an ambulance," Joey says. "Your beloved Steven or Daniel or Harry, or whatever he calls himself these days threw himself on the floor and surrendered as soon as Kristin hit the ground."

"I am so glad you came. I don't want to think about what would have happened if you hadn't. Thank you."

"You're welcome," Joey says.

"Why were you here anyway?"

"Chloe has tried to tell you about Steven all day, but you refused to listen," Joey says. "When you picked up the phone and told her where you were, she called me immediately afterwards. She knew he wasn't who he said he was, that the real Steven Elingston was killed in his home back in 2010."

"Ah. Okay. Wait. How did she know?"

He shrugs. "She looked into him. Researched him online. Who knows why Chloe does what she does?"

I look at him as Chloe hands me an icepack. "Tell me the truth, Joey," I say.

"Yeah tell her the truth, Joey," Chloe says with a sly grin.

Joey rolls his eyes. "All right. All right. I was jealous. I told Chloe to look into him, to find out who he was, and rightfully so, I might add. Who knows what could have happened you? You really should pick your men better."

I chuckle, but it hurts my head, so I stop.

Chloe helps me get to my feet. I close my eyes to try and get the dizziness to go away, and when I open them again, I look into the eyes of Phillip Elingston.

Suddenly, I don't feel so great about myself any longer. What will become of him after this? There is no family left for him anymore. Everyone else is dead, or going to jail.

Well…maybe not quite *everyone*.

Epilogue

"Thank you for bringing Phillip to us."

Kelly Elingston looks at me. She is out of her bed for the first time since the attack in her home that killed her husband and put her in a coma. She is expected to fully recover. Phillip has been staying with Salter, my dad, and me for the past several weeks until his aunt woke up and DCF could ask her if she'd be willing to take the boy.

"I figured he needed to be with family," I say. "He is, after all, your nephew."

"It'll be so good for Lindsey to have someone to play with. She still hardly speaks, but words are starting to come out of her recently. Small steps, I guess."

"I guess."

"Thank you for everything, Mary."

"It's nothing, really. I brought someone with me who wants to see you."

I open the door and ask Marcia to come in. She has been home for two weeks now and is getting better. I have found a good doctor for her and the medication is beginning to do its job. I believe I can see improvement in her every day. Meanwhile, her sister has come down from Jacksonville and has been taking care of her. Mark has moved home, and after much negotiation on my part, Carl has finally agreed to let the rest of them come back in a few months as well, if Marcia shows continuing signs of improvement. I take it as my job to help her with that.

Marcia waves awkwardly. "Hi."

"Come here," Kelly says. "I want to give you a hug."

Cautiously, Marcia moves closer, and Kelly soon grabs her in her arms. She has tears in her eyes as she holds Marcia. "You have no idea how thankful I am to you. No idea."

Marcia doesn't speak. I can sense she is tearing up as well. Lately, she has been tormented badly about how she acted when she was sick, and for her to hear that she actually did something good for someone must be a great relief. It's just what she needs right now to get back on her feet. People who love her.

"If you ever need anything, Marcia. And I do mean anything, you let me know, all right? You saved my baby's life. And mine. There is no way I can ever pay you back." Kelly lets go of Marcia and looks into her eyes.

"You're a wonderful person, you do know that, right?"

Now I am crying too.

Kelly hugs her one last time, then lets go of her, and Marcia walks over to me. I grab her hand in mine as the nurse walks in and lets us know Kelly needs her rest. Her mom has promised to come later and take both of the children with her until Kelly gets well enough to come home. Our job is done. We say goodbye and walk to the car…Marcia looking a little taller than when we came.

And rightfully so, I think to myself.

I am just so thrilled that Kristin Martin and Daniel Elingston didn't get away with any of it. The last I heard, Kristin is going to survive Joey's shot, and they'll both face prosecution for all the murders. I am working closely with Detective Brown on the case. They expect the FBI to take over sometime soon because of the murder in Denver. I don't know what my role will be yet, how much they'll need my testimony, but I am going to give them everything they need to make sure these two will get what they deserve.

The week after the shootout in Daniel Elingston's house, I went to visit their youngest brother, Peter, at the home in Rockledge. It killed me to see him, and I told Kelly Elingston everything when I came to visit her the next day. She promised me she would look into getting him to a better place. I know she even toys with the idea of letting him move into her house and be with Phillip. It's a big decision to make and requires a lot from her, but somehow, I have a feeling that she can do it.

As for Joey and me? Well, I guess time will show what happens. I am grateful that he saved me, but I still don't feel like I can trust him with my heart. Besides, he is with Jackie now, and as painful as it is, I accept it and try to move on.

I hold the door for Marcia as she gets into my car. I barely make it into my own seat before my phone rings. It's Chloe.

"I have news."

"What?"

"Your brother."

"Really?" I say, slightly skeptical. We were so certain we had traced him to Arizona, but it turned out to be a dead end. I am so glad we didn't go there, as originally planned, and make fools of ourselves.

"And this one is for real. This one I am completely certain is him."

"Great? Why are you so sure?"

"Get this. They have found Olivia. Her body was found hidden in a mattress in a motel room in Naples."

"In Naples? That's not that far from here. Has he really been this close all the time?" I ask.

"Looks like it. And it looks like he got tired of Olivia. She was probably a chain around his leg."

"And now he is free to roam."

"Exactly," she says. "It's easier for him to be on the run when he's on his own."

"That might be," I say. "But he cannot hide. Not forever at least. Sooner or later, we'll find him."

"I'd prefer sooner rather than later."

"That makes two of us."

THE END

Want to know what happens next? Go Here:
https://readerlinks.com/l/157529

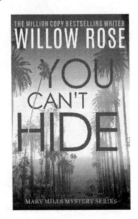

Afterword

Dear Reader,

Thank you for purchasing *You Can Run* (Mary Mills Mystery book 2). This was a tough book for me to write, because Marcia's condition was so devastating. As a writer, I have to put myself in her situation and live it with her. Imagine not knowing what you're doing half of the time, not knowing if people around you want the best for you or not, or if they're right when they tell you you're sick. It is among my greatest fears to one day wake up and realize I have been locked up for life and no one believes anything I say.

I don't think that will happen, at least not as long as I keep writing.

As always, some of the stories in this book are based on true events. So is the story of Peter Elingston, the man with Cerebral Palsy and the woman who falls in love with him. You might know of it since it has been quite a big media story, but in case you don't, here's a link to some of the articles I read about the case:

http://www.slate.com/blogs/the_slatest/2015/
09/22/anna_stubblefield_case_the_rutgers_newark_professor_is_ac
cused_of_citing.html

http://www.nytimes.com/2015/10/25/magazine/the-strange-case-
of-anna-stubblefield.html?smtyp=cur&_r=0

If you can, please leave a review. It means the world to me. And don't forget to read the excerpt following this and to check out my other books by following the links below.

Take care,
Willow

Tired of too many emails? Text the word: "willowrose" to 31996 to sign up to Willow's VIP text List to get a text alert with news about New Releases, Giveaways, Bargains and Free books from Willow.

Cover design by Juan Villar Padron,
https://www.juanjpadron.com

Special thanks to my editor Janell Parque
http://janellparque.blogspot.com/

**To be the first to hear about new releases and bargains
from Willow Rose, sign up below to be on the VIP List.** (I
promise not to share your email with anyone else, and I won't clutter
your inbox.)

- GO HERE TO SIGN UP TO BE ON THE VIP LIST :
http://readerlinks.com/l/415254

Tired of too many emails? Text the word: "willowrose" to
31996 to sign up to Willow's VIP text List to get a text alert with
news about New Releases, Giveaways, Bargains and Free books
from Willow.

FOLLOW WILLOW ROSE ON BOOKBUB:
https://www.bookbub.com/authors/willow-rose

Connect with Willow online:
https://www.amazon.com/Willow-Rose/e/B004X2WHBQ
https://www.facebook.com/willowredrose/
https://twitter.com/madamwillowrose
http://www.goodreads.com/author/show/4804769.Willow_Rose

http://www.willow-rose.net
contact@willow-rose.net

About the Author

The Queen of Scream aka Willow Rose is a #1 Amazon Best-selling Author and an Amazon ALL-star Author of more than 50 novels. She writes Mystery, Paranormal, Romance, Suspense, Horror, Supernatural thrillers, and Fantasy.

Willow's books are fast-paced, nail-biting page-turners with twists you won't see coming.

Several of her books have reached the Kindle top 20 of ALL books in the US, UK, and Canada.

She has sold more than three million books.

Willow lives on Florida's Space Coast with her husband and two daughters. When she is not writing or reading, you will find her surfing and watch the dolphins play in the waves of the Atlantic Ocean.

IT ENDS HERE

EXCERPT

For a special sneak peak of Willow Rose's Bestselling Mystery Novel ***IT ENDS HERE*** turn to the next page.

Chapter 1

It wasn't easy to tell whether the boy was dead or not. He was lying motionless on the wooden planks, his arms stretched out to the sides, and had someone entered the abandoned house on Second Street, they might have thought he was just sleeping, or maybe it was part of some game he was playing. There was no blood to indicate he had hurt himself or that someone had hurt him. There were no bruises and no wounds to indicate a crime had been committed or an accident had happened.

Outside, a thunderstorm approached, and lightning struck not far from the house, while buckets of water soon splashed on the boarded-up windows. Meanwhile, inside, there was a calmness unlike anywhere else in the world. There was just the boy, lying lifeless on the dusty floor that his mother would have told him—had she only been with him—was too dirty to be playing around on.

But his momma wasn't there. In fact, no one knew the boy was lying there, not breathing, arms spread out like Jesus on the cross.

No one would find him till many hours later.

Chapter 2

"ALEXANDER? ALEX? WHERE ARE YOU, SON?"

Mrs. Cunningham walked out of the store and looked in the parking lot. Dark clouds were gathering in the distance, and she knew she didn't have long before the thunderstorm would hit them. A crack of thunder could already be heard in the distance, and the sky rumbled above her like an empty stomach. Her worried eyes scanned the area while she wondered where the boy could be. She had told him to wait in the car while she went to grab something at Webster Hardware and Farm Supply, and when she came out, the door to the car was open, but the boy wasn't there.

Could he have gotten out of the car? Was he playing somewhere nearby?

"Alex?"

Mrs. Cunningham walked around the car, then looked in the direction of the store across the street, called *El Curiosities*. Outside on display, they had the strangest water fountains and odd figures for your yard, including a colorful life-size rooster and a cow made of metal. Alexander had been asking to go into that store ever since he heard that they had a real knight's armor in there. But he would have to cross the street to get to it. He wouldn't have done that, would he? He was only five. He knew he wasn't allowed to cross any streets.

She turned around and walked away, then looked at her watch. She had a charity event tonight and had to get home to get herself ready. Why did something like this always happen when you were in a rush?

She scanned the area around the supply store once again,

looking for any movement or a red shirt poking out somewhere in the bushes behind it, but she couldn't see any. Then she sighed and decided he'd have to have gone to the store all by himself. The temptation might have been a little too big.

Mrs. Cunningham grumbled, then shut the car door and walked up to Market Boulevard, the main street going through town. Right before she crossed the street, she turned her head for a brief second and glanced toward NW Second Street behind the supply store, where she could see that awful abandoned house towering behind the trees, the one that no one dared to approach. Not just because of what had happened in there once, but also because they feared the roof might fall on someone's head one day. Why they hadn't torn the house down long ago was a mystery to most people.

"Alex?" she called as she approached the small store across the street. She approached the big figurines, then wondered who would possibly want a metal statue of a Mexican man playing guitar in their front yard. The fountains, at least some of them, she could understand, but those figures, it made no sense that anyone would buy them, except children.

Mrs. Cunningham scanned the front of the store, then called his name again, but received no answer.

A mother and her child were looking at the huge rooster.

"Have you seen a little boy? About this tall, wearing a red shirt?" Mrs. Cunningham asked, her voice quivering slightly.

The mother shook her head. "It's just us out here. Have you tried inside?"

Mrs. Cunningham shook her head, then stepped inside the store. There were rows and rows of useless junk everywhere, and she sighed as she walked down an aisle, then yelled her son's name again and again. At the end of the aisle, as she leaned against the wall, she found the armor, but there was no Alex there either. A salesperson in a green polo shirt, wearing a nametag reading Stu, walked by and she stopped him.

"Have you seen a little boy, five years old, wearing a red shirt? He might have come in here and looked at the armor. He loves anything about knights. You know how they are…boys at that age. If anything catches their interest, they'll stop at nothing to find it, not caring at all about rules and worried mothers."

The man shook his head. "No, ma'am. I haven't seen any children at all today, except for the little girl outside with her mother."

"Oh. Okay, thanks."

Disappointed, Mrs. Cunningham walked back through the store, then took it aisle by aisle once more just to be sure. When Alex wasn't there, she rushed back outside, where her eyes met that of the mother who had now moved on to look at a big reindeer with her daughter.

"Still haven't found him?" the mother asked while her daughter giggled and touched the deer statue, petting it like it was a real animal.

"No. But if you do see him, tell him his mom is looking for him. I'll be right across the street in the parking lot in front of the supply store, where he was last seen. So, you can just call for me if you do see him, please."

"Of course. I will do my best to help," the mother said and sent her a sympathetic smile that in one way told her that she felt for her, but at the same time said *This would never happen to me. I always know where my child is.*

Mrs. Cunningham's eyes swept the area in front of the store once again before she crossed the road to get back to the car and see if Alexander had made it back yet. If he had, he was sure in for a scolding for leaving the car like that when his mother had told him to wait.

Maybe he went into the supply store to look for me, and I missed him somehow. Yes, that's it, she thought to herself. *He got bored in the car and wanted to know how much longer he had to wait.*

Happy that it was—of course—just a silly misunderstanding, Mrs. Cunningham went back into the store, and her eyes met the clerk's as she stepped through the door.

"Mrs. Cunningham, you're back already? Did you forget something?"

"Yes," she said, feeling silly for freaking out. "I seem to have forgotten my son. Is he here?"

Mrs. Cunningham locked eyes with the clerk for a few seconds, and she could tell he was searching for words. Her heart dropped when he shook his head.

"I am sorry, Mrs. Cunningham. I haven't seen him. Was he supposed to be in here? I didn't see him come in."

The blood left Mrs. Cunningham's face, and she rushed outside, now yelling her son's name in what could be mistaken for a scream, while panic settled in. She ran around the warehouse building housing the supply store, then back to the parking lot and looked down First Street, then back up at Market Boulevard. She ran up to the road and walked further down, yelling his name, then hurried back to the parking lot to see if he might have returned while she was gone, hoping and muttering little prayers under her breath.

He hadn't.

Frantically, she grabbed her phone from her purse and called her husband.

"I lost Alex," she said, barely getting the words across her lips.

"What do you mean, *what do I mean*? I can't find him. He was in the car when I went into the supply store, and when I came back out, he was gone. What do you mean, *am I sure?* Do I not sound like I'm sure? Yes, I've searched everywhere. I'm telling you; he's not here. I'm scared. Where can he be?"

Chapter 3

"I DON'T KNOW how you'll deal with it all alone," I said, holding the phone between my shoulder and ear. I reached a red light and stopped. "But you'll have to. There's no other way; I'm afraid."

"I can't believe you," Sune said, almost hissing at me. I hardly recognized him anymore. The way he spoke to me lately was so far from the way he used to adore me and everything I did. It was hard to tell that he had once loved me and I him. We had loved each other enough to have a child together. We had created a family, and now he had destroyed everything.

He was the one who had an affair with his nurse while in recovery from being shot. Once I found that out, I was done with him. I told him so numerous times when he asked me to forgive him and let him come back. It wasn't going to happen, I had said over and over. Now, Sune was with Kim, staying at her place and she had become a part of our lives. I didn't like her much—no that would be too mildly put—I loathed her. I couldn't even stand the thought of her. Yet I'd have to live with the fact that she was in my life, and—even worse—in my children's lives.

Sune had moved in with her in her condo not far from our house. I had stayed in the rented beach house and hoped I could afford to stay there until we figured everything out. But it required me making a lot of money, and that meant I had to work.

"Listen, I know you're busy with getting back to working again and spending time with your new girlfriend and all that, but you have to take your turn here. I've been taking care of all three kids for the past week, and now I'm asking for you to take them for three days. I know Julie is not your child, and therefore not your responsibility, but I also take care of Tobias when you need me to. We promised each other that we wouldn't separate the children, remember?"

"Of course, I do," Sune said, sounding less agitated. "I just don't think it's fair, Rebekka. You spring this on me the day before you leave and I'm just supposed to throw everything else I have in my hands and do as you tell me? What if I had a photo job?"

"Well, do you? Do you have a job?" I asked.

"No, not yet, but hopefully, I'll get some soon. I'm trying to get back to my life here, and that means I need to be available. Now, I won't be for the next three days."

I tried to control my anger. I could understand it if Sune actually had a job he needed to get to, but he didn't. I did, on the other hand. Why couldn't he just do this for me without complaining?

"I didn't get this assignment till yesterday," I said. "I know it's last minute, but I need to work; I need to eat too, Sune, and so do the kids. So, I have to take the jobs I can get. You're the one who wants us all to stay here in Florida so you can be with your precious nurse Kim. I don't mind it here; I actually love it here with the weather being so nice all the time and all, but when I discovered you with her, I asked for us all to go home. You didn't want that."

"I also asked you to forgive me and take me back," Sune said. "You wouldn't do that for me."

"No, I wouldn't because I can't trust you anymore and, frankly, I don't want to. But then when I asked if it wouldn't be for the best if we all went home, you said no. You wanted to stay so you could be with her. I agreed to stay, so William wouldn't lose his father, and the kids would still be able to be together, but that means I have to work as a freelancer and take whatever assignments I can get."

I paused to breathe when the light shifted, and I continued over the bridge onto the mainland.

"Don't you for one second think I like having to go do a promotional interview with some author about her next book, when I could be at home covering real stories for a real paper," I continued. "I could be writing about things that actually matter. Plus, I could be with my dad, who isn't doing too well. I'm doing all this for you, Sune. For you and the kids. So, you better help me out when I need it, okay?"

Sune was still silent and, for a second, I wondered if he had hung up. I heard him chuckle and rolled my eyes.

"You're with her, aren't you?" I asked. "You're not even listening to what I'm saying."

"So what if I am? Am I not allowed to hang out with my girl-friend?" he said, suddenly sounding like he was fifteen. Sune was the only man I knew who seemed to be maturing backward, getting more and more childish by the minute. It was ridiculous the way he acted these days, and I was sick of it, to be honest.

I exhaled, then accelerated. I hated the fact that my kids would be forced to spend time with her—the woman who had wrecked our home and caused us to split up—for the next couple of days while I was gone on the job. It was well-paid, so I could hardly have said no to it just because I didn't like Sune's new girlfriend. It was for *Metropolitan Magazine,* which wanted a feature on an author who lived inland and who had just published a book that had gone on to hit the *New York Times* bestselling list on the very first day. There were talks about a movie deal too. She was a very private person, and the magazine wanted me to do a story on her, trying to figure out who she really was. She had agreed to do an interview with me, but from talking to her on the phone, I got the feeling that she wasn't exactly excited about the idea.

"Just promise me you'll take good care of my children, will you?" I said, then hung up without waiting for his response. I felt tears in my eyes and a knot in my throat but swallowed it down along with my pride.

I hated what had happened to us.

Chapter 4

Carol watched the two girls sitting on the lawn and smiled while wiping her fingers on a dishtowel, removing flour and butter left on her hands from the peach pie she was baking for Anna Mae and her friend.

She liked to make things nice for Anna Mae when she came to visit her aunt. She wanted Anna Mae to like it at her house and hoped to be able to make up for all the bad stuff she had to witness at home.

It was no secret that Carol wasn't very fond of her sister, Joanna, or her choices in life, but she had the one thing that Carol couldn't get and that she desired more than anything in this world. A child. A beautiful angelic baby girl named Anna Mae.

Ever since she was born, Anna Mae had been the apple of Carol's eye. Her visits filled her with such profound joy that she always wished Anna Mae could stay a little longer. At one point, when her mother had been on yet another drinking bender, Anna Mae had stayed at Carol's house for five whole days, and that had felt like heaven for Carol. She had cherished the wondrous blessing of hearing a child's laughter in her home and often looked back on it as the best time of her adult life.

When Anna Mae wasn't there, the house felt so empty, so quiet. Then it was just her and John. Carol loved her husband, of course she did, but the fact that she hadn't been able to provide him with a child had come between them, and these days they barely touched or even spoke. Every time she looked into his eyes, she was reminded of her own failure, the failure of not being woman enough for him.

Anna Mae looked back at the house with her sparkling blue eyes,

265

and Carol waved with a sigh. If only Anna Mae could have been hers.

Joanna doesn't deserve her.

It was the truth; she didn't. She didn't know how lucky she was and never knew how to appreciate her daughter. Not like Carol would. She would have spoiled that girl rotten had she only been hers. Instead, she was just her niece, and she'd have to be satisfied with only seeing her once in a while when her sister got tired of her or didn't want her around for some reason. More often than not, it was because she had men in the house or was drinking.

The oven dinged to let her know the pie was done and Carol pulled it out, closing her eyes briefly when the heavenly smell hit her nostrils. She put the warm peach pie on the patio outside to cool, then went over to Anna Mae and her friend, Bella, at the bottom of the yard.

As she approached the two girls, she took in a deep breath of the warm, moist air. Spring in Florida was always so wonderful, she believed. Summers were too hot and muggy for Carol, but spring was just perfect. Up above her, the sun shone from a clear blue sky, and there wasn't a sign of thunderstorms anywhere nearby. It was going to be a wonderful afternoon, well spent with her precious niece.

"Girls, the pie is ready," she chirped as she approached them. "Let's eat it while it's warm."

But the girls didn't react. They sat in the grass, heads bent down like they were doing something very important.

"Did you hear me, girls? Anna Mae? I said the pie is done. And I have vanilla ice cream to top it off with, just the way you like it."

Carol took a few steps closer to better see what they were up to, then gasped and clasped her mouth.

"Anna Mae! W-what...what are you...what are you doing to that poor bird?"

The girls both gazed up at her, their eyes beaming with wonder and amazement, while Carol stared at the bird in Anna Mae's hands. Anna Mae was holding it between her fingers while pressing down on its throat with her thumbs. The bird was flapping with one crooked wing and trying to get loose. It was obviously fighting for its life, while both of its legs had been snapped like twigs.

"Let go of that bird, Anna Mae," Carol said. "You can't hurt a poor bird like that. Can't you see that you're torturing it? Let it go, now."

The girl looked up at her, then pressed down her thumbs hard and choked the bird, holding it tight till it stopped moving. Then she smiled and sighed... almost like she was satisfied.

"Anna Mae," Carol said, shocked. She felt the hair rise on her neck despite the almost eighty degrees out. "What did you do? You killed it! Why would you do that to the poor birdie?"

Anna Mae finally let the bird drop from her hands, and her eyes followed it as it fell to the grass below.

"It's just a birdie," Bella said, lisping slightly.

Bella was a little slow, as they put it, so it didn't really shock Carol as much to see her engage in something like this, but Anna Mae should know better. She was the smart one of the two.

"It had a broken wing," Anna Mae said. "It couldn't fly anymore. So, it had to die."

"Did you break the wing?" Carol asked. "Did you, Anna Mae? Did you break its wing first?"

The girl didn't answer. She stared at the bird on the grass, and Carol wondered what to say to her next, how to talk some sense into her. It seemed almost like she didn't feel any type of remorse at all for killing that bird. It was obvious to Carol that Anna Mae had broken the wing first. How could such a young girl act so cruel?

Carol sighed, realizing she couldn't really scold Anna Mae since she wasn't her child. She didn't want to, either, since she didn't dare risk that the girl would never come back to visit again because she didn't like it at her aunt's place. Life without Anna Mae would be unbearable.

Carol sighed and straightened her apron.

"Now, get rid of that bird before we get rats or vultures crowding the place. You can bury it in the dirt over there and then come wash up. Like I said, it's time for pie."

Order your copy today!

Made in United States
Orlando, FL
02 August 2023

35699217R00169